Tales Before Midnight

Tales Before Midnight

Ted Mason

Bartleby Press
Silver Spring, Maryland

The characters and events in these stories are entirely fictional and no reference to any person, living or dead, is intended.

Cover photo by the author
Back cover photo by Robert O. Jones

ISBN 0-910155-61-5

Library of Congress Control Number: 2004118160

Published and distributed by:

Bartleby Press
PO Box 1516
Silver Spring, Maryland 20915
800-953-9929
www.BartlebythePublisher.com

Printed in the United States of America

To Geneviève, again and always

CONTENTS

INTRODUCTION

M ost of these stories were written during the Cold War
and overseas while I was working for Uncle Sam. I
had little time to plan or write them and less to get them
published, but now I've gathered together some of the best
of them and offer them to you in this volume.

They are grouped more or less chronologically in time,
but not always in the order written, from the world of my
boyhood to the great world outside. In style and content
they range from grim realism to fantasy to humor and satire;
so I don't expect all of them to please everyone. I looked to
the classics for inspiration and measured myself against
them. The photo on the back cover, in fact, was shot at the
Lions' Gate at Mycenae in 1949, which I had the incredible
luck to visit as a student after reading the Greek tragedies at
Yale. Everything in this collection was written since then,
no doubt with varying degrees of success but always with
the classics in mind.

It wasn't easy. I had two years left on the GI Bill and $75
a month to live on in Paris, which went a long way in those
days. A first novel and many stories were written during
that cold winter of 1948-9 in my room at a *pension de famille.*
Then a second novel and more stories the next year as I
looked down the rue Jacob from my hotel room in the rue

de Seine. Those two novels are long gone, as are the Hôtel des Pyrénées, the Pension Domecq, my typewriter and my radio. The last of them was published in *Argosy* (without Blake's poem), and now it embarks on a new life, touched up and reprinted as "Tiglon."

But that story led nowhere, despite almost three years of furious effort while working temporary jobs in Bridgeport. "The Tree Climbers" and "Fellow Voyager" date from this period, the latter inspired not by Katherine Anne Porter's *Ship of Fools*, which it pre-dated, but by Joseph Conrad's "Secret Sharer."

So Geneviève and I returned to Europe on the ill-fated *Andrea Doria* to earn an honest but often stressful living in France, Germany, Vietnam, Morocco and Madagascar. One of the fruits of all this was my novel *Hostage to Fortune*. Another was a satirical novel on the US military in France, an excerpt from which appears here under the title "51 Days in June." All are signposts along the way in a lifetime of observing people and their reactions to the tricks they play on each other and life plays on them, and you can read them in any order you like. In *Hostage to Fortune* many readers identified with or admired one character or another, proof to me that I'd created believable human beings. Who could ask for more?

They say truth is stranger than fiction. But I say fiction at its best can be truer than truth. So here they are, with thanks to Jackie Pearce for her invaluable help in putting it all together, and to Robert Frost for four lines which have sustained me over the years:

> *The woods are lovely, dark and deep,*
> *But I have promises to keep,*
> *And miles to go before I sleep,*
> *And miles to go before I sleep.*

THE OLD HOME TOWN

Tiglon

Tiger! Tiger! burning bright
In the forests of the night,
What immortal hand or eye
Dare frame thy fearful symmetry?
~ William Blake

1

The news that Quassatuck was going to have a zoo came as a surprise to most of us. But that was the way Mr. Bancroft wanted it. It was to be his last philanthropy. As the leading figure in the city's brass industry for as long as most could remember, during the Depression he had funded various charities and work projects to keep us busy, and now he was to crown his munificence with the building of a zoological park along the Mattapaug river in the heart of the city.

It was a proud moment for all of us, especially for me since I, Larry Gillis, who was only a cub reporter on *The Clarion*, would be one of those covering the story. For a kid between Freshman and Sophomore year at college this could be my big chance. I might even be able to interview the man who was so unknown to us, such a legend in fact, among the people he'd lived with for most of his life that fantastic stories had grown up around his name. We imagined him (he was past ninety and spent his days in a wheel chair, with his frail body like a dry twig incased in blankets) in one of the great rooms of his estate outside the city, surrounded by subordinates and experts from zoos around the country. He would be looking at an enormous wall map of Quassatuck speckled with tiny colored lights, or perhaps a large-scale relief model of the city covering a table ten feet square—no one knew he didn't have something of the sort, and so we liked to assume he did—and pointing to an area where an old city dump was located, he would be speaking in that thin, high voice which for us was not so much a mark of his great age as a symbol of the man himself, somehow impervious to the ravages of time and decay, saying: "Gentlemen, this will be the site of the Bancroft Zoological Park."

But then, even before the dump was cleared and the few tenements bordering it torn down, Harlan Bancroft, Sr., at ninety-four, was dead. And then war came and automatically halted all work, so that for the next four years we had a huge empty lot and no animals at all. It almost seemed intended as a lesson, that even Mr. Bancroft, like all of us, was subject to the vagaries of fate.

Furthermore, it removed me from the scene until the end of the war, so that when I returned to college from the army I had lost my starry-eyed innocence and gained a degree of cynicism. I was able to look at the project now with somewhat less awe, partly due to the succession to the old man by his eldest surviving son.

Ellsworth Bancroft was a vigorous man in his sixties, with far broader experience than his father. Before the war he had hunted big game on three continents. He was a man of action, bringing to his new role as a manufacturer a knowledge of the world, a passion for its wild life, and the will to make things happen in Quassatuck, which was what we expected of him.

As for myself, I found that work had already begun

under his direction with the arrival of builders and specialists in zoo-keeping and the handling of wild animals. The freight yards would soon be full of the sounds and smell of caged animals moving into the city like cattle into stockyards, except that these animals were not headed for any slaughterhouse: they were headed for new homes of specially planned caves and pools and tree-shaded sandpits where a city of nearly one-hundred thousand would pass through iron gates and heavy wire fences to view with curiosity and exultation the wild beasts of the earth, brought into captivity and displayed here for their edification and their pleasure.

2

The prize specimen in our zoo was to be an animal dubbed a "tiglon." Now in nature the lion is the King of Beasts wherever he still lives, though for the most part this area no longer extends beyond the continent of Africa. Over the vast land mass of Asia, from the Euphrates to Kamchatka and from the Caspian to Indonesia, the King of Beasts is the tiger. Each has his domain, and never in nature have the two been known to contest the same ground, much less mate. Our tiglon, then, was a beast which could have been created by man alone. He was the result of the mating of a male tiger and a lioness accomplished in captivity. He and the very few others like him had been conceived not in the wild but in the mind of man. In the words of Ellsworth Bancroft, reversing those of St. Matthew during the ceremonies I covered on the animal's arrival, "What God hath put asunder man hath joined together." These words appeared next morning under my by-line in *The Clarion* and were copied across the state of Connecticut and beyond.

Shere Khan (Ellsworth Bancroft, an admirer of Kipling, had named him) was a strange but fine-looking animal.

Having no mane in the sense that a lion has a mane, but with thick fur on his neck and heavy, square jaw and straight ears, his head resembled that of a lion. Otherwise, he had the long, stealthy body and tuftless tail of a tiger, with the tiger's stripes faded as if washed from his fur with soap and water but still visible upon a reddish coat. This strange appearance and the fact that he was believed to be twice as ferocious as either parent brought a constant stream of visitors to his cage. Were they reassured by the fact that, like most crossbreeds, he was sterile, thus limiting to his own lifetime any threat to their safety? Probably not. For most viewers it was the forbidding walls and iron gates and fences which gave them their sense of protection and even mastery over the man-killer Shere Khan could be.

Whatever the truth, they watched as he paced his cage ceaselessly. He would advance with long and soundless strides until his whiskers touched the wall, then dropping low and turning like a swimmer under water, his face never averted from the watchers beyond the bars, he would retrace his steps, repeating the same movements again and again, always without a sound, until the onlookers themselves would grow weary and turn away.

On Sundays whole families could be seen there, munching peanuts and staring. Boys and even men would whistle or toss peanut shells at his head to taunt him and make him snarl. But never the women. Before Shere Khan they stood mute and motionless, gazing at his impotent and constricted movements as if chastened by the spectacle of their own triumph over savagery.

Sometimes they would see him in the open, for the zoo had a large outdoor quarry-like pit where the animals were released individually for an hour at a time. Once a day he would enter through a trap from his cage and quickly circle the pit's perimeter, sometimes looking beyond the high stone wall where humans moved in freedom but then always returning to the rock island in the center where he was king. Nothing could alter his aloofness to visitors; nothing could reduce his ferocity toward his keepers. And although the men who cared for him were openly disappointed that their efforts to tame him had proved unsuccessful, Ellsworth Bancroft was not. "This isn't a zoo for domesticated animals," he said. "My father's purpose was to bring together one of the finest collections of wild animals in this part of the country. If he could see Shere Khan today, I'm sure he'd be satisfied we'd made a good beginning." The number of visitors who came every day to the zoo and the expressions of wonder on their faces when they saw Shere Khan gave good evidence that they agreed with Mr. Bancroft.

3

And yet on that incredible day when Shere Khan managed to escape there was no one who could give a satisfactory explanation of how it had happened. It was not how he did it, since several witnesses saw him bound into the pit that afternoon and then suddenly, with an unbelievable leap over the wall and out among them, dart long and tawny across the grounds and out the open gate past the big brass letters spelling the name of Bancroft. Nor was it so much a question of what he had done as how the peculiar combination of circumstances—the open gate, the unobstructed passageway from his cage to the pit and the incredible leap exceeding all the calculations of his captors—could combine with the animal's first and only impulse to seek freedom. They wondered, furthermore, how it was possible that his instinct could have shown him the only path out of a half dozen which would lead to the gate. It was as if suddenly he had sprung into a maze of mirrors in an amusement park and, without so much as touching glass, reached the exit.

The truth is almost unbelievable. Not a person moved to draw the animal's attention away from his goal. They actually froze in place and stared as if this were part of the program and Shere Khan were performing a new trick for their amusement. One of the keepers, Joseph d'Agostino, who at that moment was crossing the grounds with a wheelbarrow filled with raw meat under a soiled cloth, stopped when Shere Khan sprang from the pit, the handles of the wheelbarrow still in his grasp, and gaped openly, his head turning like a mechanical toy's to follow the path of the sleek beast. And next to the pit itself, barely ten feet from where the tiglon had jumped out, Mrs. Chris Galvin held her five year-old Patrick's hand and stared without uttering a sound. Nor did Patrick even remove the green, lime-flavored lollipop from his mouth; his tongue simply paused on it, protruding pink and moist, with the lollipop cradled on its surface until Shere Khan was out of sight. Even old Art Hempel at the main gate, who for forty years had been one of the most trusted workers at the Bancroft Brass Company, even he could only remove his uniform cap and scratch his bald head at the sight.

But when it was over, then the action began, and a frantic grabbing of babies accompanied by screams and confusion followed, so that it seemed people were more afraid of a danger which had passed them by than of any real evil the present offered. The confusion itself was more irrational than could have been imagined. As soon as Shere Khan was gone Joseph d'Agostino was seen to hoist the handles of his wheelbarrow and run, pushing his tilting burden ahead of him and spilling chunks of meat wildly along his path toward the service entrance to the cages, where he bolted the door behind him, while Mrs. Galvin grabbed her Patrick with such force that she jammed the lollipop against his gums and made him cry. Only old

Art Hempel refused to panic and shook his head at the rest.

Within half an hour the entire city had the news. The afternoon edition of *The Clarion*, which was already on the presses, was called back and the front page remade, but not before the local radio station had broadcast the news to all. Housewives listening to their favorite soap operas heard the words, "We bring you breaking news..." then phoned their husbands to warn them not to step outdoors. Telephone lines were jammed, and I was sent out on the double to get the story.

The police acted too, and the fire department. Squad cars with loudspeakers began patrolling the streets advising one and all to bring children and domestic animals indoors at once and to close all ground floor windows and cellar entrances. Zoo authorities admitted the possibility that the beast might hide in the city but said it was far more probable that it would head for the woods. In any case, a search was being organized, and the people of Quassatuck could be confident the animal would be caught.

Normal business came to a halt. The streets were empty of pedestrians; the city had bolted its doors against a terror it could not see. No fire or flood or other disaster which had ever overtaken us had brought with it such a silent, invisible fear.

4

When the news reached Mr. Ellsworth Bancroft, he was in his office as Chairman of the Board preparing for a board meeting. I was already on the spot, hoping for an exclusive before the other media arrived. But his aides held me back, and before I could reach him every visitor in his outer office was unceremoniously ordered out while he retired to complete solitude at his desk, with only the intercom between him and his secretary.

Mr. Bancroft sat in his leather chair for a full ten minutes, his hands at his chin and his athletic shoulders hunched while he stared silently across the room at the closed door to his outer office. He was a different man now. There was none of the feverish movement of earlier that day, no animated bobbing of his vigorous gray head as he argued with a staff member or leaned forward to sign a paper. Now his body seemed thrown into sudden and unusual contemplation, and the energetic man of action seemed all at once to have aged ten years, as if his youthfulness were a product of his very activity and the bony frame, once at rest, could be seen for what it really was—that of a man almost seventy. Then suddenly he sat upright, turned to the intercom and within seconds the staff assistants were back in his office.

5

The city heard Mr. Bancroft's voice that evening, broadcast direct from the home his father had built a few miles outside the city. They were the first words he would say in public, and people had to wait to hear him. He'd said nothing to me or to any other member of the media waiting outside his office, but his words now were courageous words, urging calm. There was in them what might be expected from the son of Harlan Bancroft and the heir to the Bancroft Brass Company fortune. And perhaps if it had been a crisis of a different kind, people would have listened. If it had been a fire or an aerial bombardment or a catastrophe wrought by an angry god, then certainly no one would have failed to heed his words. But this was no attack by a known or unknown outside evil; it was Mr. Bancroft's own prize tiglon which had turned on the city, and suspicion and resentment were in people's minds. They heard what they wanted to hear in his voice—an anxiety not so much, they thought, for human lives as for the safety of the animal. Behind his words there seemed to be others, like, "Take care of yourselves ... but don't take any chances ... Just keep calm and everything will be all right ... Above all, try to take him alive. Don't kill the greatest living attraction our city has. Don't kill my tiglon."

Men who heard his words this way looked to themselves for help. They were not interested in the Chairman of the Board of Directors.

"He's talking like it's his tiger," said Rose Kravitz to her husband in their house on East Side Hill. "I thought he gave it to the city."

"Don't believe it," he answered. "He just wants us to pay for the upkeep. They're still his pets, and when they break loose we're supposed not to hurt them."

And Martin Stepinak at the headquarters of the local Brass Workers' Union: "He may be the biggest taxpayer, but he don't own the whole town. And he can't take us over when something like this happens."

And Ralph Conlon, in the living room of the five-room house he had bought with a GI loan. Turning off the set, he told his wife, "That guy don't tell me how to take care of my kids. You check the windows again. I'm gonna get my gun."

I heard these and other similar comments during that evening and night, and I reported them in my story. But I guess I was still green in spite of my time in the army, because the editor called me in and said, "Kid, you know I can't print these comments. I'd be out of a job tomorrow, and so would you."

"Why?" I asked, "That's what people are saying, and I have to agree with them."

"Oh, you do? And you think we can get away with criticizing Ellsworth Bancroft personally in *The Clarion*?"

"Why not? We're just reporting other people's words?"

"Listen, son, you know what a clarion is, don't you?"

"Sure. It's a musical instrument, a bugle."

"That's right, and it's made out of brass. And so is this city. And guess who owns the biggest brass company—and this newspaper. The Bancroft family, that's who. Now do you see why we do not, ever, criticize a member of the Bancroft family in this paper?"

"OK, I see," I said, "if that's the way it is."

"That is the way it is, and don't forget it. Furthermore, the people who shot their mouths off to you have jobs, and they want to keep them. Don't forget that either."

But at this late date most of the principals are dead, and I still wanted to get the truth into the record. It happened a long time ago, and I don't think it will hurt anyone if I tell it now, the way I really saw it, and as I wrote it at the time.

6

By now it was dark. And although during the first few hours not a trace of the tiglon had been seen, since mid-afternoon men had been planning his capture. At the zoo experts were considering the probabilities of the animal's whereabouts. It seemed unlikely it could have escaped to the woods without having been seen, since to get to them it would have had to cross the most thickly-settled part of town. The zoo, being situated on the river bank just above Bancroft's main plant, on the west bank opposite there is a residential neighborhood extending from about halfway up the hill over the crest toward the town of Bedford. And though the river is not high at this time of year and has never been navigable, they were convinced that Shere Khan would not cross it unless forced to. "Never fear," said one of the experts, "our tiglon can swim, but he won't want to unless we drive him to it. So our best chance will be east of the river." Ninety percent of the city lay east of the river.

In the armory a meeting of the local Army Reserve unit was being held under its commander, Colonel Mike Santoro. Colonel Santoro ran a trucking company in civilian life, but he was a WWII combat veteran and volunteered his entire command by telephone to Mayor Gilpatrick.

The mayor had seen men heading for the armory from his office window: factory workers, small businessmen, even reservists from outside town, wearing parts of uniforms thrown on hurriedly for identification in response to the colonel's urgent call. He had seen their grim, silent and efficient faces, and he hesitated. I was with Colonel Santoro at the time, but I knew the mayor's secretary, and she filled me in on his end of the conversation.

"I've got my police out patrolling the streets, Colonel," he said finally. "I don't want to turn this city into an armed camp."

"But you haven't got enough police to cover the territory, Mr. Mayor. It's dark already, and if that animal gets out of town there'll be hell to pay. You know that, don't you?"

"I know it perfectly well. I also know we're not under martial law here. The civil authority still runs the city, and we're doing everything possible at the moment."

"And I've got up to a hundred armed men at the armory right now, Mr. Mayor, and more coming. That's why I called you, to get your permission to use them in conjunction with the police. Remember, if this beast kills or maims a citizen of Quassatuck and you haven't used every ounce of force available to you, the voters will be asking why."

For a moment there was silence on the other end of the line. Then the voice said, "All right, I suppose it's the only thing to do. I'll come over right away."

The mayor was bowing to pressure against his better

judgment. It was visible in his face when he arrived. He was a careful man and a good politician, but he knew when the civil authority had to bend.

Colonel Santoro's plans were already made in detail. With the men available he was able to place an automobile with two watchers at strategic points in a giant semi-circle around the city, from the river bank behind Northside Hill along the crest leading to East Side Hill and down across the flats at the southern end of town and to the riverbank again. Finally, with a car at each of the three bridges across the river, he was confident the belt around the city was complete. At dawn it would be drawn tight on Shere Khan.

It was ten o'clock, and the downtown streets were empty. Movie theaters, snack bars, taverns, teen-age haunts were all closed and their neon signs extinguished. The only automobiles moving belonged to workers required to be on the job at night, or to reservists driving to relieve an outpost, or to the silent police, prodding with searchlights like machine guns on their turrets into the shadowed alleys and streets of the tenement district.

Farther out from the center of town the wartime air raid wardens mobilized again for the emergency and checked their neighborhoods for stray dogs and cats and open doors and windows. The responsibility was partly theirs now, and from time to time one of them would get out of his car for a closer look. But none of them found a door or a window open. And no one saw Shere Khan the tiglon.

Night enveloped the city like an enormous glass dome, sealing it off from the world and fastening it to earth with tiny rivets set at the edge of the perimeter to insure the vacuum. It was as if the city were an insect colony under the observation of some invisible, enigmatic scientist watching it for the expected and inevitable response to his stimulus.

Once a light was thrown on in a tenement near the Bancroft main plant when Angelina Denzio heard a noise in the alley below. It had sounded to her like the lid of a garbage can falling to the sidewalk, and although this was an almost nightly event and one to which she had grown so accustomed that it no longer disturbed her sleep, this time she woke her husband up and made him go to the window. And even before she heard his answer she must have known what it would be—nothing but a cat maybe and why didn't she go back to sleep and leave him alone?

For this was an in-between time, a silent intermission. The city had been darkened by the blink of an eye, and not until the eye was opened would there be light to resume the hunt. So, couched in darkness, the people and their quarry waited.

7

Dawn, and now the hunt began in earnest. With the light behind them, the sun spilled over the rim of East Side Hill like molten brass, searing the slopes and flashing red against the windowpanes opposite. Men with weapons at the ready moved on the hillside, calling across lawns and back alleys to one another. There was no need for silence now, no fear lest they be observed by their hidden enemy, since this was a creature untutored against the devices of men. Boldness was its enemy's servant.

As the circle grew smaller, the commanding view of the city was lost. From the hilltops they descended into yards and cellars of neat middle-class dwellings, the homes of doctors and salesmen and office employees. They poked through toy-strewn lawns and banged into tool sheds, their fingers on the triggers of their weapons as the doors swung inwards. And they talked in loud voices even when together.

It was past eight o'clock now, and the sun was rising in the sky. Though not a trace of Shere Khan had been seen since his escape, each man proceeded as if his own weapon were pointed at the animal's body. The task was defined now, the evil identified and isolated; their job was to locate it and stamp it out. The doubts and the panic, the questions and the recriminations of the day before were gone, and the city of Quassatuck rallied around its armed defenders.

At dawn women in dressing gowns, their hair in curlers, had already been preparing coffee, serving it from back porches and shouting encouragement as the searchers passed through. No one doubted that Shere Khan was in the trap.

At the junction of North Main and South Main Streets, the center of town, Colonel Santoro halted his men. It was eight-thirty, and they had reached before them a broad arc of land crowded tight with buildings, churches, theaters, and shops. The flats themselves were cut by an east-west artery, extending from the river at Bridge Street up and over East Side Hill. East of Bridge Street was the Green and the city's main hotels, and to the south were City Hall, the business district, the railroad yards, most of the factories, the brass mills, and the zoo.

I watched the colonel divide his men. On the west side it would be easy. A few hundred yards down Bridge Street ran the river, and across it was the red sandstone promontory called Indian Rock, a barrier to escape in that direction for the tiglon. But southward along the river stretched over a mile of mills and workshops and tenements. The men north of Bridge Street would move south into that area.

The final ring was ready to be tightened. Through normally crowded business streets the hunters began to move, past small shops and department stores and markets. Beyond the freight yards and adjoining brass mills were rows of tenements, the remains of a hurried age when scores of them were thrown up to house or at least shelter the armies of new Americans, hands and shoulders for the makers of brass.

Then one of them found something. It was a cat, or the remains of a cat—a few bones and tufts of gray fur, possibly spat from the mouth of the killer.

"He's been here," the finder shouted.

They closed in now, working faster but in silence. They filled the streets and alleys along a broad front while families cheered them on from windows above their heads. Searching every alley, they found the remains of another small animal, then nothing more. I followed them through the streets, watching their exultation turn gradually to maddening frustration as they cursed the beast which seemed to have escaped them.

Finally, the colonel brought in his forces from the North End and ordered the entire area south of Bridge Street searched again. The guards remained at their post on street corners, but by noon the southern part of the city had been gone over more than once, and still there was nothing new. Parents were warned again to keep their children and pets indoors, for the danger was not yet past; it was still possible that the animal had slipped through somehow. And again as the afternoon progressed the city began to feel the oppression of fear. The hills were raked and the downtown area gone over once more, but without success.

Then at last someone suggested Symonds's Brook.

Symonds's Brook was now part of Quassatuck's sewer system. It flowed across the flats from East Side Hill and into the river between the zoo and the Bancroft main plant. But for most of the century, since the city's rapid growth in population and importance it had been built over, walled, piped into and ignored by all but the sanitation authorities. It was a receptacle for the waste products of people and factories, and though it remained structurally sound, the stench was such that even schoolboys on summer explorations never entered it. Polluted itself and polluting the river into which it flowed, with a heavy wire screen from before the war long since rusted and torn, the tunnel was now serving as Shere Khan's last redoubt.

None of those who gathered there could tell me why he had chosen it, electing to hide in a foul hole rather than make a break for open country. Whether he had tried and failed, or whether the very instinct which should have led him to freedom was somehow missing from his makeup, they could not guess.

They simply drew lots before the open sewer; four of them would go in. And as they moved down the embankment to the ledge by the tunnel's mouth they walked gingerly, as if the noise they had made before, ostensibly to frighten the beast, had really been only to bolster their own courage. Then on the ledge they saw where their prey had vomited, disgorging bits of alley cats with which it had tried to feed itself. They knew now that the animal was there and that it was sick.

"How about a light down here?" one of them called.

They stood waiting on the narrow walk, two with wartime semi-automatic weapons, two with shotguns, and even the slow summer trickle of foul water yellowing the river seemed to run cautiously now, soberly, in order not to disturb the scene as it departed.

"Hurry up with that light, will ya," cried another. "We can't stand this stench much longer."

But it was as if the searchlight were the last thing the sick beast could tolerate, crouched here in a hole not five hundred yards from its empty cage, as if it were the light and not merely the hunters' presence against which it would utter its final protest. Because the men had already been there for a long minute, peering with sun-blinded eyes into the hole from which it could easily see their outlines, and still it had not made a sound. Only when the other arrived, the one with the light, did Shere Khan move. And then, as the beam was directed at him at last, the eyes flashed yellow and the throat brought forth the snarl, rising as if not from inside his own body but rather from the depths of some forgotten well leading to the very center of the earth, roaring out of the tunnel at them deep and terrible, as if the universe itself had been disturbed and was sending out its warning.

It did not last. Before the first breath of it had reached its height it was interrupted, broken into, dispossessed by a bright, manufactured sound like a jackhammer tearing up a street, blasting without development or crescendo, filling the air with its repeated complaints, until the mouth of the tunnel was filled with its smoky exhalations and it stopped, spent, exhausted in a dry, metallic silence.

There was a final splash in the water far up the tunnel, and then nothing more. The searchlight sent its slicing beam through the smoke, along the ancient walls dripping with cobwebs and the damp accumulations of time. Then after a minute they made their way inside, along the flowing trough, and into the reek of the animal's vomit. They did not hesitate this time, for even standing at the entrance they could see when the smoke was gone that the beast was lying motionless on its side, with its head under the water.

8

Now it is finished; the hunt is over, Shere Khan is dead. On the cindered ground above the river, next to the wire fence which separates the Bancroft Brass Company from the zoo created out of its wealth, his body lies. And all of them who hunted him are here too, standing around his form, laughing at the death they have conquered, the fear and the evil which no longer threatens their lives. It seems small to them now, this stalking terror which has cost them their sleep; and in truth it is not large, seen laid out upon the ground. Its grace is gone, its hypnotic beauty and the brutal strength of its sinews. The yellow eyes are gone too, lost in a mass of chopped and formless meat which once housed all the cunning of its nature.

Now from behind the crowd a figure in gray has approached, walking slowly across the cinders, coming as if to give the last rites of some unconsecrated church. It is a man, tall and heavy-boned, his body still resilient despite the age which more than ever seems to define him. And as he draws near they step aside, making room in silent curiosity. They hear him speak as he comes among them, hearing his words to a subordinate before he has quite arrived in sight of the body.

"Perhaps, if the skin isn't too badly damaged," he says, "...or the head ... That would be something, at least."

Then he stops and gazes downward; and after a long moment slowly turns away. "No... I'm afraid not," he says, and is gone, an old man.

And some of them go too, satisfied now with the sight and knowledge that it is finished. And some of them linger to tell how it happened, who it was who thought of the sewer, and how the eyes looked from outside the tunnel as they fired, recounting in ever-expanding form the story of what has been an exciting day in their lives.

For it has been a day, and more. Already evening has come to them standing there, evening in Quassatuck. Over the rooftops of West Side Hill the sun has set, and a sky the color of rolled brass hangs over the city where Shere Khan, a creature of man's imagination, bastard hybrid half a world from his home, has yet for one day, even here in Quassatuck, proved himself the King of Beasts.

PONKATOKET'S PROFILE

M ost people in Quassatuck know something about our Indian Rock. Some even know there's a story, or a legend, telling us not only how it got its name but how it got its face too. Beyond that there is controversy, or just plain ignorance. Which is why I, Larry Gillis, reporter on the Quassatuck Clarion, have decided to try to set the record straight.

The Rock does have a face, you see, and it's clearly the face of an Indian. There is a kind of rough-cut profile looking south across the Mattapaug River from above the pile of loose red sandstone which supposedly fell on the day the features were laid bare. It doesn't take much imagination to visualize it. It's set just under the cliff top, where a tree-covered knob slopes downward to the west to complete the illusion of the old woodland Indian's crest of hair and single trailing feather. Furthermore, from the brass mills in the south end to Northside Avenue just across the river the view is good enough so that anyone looking at that long, jagged nose and slanting forehead, with the tight, lean lips and the rock-hard jaw, would say it was an Indian. Some even know the story well enough to call the Indian Ponkatoket.

So the question isn't the face itself but how it got there.

And that is why I wanted to write a feature story on the subject for *The Clarion*. My editor jumped at the idea, since the legend was an embarrassment to the town fathers, who wanted the story discredited and forever laid to rest. Why? Simply because it claimed our city of Quassatuck was living under the Sachem's curse.

No one believes in curses these days, you'll say. True enough. Yet even if only a few are believers, their words can damage a town's reputation at a time when Quassatuck needs all the boost it can get.

So here's the legend. To understand it you have to go back to a time when this city of brass was nothing but open fields rimmed by wooded ridges on all sides, with a small river cutting through from north to south. No profile, no face, no white men at all—just a tribe of Algonquin hunters who may have been there from the beginning of time, for all anyone knew. But their time was destined to come to an end in the year of blood which the white man, in honor of his god, called sixteen seventy-six.

Ponkatoket was their Sachem, the story goes. But the Reverend Joshua Symonds knew nothing of that, nor did Captain Amos Tate, his military commander. All they knew was what the scouts of the year before had told them, that there was a place several days' march up the river where the Lord had seen fit to put down some fairly fertile farm land. There was plenty of water from the river and from a brook emptying into the river from the east. And miraculously it was said to be almost bare of trees and without too many rocks beneath the soil.

This was enough for Symonds. Life in New Haven had been hard for him since the Restoration of 1660, which ended Cromwell's Puritan rule in England and in the colonies. Symonds's responsibilities to his congregation had forced him to stay in place while the regicide judges Whalley and Goffe hid in a cave on West Rock. But when news of the Lord's bounty had come to him, he hadn't hesitated a day. Now, the following summer and after a hard march during which two of his people had died, he stood on the south rim of the basin, with his hand extended toward the flat land before him, and spoke these words:

"Here, friends, we will build a new Jerusalem and raise a bulwark against the Kingdom of Antichrist!"

Joshua Symonds was a stubborn man. Persecution and exile for his beliefs had hardened his mind; for how else could he hold to doctrines others claimed were false? Restless already in Cromwell's England, he was ready to move on again rather than accept the new king's softer view of the world. So there was even less chance that such a man would permit the force of his will to be deflected by a heathen chieftain occupying the other end of the basin he, Symonds, had promised his flock.

The Sachem had surprised him, it seems, in those first days by coming down himself to their camp with a delegation of his braves across the brook dividing the flats in two, until he was face to face with Symonds and Tate.

"You are of those who live by the long river?" he asked, referring apparently to the Connecticut colony at Hartford.

"No, we come from the sea."

"And you wish to plant corn?"

"Yes."

"The land is good for corn. You plant corn on this side of the brook. My people will hunt on the other side. That way we will live in peace."

They smoked the pipe. But Symonds and Tate knew of the troubles in the Plymouth Colony, where Metacomet, son of Massasoit, dubbed "King Philip" by the English, was making war a generation too late to drive the white man from the continent. And they were preparing to defend themselves should the fighting spread this far to the west. Furthermore, both were immediately suspicious of an Indian so ignorant of the value of land that he would offer to give up half of such a basin to strangers. So Symonds insisted on a transfer of ownership by payment, and in writing, to which Ponkatoket, with an enigmatic smile, agreed.

But in the building of his New Jerusalem there were no plans in Symonds's mind for sharing with the heathen. So even after payment was made Symonds knew this to be a transaction only half completed.

Nevertheless, as a bargain it might have lasted for some time but for the war with King Philip. As it was, however, Symonds saw that his own position was anything but strong. Outnumbered two to one by the Indians and without a stockade, another man might have been conciliatory. But not Symonds. Before long, in pursuit of game the savages began to trespass on land bought and paid for by the settlers. And for this Symonds summoned Ponkatoket for an explanation.

The enigmatic smile returned to the Indian's face.

"I am sure you know of Metacomet, the one called Philip," Symonds told him in a confrontational tone.

"I am of the generation of Massasoit," he said. "The one you call Philip is a boy."

But something in the smile enraged Joshua Symonds.

"Do not laugh at me, Ponkatoket, while you send your braves to spy on us and prepare for war."

The smile left the Sachem's face, and the jaw hardened.

"The white man and I have smoked the pipe of peace," was all he said. And no threat of Symonds or Tate could get another word from him. They watched him cross the field where the summer's corn had been harvested and saw him ford the brook without slackening his pace and reenter his village.

"Our position here is untenable," Amos Tate warned Symonds. "If we are attacked, we'll have no chance to defend ourselves. Besides, he controls our water supply from both the river and the brook."

But now a look of mystic certainty came into Symonds's eyes. "We shall not be attacked here," he said. "The Lord has placed us among these heathen to test our faith. We shall trust in His power."

They trusted, but they took steps to defend themselves. By the time of the first snowfall Tate had brought them to as near a state of readiness as any man could. The crops were harvested, a kind of stockade had been erected, and with a little help from the Almighty they expected to last out the winter.

Yet doubt continued to haunt the mind of Joshua Symonds. On almost any winter's day he could watch the Indians tracking game or setting traps in the snow, and on the Sabbath they desecrated the day by dancing and hurling their heathen cries at Heaven. This blasphemy Symonds considered a greater threat to his community than the force of arms.

Incidents occurred. A settler accidentally shot an Indian while hunting rabbits. He was seized and only managed to escape with his life, losing gun and powder horn in the confusion. Ponkatoket protested and was dismissed with a curse by Tate, who feared the advantage a firearm would give the savages. Then a quantity of corn disappeared from the stockade, and though it was proved that the guard had been asleep, the same guard swore it was Indians who had stolen it. And when Tate demanded entry into the Indians' village to search for the corn, Ponkatoket denied him the privilege, merely repeating the words they had come to know. "I have smoked the pipe of peace with the white man."

For several months the community had felt itself without a spiritual leader, for Joshua Symonds had become preoccupied with the conflicts within his own soul. A dark pessimism filled his sermons. His words seemed addressed not to his flock but to an angry God. They sensed only a wariness, even an evasiveness, in his words to them.

Finally, however, with the coming of spring and the breakup of ice in the Mattapaug River, the pressures within Symonds broke through, and he seemed to come to a decision. "There is an accursed thing in the midst of thee, O Israel!" he cried. "Thou canst not stand before thine enemies until thou takest away the accursed thing from amongst thee!" And with this warning from Scripture, he declared a day of general fasting to permit each member to search deep in his soul for the evil which had given the heathen power over them, after which he declared them purged and ready to attack the evil without.

If Symonds had had his way, the attack would have taken place immediately, while the settlers were aflame with the fervor of his sermons. But Tate's more realistic counsel dissuaded him.

"They still outnumber us," he warned. "Let us wait at least until the others arrive."

The others were a group from the Connecticut colony who had begun their journey from Hartford, and since the prospect of an almost doubled force was a strong argument, Symonds agreed to wait.

But half of the new ones never arrived. They were massacred along the way by a party of King Philip's men. And with this news the light of mystic assurance glowed once more in Symonds's eyes. "We can wait no longer," he said. "God's will has been made manifest to us."

There were two parties, the story goes, in the force which the settlers gathered that evening. Symonds led the first, and Tate led the second. And according to the account, the routes they took are commemorated today in the very names of the streets which follow them: Tate Street, which leads up the west bank of the river under Indian

Rock, and Symonds Street, which runs north past the Green and into the old residential district on the north ridge. At a signal the parties were to converge on the the village and set their fires.

They worked rapidly and well. A good half of the huts were in flames before a single Indian could give warning. It is doubtful that few were able to escape, and Ponkatoket himself was taken prisoner. At noon the following day they stood him with hands and feet bound on a tree stump in the charred ruins of his village and judged him. His ancient face, with the Rock outlined in the distance behind it, seemed even then to be engraved in the stone. And with his voice low at first and rising slowly, he spoke to them and gave them this curse.

"It belongs to you now, white men," the story has him say. "You have taken for yourselves what none of us had ever thought to claim, and where we welcomed you when you were weak.

"But hear me now, O men whose blackness of dress cannot hide your blackness of heart, for this is my curse. My people are dead, and though you kill me too, we will remain here to watch you betray each other as you betrayed us. Son against father, brother against brother, generation after generation, until the blood of treachery is thin in your veins and you are destroyed by others stronger and more treacherous than you. Hear my words, for this is my curse on those who would possess for themselves what all were meant to share."

They killed him quickly, the story goes, without torture. And being practical men, they set out immediately to occupy and clean up the burnt village. For they had already agreed on this as a better site for their New Jerusalem than their original settlement south of what we now call Symonds's Brook. In fact, it is said that the northeast corner of the Green, where hundreds of people now pass every day, is the exact spot on which Ponkatoket was judged and stood, just as it remains the heart of the city today.

But then the rain began to fall. And before they realized it was more than the ordinary cloudburst rolling up and down the valley at this time of year, Symonds's Brook and the river itself were mad torrents, and they were seeking cover anywhere an Indian hut was left to cover them. But the storm, instead of passing, grew only worse, with flashes of lightning illuminating a gray wall of water and the crashing of thunder beyond the ridge.

In fact, it was morning before the last thunderclap had struck and the rain had subsided and they were able to look out into the sunlight of the new day and see, high above the cinders of the Indian village and set like a brooding god in the naked rock, the same ancient profile which the day before they had destroyed, graven deep in the red sandstone now and for all time.

"Idolatry!" Joshua Symonds cried when he saw the awed faces of his flock. "It means nothing. It is an accident, a coincidence. How could a savage accomplish any such feat? And why are you gaping at it like fools? Do I have to destroy it myself to prove to you it means nothing?"

Which is what he supposedly set out to do. And here the legend becomes even more preposterous, for it has Joshua Symonds, that dour Puritan divine, attempting to scale the face of Indian Rock and knock away the features of old Ponkatoket with an axe. What's more, it is anything but clear as to what happened next, whether the trouble was overexertion or whether he simply lost his foothold as he hacked away. It only quotes a purported document of the time (which nobody has ever located) stating that, before the eyes of his entire congregation, the Reverend Joshua

Symonds "did receive such a blow to his chest as did send him backward down ye side of ye cliffe, which, if ye same blow had not already done so, did kill him outright."

And that is all, if you can believe it. I didn't, but some may yet, and that is why I set out to disprove it, lay the ghost of Ponkatoket and free the city of the false curse put upon it.

I began my search at the Public Library, where many dusty old volumes talked of everything but a curse. In fact, they followed the legend up to the signing of a deed ceding the entire basin to the settlers (a deed never found, incidentally), after which a benevolent Ponkatoket was said to have moved on with his people. The face on Indian Rock was left as a simple memorial of his time there, even a blessing to the new owners of his village of Quassatuck— a name the settlers gladly gave it as a token of their gratitude.

This version of our origin is, of course, the one preferred by succeeding town fathers. But disproving the other turned out to be less difficult than I had feared. I moved on to the Quassatuck Historical Society, where among dusty boxes of unsorted records in the basement I finally found what I was looking for—a ten-page manuscript left with the owner of a boarding house by one of her tenants. It was all there on paper, carefully written down in a painful scrawl in one of those blue and red-lined ledgers clerks were using before the advent of the typewriter. The author apparently was someone more used to writing figures than complete sentences, much less historical accounts, and it bore no signature. Attached to it, however, was a note in another handwriting which said: "This was found in the room of one of my boarders, Mr. Dudley Fenwick. He left town six months ago without no forwarding address. As he has not come back to claim it, I am giving it to you. I can't speak to the truth of what it says, though it may mean something to you." The note was signed by the landlady and dated 1885.

With this I was well on my way, and before long I'd learned a lot about Mr. Dudley Fenwick. It seems his family, which went back to colonial times though not to the original Symonds party, had owned a small machine shop before the Civil War. Dudley was the eldest of three brothers. The other two, in their own words, had gone off "to fight Johnny Reb" and had left Dudley to run the business and care for their mother. After the war the brothers had sold their share of the property to Dudley and had gone west, vowing not to stop while there was land in front of their feet. They'd left him the very things he thought they'd been fighting for: the old frame house on the hill opposite Indian Rock and the machine shop which even in wartime he hadn't managed to make profitable. Far from any thought of returning to a smoky mill town in Connecticut, they intended to free themselves for good.

So Dudley stayed and proved that he was no better a businessman after the war than during it. Having borrowed heavily to buy out his brothers, within five years he'd seen the machine shop go bankrupt and its equipment go for a song to Nate Jessup the brass manufacturer. Then a few years later the old house also went to Jessup for half its value, whereupon Dudley took his mother to live in a rooming house on the south side of town in an area any fool could see was destined for industrial expansion. And sure enough, Jessup's new rolling mill went up a few yards from their door.

But this time they didn't move. Dudley by now was working as a clerk at the Bancroft Brass Company (Jessup's deadly rival, it was said, though the two were brothers-in-law). And since the street car to his job went by the front door, he and his mother just stayed. It was hot in the summer and cold in the winter, and the air wasn't what they'd known in their old house on the hill. But they didn't have much choice. He was almost sixty by now and was known as a recluse and generally antisocial. He was on speaking terms with almost no one, and was convinced they were all out to cheat him. In any case, a few days after his mother was buried he left the manuscript and walked out the front door and was never heard from again.

So it wasn't hard to imagine how Dudley Fenwick had twisted the legend of Ponkatoket's Profile to make it a vessel for his accumulated resentments against society in general and Nate Jessup in particular. The old sachem's curse on Quassatuck was in reality nothing but Dudley Fenwick's curse on Jessup and anyone else who might have cheated him.

With that I'd solved the mystery and thought myself the savior of Quassatuck's fortunes and its good name. I wrote it up as a Sunday feature for *The Clarion* and handed it to my editor, sure I'd receive a commendation and thanks from City Hall. I waited a week, then two weeks, before I ventured to ask my editor what he thought of it. After all, it wasn't news, just a feature, and there was no pressure to publish it right away. So my query when it came carried no anxiety at all, only impatience that the congratulations I expected were a bit late in coming.

"Nothing wrong with it that I can see," he told me with a more friendly smile than I usually got from him. "It's clear, well-written, and shows you've done some digging to get at the truth. I just thought I'd pass it up the line for the bosses to see. I'm sure it'll be what they wanted."

"When do you think I'll know?" I asked.

"Can't say. Depends on how much time they'll have to read it. They're busy men, you know."

"I know they are. But you told me they really liked the idea. In that case I'd think they'd want to see it published."

"They do. I told you that. Now don't get excited. You'll know as soon as I do. In the meantime, you've got other items piling up on your desk. I suggest you get busy on them."

Was I getting the run-around? It looked that way. But for the life of me I couldn't figure out why. I went back to my desk, but the thing bothered me, and I had to tear up another story I was working on three times before I got it right. What was it the town fathers didn't like?

I must have agonized over Ponkatoket's Profile for two weeks before I mentioned it to co-worker Pat Gorman, an old hand at the game who knew where most of the bodies were buried.

"Sure, I've read it," he said, "and it's a damned good job. No, I don't know the truth behind the delay, but if I were you, I'd ask myself a question or two. For instance, what's your headline? NO CURSE ON QUASSATUCK? Or SLANDER ON CITY EXPOSED. Maybe just the mention of a curse is bad luck. I'll bet you half of the town has never heard of a curse, so why bring it up in the first place?"

"But they encouraged me," I said. "They wanted the truth, and I found it for them. It was just a disgruntled loser named Fenwick. What's wrong with that."

Gorman heaved a sigh. "OK, Larry, let me give it to you straight. But if you say I told you, I'll deny it and call you a liar. Reason Number One: It shows Nate Jessup for what he was: a coldblooded SOB with grandiose ambitions for himself and his family. You've seen Overlook, haven't you? It's the biggest, gaudiest pile of junk of any of the houses on Northside Hill. He bought and tore down an old farmhouse and broke Dud Fenwick's heart just so he could have the best view in town of the Indian Rock."

"But Jessup is dead, and so are all the other Jessups."

"Maybe so, but they were top dog once, and they were related to the Bancrofts. These people stick together, in death as in life. Then there's the curse."

"What about the curse?"

"Your research didn't go that far, did it? Fenwick's curse was on Jessup, not on the town. And Jessup had a stroke within a year of moving into his new house. He died in a nursing home. So anyone reading your piece and knowing what happened to Nate Jessup would say the curse did work. What do you think?"

I was dumbfounded. Instead of refuting the curse, I was actually reinforcing it. If I'd looked deeper, I might have found more about the Jessups. The name may be gone, but who were the other ones, and what happened to them? Were they victims of the curse too? No wonder my piece would never appear in *The Clarion*. I'd uncovered something no one wanted to talk about, or have known.

Yes, I told myself, but the story should be told anyway, as a part of the history of Quassatuck.

So here it is, at least a part of it. And we don't know any more about a curse than we did at the beginning. Can a city like Quassatuck live under a curse, or not? Of course it can. The histories of half of the cities on this globe testify to that fact.

So bear up, Quassatuck. You're no worse or better off than any other town. You may not be "a bulwark against the kingdom of Antichrist," but the others aren't either. So it's time for you to join them and work together for the common good. We're all part of the same universe.

Besides, in the years since these events took place the legend has occasionally come back to life, once when the local TV station got the idea of interviewing passersby live and at random at the northeast corner of the Green. The first person they asked was a man one look at whose face would have told me to pick someone else. But this interviewer, a novice just as I'd been once, went right ahead anyway.

The man obviously was in a hurry and in no mood for levity. But it was too late. "What curse? What face?" he asked as the direct feed was picked up by half of the TVs in the city. "I've lived here all my life, and there's no face in that rock that I can see—and no curse that I know of. Now if you guys on TV would stop digging up folklore and find a way to bring business back to Quassatuck, instead of spinning tales for a tourist trade that doesn't exist, you'd do us all a favor. As for your program, I never watch it. Haven't got time for such nonsense."

THE TREE CLIMBERS

Frenchy out of Maine

Frenchy come down out of Maine about the time we was fixing to clear the lines for the electric light company. He walked into the yard one morning just as we was getting the trucks out. He was a little guy, no higher than your shoulder and he come all dressed for work, with boots on and gloves and his belt with a hook on it. None of us had ever seen him before.

"Any of you fellows know where the boss might be?"

"Back there in his office," I told him.

"Thanks." He hoisted his pants up and walked back across the yard. I ought to say he bounced because when Frenchy walked it was with a bouncing step like a bird trying to fly for the first time.

"Looks like he might make a good climber," I said to Whitey.

"Then he come at the right time," Whitey said. "The old man needs a good climber for this job."

Now this was in the days before cherry-pickers, so the old man needed good climbers for most every job. He had a contract to trim trees where there was wires so the first ice storm wouldn't knock branches down over the lines.

Well, a couple of minutes later him and Frenchy come walking out of the office together, the old man slow and heavy and Frenchy small and light and hopping alongside him.

"Maybe I can work you in somewheres," the old man's saying. "Come back in three or four days, say Monday morning. By that time I may have room for you."

"Monday's next week," says Frenchy. "I'm ready to work today. That's what I come in early for."

"Well, I ain't got no place for you today."

The old man thought he had Frenchy where he wanted him, so he was going to let him wait a few days and save on his pay.

But that didn't satisfy Frenchy. "I come because I heard you needed a climber right away," he says.

"I'm gonna need one, that's right. Come back on Monday. There'll be plenty of work then. I can't use you when there's no work, can I? I ain't got that kind of money."

The old man was talking poor now. That's how he got to be one of the richest guys in town.

"Well," says Frenchy, "I guess I'll be movin' on to some place else then. I can't be waitin' till next week for work." And he started to walk off.

The old man stood there watching him go. You could see it hurt him, but he hated to let anyone talk him down, especially in front of us. Finally he calls him back. "Hey, wait a minute. I'll see what I can do."

Frenchy stopped and turned around slowly without making a move to come back. The old man called Mac the foreman, and the two of them talked together, low so none of us could hear. Then he motioned to Frenchy with his head. "Come on back."

Frenchy walked over to him slow and easy.

"You got your lunch?"

"Right here." Frenchy held up a paper bag.

"Then you go with Mac today. We'll see how you make out."

And the old man turns and goes back to his office so the rest of us can't watch him after he's caved in.

And that's how Frenchy come to work for us. We was sure he wouldn't give us no trouble as a climber. But he'd made the old man look bad, and so we figured Mac would have to put it to him the first day. It turned out we was right on both counts.

Frenchy sure did know how to climb a tree. We had half the streets in town to cover, and that meant mostly small maples and sycamores along the sidewalks where they grew up into the wires. Sometimes they was young trees that just had to be cut back every year so they'd have to find a way out and around the wires if they wanted to keep growing. And sometimes they was big trees and the wires was just growing through the middle of them, so that when we cut back the branches around the wires you could stand down the street and see a hole big enough to drive a car through.

"All right, Frenchy, pick a tree and a pole for yourself," said Mac.

We had seven poles on that truck. One of them was just a hook to pull down branches hanging in the trees, but the others all had cutting edges that you worked by pulling the string at one end to shut the blade at the other end. Three of them was ordinary pruners, and the other three we called bullpoles because they had more leverage and could cut a heavier branch.

Frenchy took one of the pruners and worked it in his hands, and then he took the longest one, which was about twelve feet, and tried it and said:

"Think I'll use this here one for a while."

"Why don't you take a pullpole, Frenchy?" says Whitey. "Some of them branches is pretty tough."

Frenchy worked the blade on his pruner back and forth. "This here one looks pretty good. Think I'll just try it a while."

He walked over to a Norway maple and hung his hook on one of the branches as far up as he could reach. Then he give a jump and swung himself up onto the lowest branch. It wasn't a jump that any of us couldn't do if we had to, but Frenchy made it look so easy that I and Whitey had no doubt he could climb a tree—at least a small one.

"How much clearance you want around the wires?" he called down.

"Make it about two feet, and watch out for the primaries," Mac said.

"Right," said Frenchy, and that was the last time he said anything while he worked in that tree.

When he come down the wires was clear all around, and the tree was trimmed back so that it looked like a cake with a big piece out of it. Frenchy was standing on the ground pulling down the cut branches with his pole.

"You can leave all them hangers there," Mac told him. "Henry'll pull them down and pile them. That's what he's here for."

Henry was a guy that had been working on trees only a short time and didn't seem to know much about them. He was a coal miner from Pennsylvania that had got sick working underground and switched to trees. But the old man wouldn't let him climb no more because he'd had a couple of falls, and so he just stayed on as ground man, walking along under the trees and pulling out the hangers and piling the brush so we could pick it all up easy and load it on the truck. And even for that Henry wasn't much good, and none of the crews liked to have him with them if there was a hard job to do.

"OK, I'll take that there sycamore down the street," said Frenchy.

"Wait a minute," Henry said. "Lemme bring you the ladder. That's what ladders is for."

"Don't need no ladder for that there tree," says Frenchy.

Henry looked at him a minute and said, "Kid, what're you tryin' to do, talk me out of a job?"

Frenchy grinned. "Go ahead and bring me a ladder if you want. Maybe I'll need one, at that."

That's how it was all the rest of the morning. At noon, Mac said to Frenchy, "Let Henry do some work for you, even if you don't need him. He ain't got much else to do. Only watch out he don't make no mistakes and give you trouble. He's pretty dumb that way."

"Don't worry," said Frenchy. "I'm used to that. Got a kid brother up in Maine worked for me as ground man. He always give me trouble. Fell outa a sugar maple when he was small and ain't been the same since. I left him home till I been down here long enough to see what's what."

"Then you know how to handle Henry," says Mac. "Ever use a power saw?"

Frenchy's eyes lit up. "Sure have."

"Then I got a good job for you this afternoon. There's an old elm on the corner of Main Street that's got a branch hanging over a building. Maybe you can take it off for us. No one else wants to try."

Mac was testing Frenchy now, the way the old man must have told him to. He could see Frenchy was good in a small tree and he must have figured if he could handle this elm he could do most anything. Only Frenchy didn't know how big this elm was.

"Ellum?" he says. "Sure, I climbed plenty ellums up in Maine. We grow 'em big up there—the ones that's left after the disease, that is. Easy climbin' if you're crotched in right."

"This one's pretty big, Frenchy."

"That don't matter, once you're up in it."

"OK, take a look at it this afternoon and tell me what you think of it."

When we'd finished eating and got back on the truck, Mac drove us to where this elm was. There's still a few elms in town even though the Dutch elm disease got most of them, but I'd never seen a bigger one than this one. It seemed a good eight feet around the trunk, and you had to go up pretty close to twenty feet before you come to the first leader.

When he seen it, Frenchy whistled once through his teeth and took a walk around the trunk. He walked twice around it, with his hands on his hips, looking up. Then he whistled again.

"Yessir, that there's a purty big ellum."

"Bigger than any you've ever seen up in Maine, I'll bet."

"Wouldn't say that," says Frenchy slowly. "Nope, wouldn't say that. But I will say it's the biggest ellum I ever seen down here."

Mac looked at him. Frenchy was a lot smaller than Mac, so maybe Mac didn't think too much of the old man's idea of putting it to him the first day.

"Tell you what I'll do, Frenchy," he said. "Seeing this is your first day on the job, I'll send one of the other boys up. I shouldn't oughta send you up in a big tree anyhow till you've had time to get used to the lines."

Frenchy turned on him. "You got plenty of lines here, ain't you? Well, I'll just pick me out one I like and go on up. What's wrong with that?"

"Better not, Frenchy," says Mac. "You might get hurt. How do I know you can climb a tree that size?"

"I'm gettin' climber's pay, ain't I?"

"Yeah, but that ain't for trees this big." Mac was on the spot now. Seeing that big elm made him think twice. A man could get killed in a tree like that if he didn't know his business. "How about if I let you take the next one?" he said finally. "I'll give this one to Whitey."

Now Frenchy got mad. "Well, if this ain't the craziest outfit I ever see. You tell a man to climb a tree, an' when he gets to it you change your mind. Think what I better do is collect my pay this evenin' and move on to where they know what they want."

"Now wait a minute, Frenchy," says Mac. "I didn't say you couldn't climb it. I just said you don't have to."

"Well, I'm ready to climb it. What you got to say about that?"

"OK, OK. Don't get excited. Climb it if you want to. It's your funeral."

So Frenchy got his chance to climb that big elm. He picked himself a good climbing line out of the box on the side of the truck, untied it and tried it in his hands to make sure the rope was soft. Then he tied himself a saddle out of one end and took and hung the rest over his shoulder. Next he got himself a hand saw and a paint pot to paint the cut with and clipped them both to his belt. Finally he looked up at the tree again and said, "You ain't got a ladder long enough to reach that there first leader. You better back the truck up against the tree."

The truck had a fireman's ladder on it that you could turn at any angle and run up further than the other ladders would go. It wouldn't reach high enough to get him into the tree but from the end of it he could throw his rope into a crotch. So while Mac moved the truck into position and Henry ran the ladder up as far as it would go, Frenchy took another walk for himself around the tree. He stood back looking from all angles at the leader that had to come off. It was a big one, and it was dead at the end. It looked like a good windstorm might drop pieces of it down onto the wires underneath. It'd have to come off, right back flush against the trunk, even though some of it was still alive.

"Watch out that leader don't break under you," I said.
"It won't break," he said. "A live ellum don't snap off.
Just kinda splits and twists off."

"Here's your power saw," says Mac.

Henry untied the saw from the back of the truck and
brought it over. Frenchy looked at it. "I seen that kinda
saw before," he said. "Used 'em many a time up in Maine."

It was a small saw with the chain running out about a
foot from the motor. It had a handle on each side so you
could work it from any angle, and at the back it had a grip
like a machine gun with a trigger to make the chain run.
Mac took the can of gas and filled the tank.

"We'll send this up when you're ready for it," he said.
"you better leave a butt about two foot long so's you won't
rip the bark on the trunk. You can flush it off afterwards."

"You tellin' me how to take a leader off a tree?" Frenchy
asked.

"I'm telling you I don't want the bark off the trunk,"
said Mac, getting hotter. "And I don't want no stubs
dropped on the sidewalk neither. You got plenty rope to
let down easy everything you cut."

Frenchy smiled. "You watch how we do it up in Maine."

He climbed the truck ladder and took the line off his
shoulder. Then he took all the loops, one at a time, in his
right hand and, still holding the saddle in his left, hooked
his leg over the top rung and give the rope a toss. It sailed
right over the leader he was aiming at. Then he flipped the
line to make the rope move over the leader and let down
the end. When he saw he still couldn't reach it, he yelled
down: "Shoot me up that there hanger pole, will ya?"

I tossed him the pole. He reached out with it and pulled
the end of the rope in and dropped the pole down to me
again. Then he got into the saddle he'd made out of the
other end of the rope and pulled it on like a woman pulls
on a corset. After that he put a slip knot into the rope in

front of him and tugged on it to see if the rope would hold him. Then he jumped off the ladder.

He hit the trunk with his feet, worked the slip knot between his fingers and pulled himself up to the leader. A couple seconds later he was standing in the crotch, and by that time we knew Frenchy could climb any tree.

He tossed his rope over another leader higher up to hold his weight while he walked out on the one he was going to cut. Near the end of it he kicked at the dead ends and knocked them off. They bounced down onto the street and crumbled into powder as they hit.

"I told you not to drop no stubs on the sidewalk," said Mac.

"Them ain't stubs," said Frenchy. "Them's just rot."

"Take off the small branch first," yelled Mac. Mac was sore, and he was worried, but he still wanted to show he was boss. So he ignored Frenchy's back talk. "Here's a hand line," he said.

He tossed the line over the leader in front of Frenchy's feet. Frenchy took it and threw it over the leader above him and tied the end to the piece he was going to cut. Then he cut it with his hand saw, and Mac let it down to the ground. They did the same with another branch, Mac still holding one end of the hand line to let it down. When Frenchy was ready to make a big cut with the power saw, Mac said, "Tie the hand line around the end of the leader. I'll send up a bull line for the butt."

He tied the heavy bull line to the hand line, and Frenchy pulled it up and tied it where he was going to make his cut.

They worked pretty good together, the two of them, even though they argued a lot. I and Whitey and Henry stood there watching. We had flags out in the street so no cars would come by, and people began to stop and look up at Frenchy. A guy coming out of the drug store stopped, and then a woman with a kid, and pretty soon there was a crowd, all watching Frenchy up in that big elm.

Mac sent the power saw up on a rope, and by that time there was so many lines hanging down from that tree that a kid asked me how we knew which one was which. "On this kind of job, sonny," I told him, "you got to know what you're doing." The kid looked at me with admiration, and I knew then we was a good crew.

The power saw made a noise like an outboard motor, and that brought more people to watch. By now we had one bull line wrapped around the trunk near the ground, with me and Whitey holding it. The other line was around a tree across the street, so Henry could help let the butt down easy. He even had a couple of wraps around his arm, but I thought nothing of that. He didn't look too sharp but he was paying attention for once. As for Frenchy, he had a good grip on the power saw, with the weight of it hanging from the limb above. Then he started his cut.

The saw eating into the wood made a racket like an airplane. The sawdust come down like snow, and up above it you could see Frenchy, his legs wrapped around the leader like he was on horseback, leaning into the cut.

It was a quick cut. The lines sprung tight when the leader dropped, and all of us dug in our heels and hung on.

"OK, let it down easy," says Mac. "Hold on tight, Henry."

We let the butt down slow until it hung straight up and down. Then Henry loosened his line too, and in a minute that whole leader was on the ground. It was as big around as Frenchy himself and four times as long, and there was Frenchy sitting and swinging his legs on what was left of that big leader, riding it like it was a hobby horse. He was grinning like a kid.

"That's the way we do it up in Maine," he called down to the crowd. One of them cheered and waved and then all of them waved, and Frenchy waved back.

"Take it easy, Frenchy," Mac yelled when the cheering stopped. "You still gotta flush off that stub."

"I know it. Send me back that there line so I can put a tie around the stub."

Mac untied the end of Henry's line from the leader and tied it to one of Frenchy's lines. Frenchy pulled the line up, and Mac called over his shoulder to Henry, "Better take a couple of good wraps around your tree. That stub'll be heavy."

"Sure," says Henry. But none of us was watching him; we was watching Frenchy put a tie on the stub and swing himself back against the trunk to make his cut. And that's where we made our mistake. But you couldn't be watching Henry all the time, and you didn't want to miss seeing what Frenchy was doing.

Frenchy had the power saw going again and was flushing off the cut. Now when you do that, you got to cut straight along the line of the main branch so that afterwards it's just as smooth as if there never was a branch there. You can't leave a lip of wood sticking out, and you can't let the stub rip the bark off the trunk. So you've got to work slow. But Frenchy was showing how fast he could do it, and that's why Mac and us and maybe Henry wasn't paying attention to anything else.

Then Frenchy give the yell we expected: "Here she comes!"

And like the rest of us he was expecting to see happen what was supposed to happen: the stub dropping a couple inches and coming tight against Henry's bull line and the tree where he had it wrapped around the trunk.

But that's not what happened. The stub dropped all right, and the line come tight for a minute. But that stub must have weighed a couple hundred pounds, and so instead of stopping there it bounced once and just kept right on going. We seen Frenchy's mouth come open as he looked down the line, and when we looked over at Henry we could see why. Either Henry didn't take enough wraps around that tree trunk, or else he didn't take none at all. But one thing he did do was take a few wraps around his arm. So what we seen was Henry come sliding across the street with his heels out, trying to stop that stub, and the stub that weighed a good deal more than Henry coming down and pulling him up at the same time.

The stub didn't weigh so much more than Henry that he went up fast, but fast enough so that I missed him and fell flat on my face when I tried to grab him. Mac was yelling, "Drop, Henry!", but that was the one thing he couldn't do on account of how the rope was wrapped around his arm. And maybe that was a good thing too, because if he had, the stub on the other end of the line would have dropped on top of him.

As it was, it didn't take the stub long to pass Henry on the way down, and before you knew it there it was on the street and Henry was hanging from the line forty feet up and swinging back and forth in front of Frenchy's face.

"Here, grab ahold of me and come down against the trunk," we hear Frenchy say.

And Henry answering back, "Hell, no. I ain't no tree climber."

And Frenchy: "Well, now's your chance to learn."

And Henry, real stubborn: "I'm stayin' right here."

"That's just what you ain't doin'," Frenchy says. And the next thing we see there's Frenchy swinging out on his own line and grabbing the bull line just over Henry's head. Then he lets his own line go slack and yells, "Hang on, Henry!" and down comes the two of them the way Henry went up. Frenchy was light, but together with Henry he weighed more than the stub, and so a couple seconds later they both pass it on its way back up again. And when they reach the sidewalk, there's that stub right up where it started from.

Henry had a pretty sore arm after that, and Frenchy was a kind of hero. People cheered and clapped their hands at him.

"I'll bet that's one thing you never done up in Maine," says Mac when we had the stub down again.

"I wouldn't say that," says Frenchy, "but I will say up in Maine I never had no audience watchin' and applaudin'."

So from that day on Frenchy was part of our crew. It was also the day Henry quit to go back to coal mining in Pennsylvania, which left a job open as ground man for Frenchy's brother Bub. But that's another story.

One more thing, and we didn't know if Mac was putting it to Frenchy or not when he said, "So now all you gotta do is climb back up there and paint that cut."

But Frenchy didn't bat an eye. "I'm goin'. But I ain't messin' around with no truck ladders and all that foolishness. You fellows just untie the line from that there stub so I can make a saddle out of it. Then you can haul me up to where I can paint the cut and then let me down again— easy."

And that's how we done it. And Mac never put it to Frenchy again after that.

Brother Bub

Frenchy loved that power saw. He loved the yellow cover and the roar like an outboard motor, and he loved the feel of the weight in his hands. Whenever there was a good-size cut to make with the power saw or a big leader to drop past some wires, it was always Frenchy got the job. He'd look it over first from the ground, walk around the tree two or three times, judge the weight of the leader and its angle from the trunk and then decide just how he wanted it to fall and what he'd have to do to make it fall that way. He never made up his mind before he finished his calculations, but once his mind was made up not even Mac could change it.

Mac was foreman, and he knew how to take down a tree. But he never insisted on having Frenchy do it his way. They might argue about it for a while, but it always ended up with Mac letting Frenchy do it the way he wanted. Then, just to have the last word, Mac would say, "OK, do it your way. But you bust them wires it'll be your neck."

"Ain't bustin' no wires," Frenchy would tell him, "not if I put a bull line in that there crotch. You just get that power saw up to me when I call for it, an' I'll show you how we do it up in Maine."

Then Frenchy would walk around the tree one last time to make sure he was right, and finally, without once taking his eyes off the tree, he'd spit, untie his line, make a saddle out of one end to throw over his shoulder and whistle for Bub to bring the ladder and the saw.

Bub was ground man, and he was Frenchy's kid brother. But to look at them, you'd never know the two of them was anything to each other at all. Frenchy was small and he was quick, and he did everything with his arms. He had the strongest arms for his body of any man in the outfit. But with Bub it was the other way around. Bub was a big guy that couldn't climb a tree to save his life. Frenchy told us once when they was kids up in Maine Bub fell out of a sugar maple on his head and that was what was wrong with him. It may be Frenchy was just kidding about that part, but there wasn't no doubt Bub was dumb. He was the dumbest guy on the crew and then some. When he come to work a couple of weeks after Frenchy, the old man seen how dumb he was and didn't want to hire him. But Frenchy wasn't scared of the old man.

"Bub goes with me," he said. "He come down here because you been sayin' you ain't got men enough. Well, him 'n me is together. If he don't work, I don't work."

The old man was hard up for climbers right then. It was October, and he had work to do on maples before they filled up with sap and couldn't be cut. He knew he couldn't do it without Frenchy, and so he had to hire Bub too as ground man. A ground man don't need much brains, he figured, and what little Bub had might be enough, at least if he put the two of them together.

Frenchy and Bub was funny to watch. They worked together and they lived together, and still they didn't get along. Frenchy would come to work some mornings with Bub following behind him and neither one of them saying a word. Then Bub would start talking to us loud and friendly while he was getting the truck out, and Frenchy would say to him, "Go lay down in the back of the truck. Ain't no room for you up in front." And afterwards one of us would say, joking, "Maybe we better tie Bub down with the ladders back there so he won't fall out and land on his head and hurt himself."

Frenchy would just snort at that. "Can't think of anythin' that'd do him more good," he'd say. "Might knock some sense into him."

As a general rule, Frenchy wasn't really mad at Bub all the time. He got mad when Bub got them both into trouble, but afterwards everything was all right again. It was just that Bub did something stupid so often that Frenchy hardly ever had time to start feeling good afterwards before he'd have to get mad all over again. The time Bub let go of the bull line and the big stub dropped onto the sidewalk from thirty feet up and cracked the cement was bad enough. The only one in the way that time was Bub himself, and he come so close to getting hit on the head that every time after that Frenchy told him it was too bad the stub missed. But then the time Bub was chopping up a leader Frenchy had just dropped and chopped through Frenchy's line by mistake, so that when Frenchy went to haul it up to make another tie all he got was about fifteen feet of rope with the end cut clean, well, that time Frenchy really was mad. It was his best line, and he'd been working on it for a month to make it soft, and now he had to splice it. Him and Bub didn't say one word to each other for the rest of that day, and that was why the next afternoon, when something really did happen, Bub was standing there the whole time and didn't dare open his mouth.

It was getting toward the end of October, and most of the leaves was on the ground. We was working along a street that was pretty well out of town, and the trees was mostly maples, with a few sycamores and now and then an elm. Frenchy's job was taking a leader off an old maple that was growing up past the wires. We'd already cleared the wires, and the tree had a hole in the middle of it that looked like a cannonball had went through it. But there was this leader now growing out over the street, and somehow, in a storm maybe, it had split and had to come off.

"You mean we brung out the power saw for just that there one leader?" Frenchy asked Mac when he seen the tree.

"You wanta take it off with the hand saw?" Mac asked.

"Didn't say that. Just askin'. Don't worry, the old man'll get his money's worth outa me."

Frenchy knew any big leader was a job for the power saw, at least officially. And he knew the old man got paid more every time he had to use an extra piece of equipment on a job. So he didn't mind if the old man cheated a little since he loved that power saw anyhow. With it he felt the way another guy would feel behind the wheel of a new car. Only with a power saw a guy has got to be careful, and his ground man has got to know what he's doing.

It wasn't a big maple compared with some in town, but it was an old one, and the trunk was ragged. There was a big pile of leaves under it that had been raked up to the trunk, and in the middle of the leaves was some brush we had cut that morning trimming, mostly short branches and suckers you take off with a pruner.

"How about one of them ladders?" said Frenchy, not naming anybody since he was still mad at Bub and hated to have to talk to him.

"Which one you want, Frenchy?" Bub asked him. "The big one or the small one?"

"Which one do you think I want?" said Frenchy. "Can't you tell how high them branches are, or have you went blind or somethin'?"

The branches was low enough so that the short ladder was plenty long enough to reach them. They was low enough too so Frenchy could've got up by jumping for them. I've seen Frenchy shinny up ten feet of trunk and I've seen him crotch in from the ground and pull himself up on a rope. But this time I guess he just wanted to get some work out of Bub, and Bub was trying real hard to please him. It was like he knew that Frenchy, being his older brother, had a lot of responsibility and deserved nothing but the best. So he got the big extension ladder off the truck instead and set it against the tree.

"This one do, Frenchy?" he asked.

Frenchy didn't say nothing. He just looked at Bub, pitying like. Then he looked at the ladder and said, finally, "Yeah, this one'll do. Now go get the power saw and set it down here on the ground."

After that, Frenchy paid no more attention to Bub. When he had a tree to work on, he never noticed what anyone else was doing. He was what you'd call totally absorbed. He set the ladder against the trunk like he wanted it then hoisted up his pants and climbed into the tree.

"He sure is feelin' mean today," said Bub to me as soon as he thought Frenchy couldn't hear him.

"And you better watch your step he don't come down and take it out of your hide," I said.

Bub looked at me serious. "He could do it, too. I know 'cause he's done it to me more'n once."

Coming from a big guy like Bub, this sounded funny, but it wasn't. He was good-natured, but all it took was one yell from Frenchy, and he did everything wrong. He made more mistakes when Frenchy was watching him than when he was doing a job by himself. But it didn't seem to me he could do much damage today since he was only the ground man on this crew.

A minute later me and the other boys was up trees off on our own. I was in a small sycamore, and between trying to keep the suckers out of my face and keep from slipping on the bark, I didn't have time to look at Frenchy and Bub. So when I come down, Frenchy was just letting the power saw down to the ground. It was hot, and the chain of the saw was covered with sawdust. The big leader was laying in the gutter with a stub next to it where Frenchy had flushed off his cut. Frenchy was still up there in the tree, painting the cut so the sap wouldn't run out. The ladder was back on the truck.

"You know what this guy done?" Frenchy called down to me.

"Who?"

"This dumb brother of mine. I tell him to tie the power saw on the end of my line and pull it up to me. He gets it halfway up and starts lettin' it down again. 'What you lettin' it down for?' I says. 'Ain't no gas in it'" he says. He's tryin' to send me up a power saw without no gas in it."

I had to laugh, but all the time he was talking Bub was pulling at my arm. As soon as Frenchy stopped, Bub whispered, quiet so Frenchy wouldn't hear, "That ain't what happened at all."

"No? Then what did happen?"

"Sh-h-h. Not so loud. They was plenty of gas in it to start with. Only I forgot to screw on the cap, so about halfway up all the gas spilt out. I had to haul it back down and fill it up again. See on the trunk here?"

I looked at the trunk and whistled. What I'd been thinking was sap from Frenchy's cut was nothing but gas. It started just below the first leader and reached down to the pile of leaves. "You better not say nothing to Frenchy about this," I said.

"I ain't goin' to."

Frenchy called down again. "Get me my bull pole. This here tree ain't finished yet. I got trimmin' to do yet."

Bub run over to the truck and got the long pruning pole Frenchy used and managed to toss it up to him without doing anything wrong. Then, as I'm walking back to my next tree, I hear Frenchy call down again.

"Now go look in my coat pocket and toss me my cigarettes."

Bub don't answer for a minute. Then he says, "What do you wanta smoke for, Frenchy? You know it ain't good for ya. Besides, you're comin' down in a minute, ain'tcha?"

"Don't give me no trouble now," says Frenchy. "Just do what I tell ya. If I want to smoke, I smoke."

I watched Bub toss up the cigarettes. Then I started my own trimming. It was no more than a couple of minutes after that when I started to smell smoke. Someone burning leaves, I says to myself, and didn't think no more of it. Then the smell got stronger, and a minute later I look over toward Frenchy in his tree, and I can't even see the tree, much less Frenchy, on account of the smoke.

Well, it was maybe a hundred yards from my tree to his, and I figured he must have come down to burn leaves for some reason, although there's a city ordinance against it. So I decided to come down and see for myself. But by that time I could see the whole tree trunk was on fire, and the smoke so thick in the branches you couldn't tell whether Frenchy was up there or not. As for Bub, he was just standing there jumping from one foot to the other and looking miserable.

"What happened?" I asked him.

"I told him not to smoke. I begged him, but he wouldn't believe me."

"You mean Frenchy set that fire?"

"T'warn't me, so it musta been him. He musta dropped a match in them there leaves."

"You mean Frenchy's up in that tree and you didn't tell him the tree's on fire?"

Bub just looked more miserable than ever. "He must know it by now, don'tcha think?" he whined.

"Frenchy!" I yelled up into the white clouds of smoke. "Come on down!"

"He can't come down," wailed Bub. "He dropped his rope when he finished with the power saw."

"Then why don't he jump? Hey Frenchy! Jump!"

"They ain't no way to jump," said Bub. "He can't see enough in that there smoke to jump."

All I could hear now was the fire crackling and the sap popping in the maple tree. "I better get Mac," I said.

It was all I could think of doing. Mac was in the next street with the truck and the two ladders on it, working in a small maple.

"You better come quick with the truck," I said. "Frenchy's tree's on fire."

"Whaddaya mean, on fire?" said Mac.

"Yeah, and Frenchy's in it."

Mac looked at me hard. "Are you nuts?" But he come anyhow, and a minute later the truck was up close to Frenchy's tree, but not so close there was a chance it would catch fire.

"You seen Frenchy yet?" I asked Bub.

"Ain't seen nor heard him neither. But then, Frenchy never was one to say much when he was mad."

But Mac knew what to do. "Get that ladder off the truck," he told Bub, "and set it up against the tree trunk. Never mind if it starts to burn." Then he called up to Frenchy, "You come down that ladder as soon as you see it against the trunk."

Right then was the first words we heard Frenchy say. We couldn't see him, but we heard his voice coming out of the smoke, and it was kind of low and strained like he was mad he even had to talk at all.

"I ain't climbin' through no fire. I ain't crazy like you."

"There ain't no other way down, Frenchy."

"Maybe there ain't; maybe there is."

And that's when we seen Frenchy come out of that tree.

Like I said, all the wires passed right through the middle of the tree. That's why we was there, to trim back the branches. Well, the phone cable was the lowest-hanging, though it was still a good distance from the ground. And right then it started to bob up and down, and what did we see but Frenchy coming down along it and out of the smoke, swinging on it and moving along like a monkey in some Tarzan picture. I remember thinking what a good thing he was small and light or the cable would bring him down with it. But he made it, dropping into soft turf.

Frenchy wasn't saying one word that whole time. His face was smudged black, and his boots kind of smelled like burning rubber, with smoke coming out of the holes. As for Bub, he kept as far away from Frenchy as he could, watching me and Mac slap his brother on the back and tell him how lucky he was.

But that maple tree was in bad shape. The fire was out already because we'd raked all the leaves back from the tree trunk and the little gas there was against the trunk was consumed in no time. But the trunk was black and cracked and running sap, and altogether we figured the old man was gonna have a pretty big fine to pay, and we wondered what we were going to tell him.

Bub hadn't said a thing, but toward the end of the afternoon he looked up through the branches of the tree we was working on then, and said, sort of quiet and wistful: "Now if we had a good rainstorm, like we get 'em up in Maine, maybe we could tell the old man the tree was hit by lightnin'."

Frenchy looked at his kid brother real hard and said, soft and low, "You wait till we get back home, son. That's when you'll see lightnin', and there won't be no rainstorm to go with it."

So when they come in to work next day, it looked like Bub was up in the tree when it caught fire instead of Frenchy. But believe it or not, it did rain that night, and there was thunder and lightning, and people going to work saw the tree and said it must have been the lightning. And the old man believed it!

Later I asked Bub why he let Frenchy hit him when he was plenty big enough to defend himself.

"Maybe I deserved it," he said finally. "Feller Frenchy's size can't usually find nobody smaller to take on. This way I kinder take care of him too, and it stays in the family."

And maybe someone up there is taking care of them both.

Whitey's Christmas

When Whitey come to work that Tuesday morning, just about every guy in the outfit knew he'd spent the weekend in jail. They also knew the only reason he was out was the old man had paid his fine.

It was not showing up on Monday that started the talk. Whitey was always there on Monday, not so much because he wanted to be as because he couldn't afford to lose a day's pay. He was a guy with a family, and no matter how hard he worked he never seemed to get ahead. Losing one day's pay put him so far behind it was weeks before he was able to buy anything again.

The old man give Whitey a good rate of pay, for a tree-climber, and Whitey worked hard to earn it. He come in Saturdays whenever there was a job, and on Sundays he went out himself looking for a hedge to trim or a limb to come off. Yet he had never been able to get himself out of debt. His wife was expecting their third kid, and he was still paying money on his color TV. He'd been paying for a washer too, but a couple months earlier he'd made the last payment, and having a little extra money, or else owing a little less, made him feel so good he decided it was time to get a new car. It was getting so bad that every week now he showed up in the old man's office asking for twenty bucks against his pay. Usually he got about half of what he'd asked for.

Whitey actually believed that some day he'd have a lot of money so he wouldn't have to climb trees. It was what give him his hope and caused him his trouble, both at the same time. When things go wrong with a guy like that, there's bound to be an explosion, and that's what happened to Whitey that weekend.

It was a bad time of the year for work, and staying home with the wife and kids had brought on a fight, and so he just went out and got drunk. The cops picked him up in a brawl and let the old man know they had him. The old man paid the fine because Whitey was a good climber, but he swore it was coming out of Whitey's pay. So just for good measure he let him stay in jail till Monday. Even though he needed Whitey, he didn't need him every day, and this was the best chance he'd had to teach him a lesson and save himself a day's pay at the same time.

So Whitey was looking grim when he come in that Tuesday. It was December, and it was cold. Standing in the back of the truck, both of us kept our gloves on and stomped our feet. We was trimming trees along the main road that day, and so we had to move fast on account of traffic. Whitey would climb a big pin oak and get out over the highway to cut a low-hanging branch, and I'd do the same in the next tree while Bub would put flags out on the road, and that way we'd keep warm.

All during the first part of the morning Whitey had nothing to say. Then about ten-thirty, when the sun had burnt the frost off the fields and we was changing trees, he said to me, as if I owed it to him, "Lend me a couple bucks, will you? I gotta buy my lunch."

I knew he had a lunch box, but I give it to him. I didn't expect to see that money again.

"Can't borrow off the old man this week," he explained. "I'm in hock to him till after Christmas."

"Maybe he'll let you work weekends."

"Not him. Not unless there's an emergency. He give me a line about laying off guys on account of winter. No Saturday jobs at all."

"At least he can't lay you off as long as you owe him money."

"That don't help. First place, I know he's telling the truth. I can't even get work on Sundays myself."

We was in the back of the truck now, going away from town toward a place where there was more oaks growing over the wires. A little distance up the road we passed the city reservoir at a spot where the road cuts over the water on a viaduct.

"Trouble is," Whitey was saying, "I don't know nothing outside the tree business, and people ain't planting trees or trimming them either this time of year."

He was looking at the reservoir. It spread out in both directions, with islands in the middle and a high fence around it and every inch of the ground covered with evergreens.

"Look at them spruce," he said. "Ain't they beautiful? And look at that one over there. Wouldn't that one make a Christmas tree though?"

Suddenly his face was glum again. "That's another thing. How'm I gonna buy Christmas presents for the kids this year? I ain't even got enough to buy them a tree."

"Why couldn't you make some money selling them?"

"Selling what?"

"Christmas trees. Why not?"

"You kiddin? That's a big business. Where would I get any Christmas trees to sell?"

We was past the reservoir now, riding over the top of a rise. I didn't even have a chance to give Whitey an answer. He turned around like a top spinning and looked back where we'd been.

"That's it! Christmas trees!" he said.

"Where?"

"Back there at the reservoir," he said. "Some of the most beautiful Christmas trees you ever seen, sittin' right there waitin' to be took."

"Now wait a minute, Whitey," I said. "You can't take them trees."

"Why can't I?"

"Well, in the first place, they belong to the city."

Whitey was just laughing at me. I'd never seen such a change in him. One minute he was in the dumps, and the next he was the liveliest guy you'd ever want to see.

"Then how about the fence they got all around the place?" I said, seeing I hadn't made an impression the first time.

"One strand of barbed wire at the top," he said. "That oughta be easy to get over."

"But don't you think they're just watching for guys like you to come along and try to make a fast buck?"

"Not at night, they ain't. They couldn't watch all of it anyhow. That's a big reservoir."

I could see this was a losing game, but I still tried to talk him out of it.

"Where would you sell them? You'd get caught trying to pass them off."

"You know Al Tedesco, the bartender? His brother's selling them. He'd take all I could bring him."

"But you couldn't get enough trees into a car to make a profit, Whitey."

I thought I had him there, but he just laughed at me, "Maybe not the first trip. But I'd get enough, don't worry." I could think of just one more reason, and I was counting on it to stop him. "OK, supposing you go in over the fence and cut some trees. It'd take you maybe an hour to cut a good load and drag them over to the fence. All that time your car's sitting on the side of the road, next to the fence, where anybody can see it. There's no place to hide a car around there."

Whitey was still smiling. "My wife wouldn't even let me take my car out alone at night," he said. "That's why I'm gonna need you to drive me in yours."

There was no use trying to talk Whitey out of it.

I had an old car, and although it wasn't much good, it got me around and had plenty of room in it. I didn't mind getting the inside of it dirty, but on the other hand I wasn't as hard up for money as Whitey, and I didn't want to take risks.

"You ain't takin' risks," Whitey told me. "You ain't even committing a crime. All you're doing is picking me up by the side of the road."

"Sure, you and them spruce," I said. "What do you call that? Receiving stolen goods, that's what."

"G'wan, you ain't receivin' nothin'. It's Al Tedesco's brother that's receivin' 'em."

"Well, I'm some kind of an accessory anyhow."

"Don't worry about it," said Whitey. "If there's trouble, I'll handle it. You get part of the profits and take no risks. What more could you ask for?"

Well, Christmas was less than a week away, and I had a date that night that I couldn't break. So we decided on the night after, and around eight o'clock I picked Whitey up a block from his place and started out to the reservoir.

"Good thing it didn't snow this afternoon, Whitey, You'd be leaving tracks everywhere."

"Well, it didn't," he said. "No, sir. Everything's workin' out perfect. I got it fixed up with Al Tedesco so we'll bring the trees right into his brother's back yard. Then I'll have some money to make up for last weekend, and the kids'll have some presents for Christmas."

I was going to tell him I thought his wife would find some way to buy presents for the kids, but I didn't say it. There was plenty of things they could use the money on, even if they had presents. And it looked as though he'd have it. The night was perfect for it. No snow, no moon. Just cloudy and dark.

When we got to the reservoir, Whitey pulled out the hand saw and a length of rope and said, "Pull over here by the side of the road."

He opened the door and jumped out. "Be back here in an hour," he said. "If I'm not here, don't stop. Just drive on awhile and turn around and come back."

He tossed the saw and the rope over the fence and climbed up the wires. At the top he was about seven feet off the ground. He give a jump and rolled over when he hit. Then he looked through the fence at me and said: "What are you waitin' for? Get outa here!"

As I drove off, he disappeared into the small forest of pine and spruce and fir that was around the reservoir. I rode around for a few minutes and then come back into town and stopped at an arcade. I shot at the ducks for a while, and then I went across the street and had a beer, wondering all the time what I ever let Whitey talk me into a fool thing like that for.

After one more beer it was time to start back to the reservoir. I emptied out the back seat and tried to figure out how we could ever get trees over four feet long into it. Finally I decided we'd have to let them stick out the windows, and so I opened up both back windows.

The reservoir looked quiet when I got to it. There was no lights anywhere, and I couldn't hear a sound. I looked at my watch. It was just an hour since I'd left Whitey, so I drove up fast and tried to stop at exactly the same place as before, I don't know how it happened, but just as I was putting on the brakes and almost had the car stopped, all of a sudden there was light everywhere, and I could see all of them standing there in front of me. There was the fat cop I'd seen in town a few times, and a guy that must've been from the water company. And there was the police car pulled up against the fence and another cop inside that had just put on the lights. And in the middle of all them guys, standing next to the biggest load of fresh-cut trees I ever seen off a ten-ton truck, was Whitey.

"Whadda you want?" the fat cop asked me.

"Nothing," I said. "Nothing at all. I seen your car and I thought you was in trouble, is all. I was going to give you a hand."

"Yeah? How do I know you ain't with this guy?"

"With what guy?"

"How about it, you?" one of the others asked Whitey. "This is the guy you was waitin' for, ain't it?"

Whitey answered loud. "Him? Whaddaya mean? I ain't never seen that guy before in my life."

"Kinda cold in back with the windows open, dontcha think?"the fat cop asked me. "You always ride that way?"

"Yeah," I said, trying to smile. "Fresh air, you know."

"Go on, beat it before we run you in, too," said the other cop. I looked at Whitey. There he was, caught with all them Christmas trees and not blinking an eye, just looking me square in the face and his look telling me to beat it.

I left. And I didn't sleep all that night from thinking of Whitey back there with the cops, and all them good trees gone to waste. I was going to call his wife, but then I figured I'd let him do that, and anyway I wasn't supposed to know about it. Besides, when his wife found out, I didn't want to be nowhere around.

When I got in to work the next morning, the old man was standing in the yard as usual, sending out the crews. He had four trucks out that day, but he was short handed on men, and I wondered whether he knew anything about Whitey. It was plain enough Whitey wasn't in the yard.

I didn't have to wait long to find out. The phone rang, and the old man went into the office to answer it. I sort of edged over to the door where I could hear better what was going on.

"Again!" I heard the old man say. "He can't be! It's the middle of the week, and he hasn't got no money."

There was silence for a minute, and then the old man really exploded.

"Christmas trees? With my hand saw? Well, I don't know nothing about that. No, I don't need him today or any other time either. Let him rot!"

Then the old man come storming out of his office, bouncing mad.

"Count every tool on these trucks!" he yelled. "By God, if there's any missing, I'm gonna raise hell. Any man that takes one of my tools home is gonna pay me for it."

This time it looked as though Whitey was going to stay in jail. I went to see him that evening, and he was the saddest-looking guy in the world.

"You don't think there's a chance then?" he asked me.

"It don't look that way. Not after what I heard him say this morning."

He sat down, moaning. "How do I get myself into so much trouble? I owe him money already for payin' my fine. And now I'm losin' another day's work tomorrow. And the day after that's Christmas, and my little kids is home alone without their pa."

"Jeez, Whitey," I said. I couldn't say no more because he was almost in tears.

"If he'd just bail me out this once, I swear I'd never give him no more trouble again. Ain't he a hard-hearted man though?" By this time I was almost crying myself. And when I left him, I knew I wasn't going to enjoy Christmas a bit myself. I worked all through the next day without even noticing the weather, which was getting warmer and cloudy in spite of the predictions for a cold and dry Christmas. That night I went home thinking maybe there would be some snow to make it a white Christmas, after all. But then I started thinking about Whitey, and I never even noticed the weather again.

About eleven-thirty the telephone started ringing. I wasn't going to answer it at first, but it kept on ringing, and so I finally picked up the receiver. It was the old man. "Get down here right away," he said.

"What for? Is there some kind of trouble?"

"Whaddaya mean, what for? Don't you know we're in the middle of an ice storm? There's lines down all over town. Hurry up. I need every man I can get."

"Aw, look, boss," I said. "It's Christmas Eve."

"Christmas Eve, hell! You get down here tonight, or you can start looking for another job next week. This is an emergency."

There wasn't much I could do. I got dressed and put on my boots and my cap and started down to the yard. The boss was right about the weather. It had snowed a little in the evening, and then it had turned to rain. But now it was getting colder, and the rain was turning to ice everywhere. When I got there, the place was all lit up, and the old man was sending out crews as fast as he could get them together. When he saw me, he yelled:

"You get on the back of Rush's truck. Rush, you drop him off at the corner of Maple and Grand. There's a primary down there, and they need another man bad."

So I bounced around in the sleet in the back of Rush's truck while he skidded through town. He dropped me off where the old man had said, and I walked over to where I seen one of our other trucks. It was Mac's.

"Well, I hope we didn't disturb your sleep," he said. "How about getting a line out for yourself and going up that elm over there? And when you get there, watch out for that primary."

The place was a mess. The primary was lying on the sidewalk, sizzling, and a couple of other wires was down too. A crew from the electric light company was working like beavers trying to get them repaired.

I looked at the elm. It was covered with ice, and two big leaders was bent over with their ends snapped and hanging on the telephone cable. An extension ladder was already leaning against the trunk, and so I went right up. I was just crotching in with my line when I heard a voice yelling at me from somewhere higher up in the tree.

"Hey, is that you over there?"

"Yeah," I answered. "Who's that?"

"It's me. Right over here. Can't you see me?" I looked hard. Then over on the end of the leader, with his arms and his legs wrapped around it and icicles hanging down from the collar of his jacket like a beard, was Whitey. "Whitey! How did you get here?"

"I rode here in a car. How do you think?"

"Then the old man bailed you out?"

"Come down for me himself and drove me back in his car. He's a great guy, the old man."

I started to laugh. It must have hurt the old man like poison to have to bail Whitey out of jail. Nothing short of this ice storm would've made him do it.

"Boy, are you lucky we got an ice storm on Christmas Eve," I said to him.

He yelled back at me. "Hell, this ain't Christmas Eve. We're gonna make some money today,"

"How do you figure that?"

"Brother, this is Christmas day," said Whitey. "We're gonna be here all day, and for every minute of it the old man's gotta pay us double time!"

Rush

The old man had a fleet of maybe half a dozen trucks working on contract with the electric light company to keep the trees trimmed around their wires. His outfit and another one handled all the towns for ten or twenty miles around. But the other outfit was after his contracts, and so the company played one against the other and kept the old man wondering when he was going to lose out. The idea was to keep him on his toes, but you wondered if it sometimes didn't have the effect of freezing him like a scared rabbit so that nothing at all got done.

The work meant a lot of mileage on his trucks, and that meant gas. And between sending a truck out with a crew in the morning and getting it back at night there was a lot of money laid out without any work at all getting done. So when the old man said he didn't want any more gas wasted, that he was keeping track of the mileage and that he wanted to know every place a truck went during the day, we knew he was getting suspicious of Rush. Because Rush's truck ran up more mileage than any truck in the outfit.

Rush was a long, skinny guy from somewhere in the mountains of West Virginia. He was kind of slow and had big blue eyes and an innocent expression, and he just couldn't understand how any man could think wrong of him.

"I ain't wasting gas, boss. Honest, I ain't," he said to the old man. "I just been driving out to where you told me."

"I ain't accusing you of nothing," the old man said. "I'm just telling you to keep your mileage down."

"But boss, I swear I ain't taking that truck nowhere but on the job."

By this time the old man looked like he was sorry he ever brought the subject up. Rush wasn't much of a climber, but he was the most sincere guy in the outfit.

"Look, Rush," he said, "just forget I said anything, huh? Do like you been doing and keep your mileage down, and everything'll be all right."

"But boss, I ain't lying to you, honest," Rush whined. Well, the only way the old man could break it off now was by hitting the roof, and that was what he did. So when Rush finally got into the truck, he was quiet, but he was hurt, like a kid that's been accused of something he didn't do. And when Rush felt like that, he took it out on the truck. He was a fast driver anyhow. When you rode in the back, you didn't stand up. You just sat on one of the old cushions with your back tight up against the rear of the cab and held on with both hands. That way you didn't stand so much chance of getting thrown over the cab when Rush put on the brakes. But when Rush was upset, like he was today, the only thing you could do was shut your eyes and pray. It was so bad today that Whitey, riding in the back with me, let out a yell when one of the turns threw him off his seat.

"Hey, I got a family. I can't afford to get killed!" Whitey was a guy that was in trouble a lot and worried about it even when he wasn't. He didn't like riding with Rush any more than I did, but today he looked like he might get desperate. When we took a bump that lifted him up off his cushion and sat him down on the floorboards, that did it.

"Listen, this is the last time I ride in this truck with him," he told me. "I'm tellin' the old man tonight."

"You can't do that," I said. "The old man won't do you any favors. If you tell him, he'll just have to talk to Rush again, and that'll make it worse."

It was always the same with Rush. You hurt his feelings, and he took it out on the truck. Whitey had told him to slow down just a few days before, and instead he just drove that much faster. Not out of spite either, because Rush was too gentle to do anything out of spite. He probably didn't know he was driving faster than usual.

"I know that," Whitey said. "But there oughta be some way."

Whitey knew there was one thing no guy in the outfit ever did, and that was complain to the old man about another guy. Anyone that did that didn't last long. It was something you had to fix up among yourselves.

"Well, I can't think of any other way," I said, "unless somebody else complains about him."

"Who? There ain't nobody else."

"I don't know. Somebody along the road, maybe. Somebody that don't like the way he drives past their house or something. The old man gets plenty of complaints about the way the trees are cut."

"Say, that's an idea," Whitey said as the truck lurched again. "If somebody complained to the old man over the telephone, maybe this hillbilly'd believe we're tellin' him the truth."

"Except you may have to wait a long time for that."

"I dunno. It's an idea."

We worked all day without Whitey saying much, and on the way home he just hung on and gritted his teeth. When the truck stopped at the red light where Whitey always got off, he just jumped off the back and started across the street, waving at me and saying, "Safe for another day."

That was how we did it coming home from work. We didn't have to go all the way back to the yard, and so Whitey jumped off near where he lived and I got off a little later. Rush was always left to take the truck in alone, so we never knew what he did with it after we got off. That was why, when the old man started complaining about the extra mileage, we couldn't tell him anything about it. Only it didn't seem Rush could be going very far, since the yard was close to where I got off.

But next morning the old man was hopping mad again. "Rush, c'mere!" he yelled across the yard.

We watched Rush run over to him, loping like some longlegged animal and then bringing his hands down stiff to the seams of his pants like he was standing at attention. The old man's face was red as he started talking, and it got a lot redder before he was through. And all the while Rush was just standing there listening, except that slowly his head was going forward and his eyes opened and his lower jaw dropped. Then when the old man was finished, we heard a screech come out of Rush like a sick bird.

"Boss, I don't drive fast. Honest, nobody *never* complained to me about my driving."

"Well, they complained to me, by God!" the old man roared. "I got a phone call last night that burned my ears off, and I don't want to get another one. You hear that?"

I gave Whitey a long look. He just gazed back at me, and his face was all innocence. He made a motion as though he knew nothing about it, but I didn't believe him, and I was sorry to see Rush in trouble on account of Whitey. Just the same, I kind of wished I'd been there to hear Whitey give the old man hell over the telephone. It wasn't often that Whitey talked up to the old man. Or anybody else, for that matter.

Rush had his right hand raised in the air now. He brought it down just long enough to cross his heart, and then he raised it up again and stood at attention and said, just like a Boy Scout, "Boss, I swear I never run your truck over the speed limit. I hope to die if I did."

The old man took a deep breath and scratched his head.

There was no use trying to tell Rush he was wrong when he thought he was right, and Rush was just plain convinced he didn't drive fast. No man could lie like that with a straight face.

"OK, OK," the old man said in a tired voice. "Just don't ever let me catch you speeding, or you're through. Now get me your mileage."

Rush gave it to him, and we got into the truck. I was riding in the front seat that morning, and as soon as we was on the road Rush said to me, "You don't think I drive fast, do you?"

"Sure you do, Rush. You oughta see the way we get thrown around in the back."

"But that ain't my driving. That's the truck. This truck'll throw you around no matter who's driving it."

You couldn't talk him out of it. "Have it your own way, Rush. I say you drive too fast, and you say you don't." But then I dropped the subject because I could see how it affected him. His mouth clamped shut, and his hands tightened on the wheel, and at the same time, I guess without him noticing it, his foot went down on the accelerator. He was mad, and that was just the way it affected him.

We went to where we was working and started trimming the trees. It was a day like any other, and after we'd worked up and down the streets all morning, we knocked off for lunch. Rush and Whitey hadn't said a word to each other all morning, partly because they'd been working separately and partly because they had their own thoughts. Rush was beginning to burn again about his fight with the old man, and Whitey looked like he was feeling guilty about what he'd done. Then all of a sudden, while we was sitting in a booth, Rush looked across the table and said to Whitey, in an innocent way but very sincere, "Whitey, you don't think I drive too fast, do you?"

Whitey jumped. It must have been exactly what he was thinking, and what he'd been thinking all morning long.

"Why should I think that?" he answered, looking suspicious.

But Rush went right on without noticing how Whitey took it. That was what was the matter with Rush, I guess. His own ideas was so firm in his mind he couldn't see you didn't necessarily agree with everything he said.

"Well," he was saying, "the way the boss went after me this morning, you'd think I was trying to kill all of you and wreck his truck. You don't think I'd do a thing like that, do you, Whitey?"

"I don't think nothin'," said Whitey.

"You know what he said?" Rush went on. "He said someone called him on the telephone last night and told him the truck was going by their house sixty mile an hour."

"Yeah?" Whitey said.

"That's right. You know that warn't true, Whitey. I wonder who'd go and tell the boss a thing like that." Whitey slammed his spoon down on the table and stood up. His food was spilled all over the table.

"What's the matter? You think it was me that called him?"

Rush looked really surprised now. "I didn't say that, Whitey. It couldn't be you. You're riding in the back of the truck all the time."

"Nuts! You think you're pretty wise, don'tcha? Innocent, my neck." And Whitey got out of the booth and left us sitting there.

Rush just looked after him with wide-open baby-blue eyes. "Well, whatever could be eating Whitey?" he asked. "I didn't say nothing, did I?"

I lied to him. "Whitey's just fighting with his wife again, is all. Leave him alone. He'll be all right."

"All I did was mention that telephone call the boss got last night. Why should that get him mad, I wonder?"

"Don't worry about it, Rush," I said. "Just forget it."

But Rush didn't forget it. I could see it was bothering him more and more as the afternoon went on. He was such a mild guy that you could say almost anything to him without him getting mad. But you had to be careful not to accuse him of anything. It was like that now, and he had all afternoon to think about what Whitey said to him. As for Whitey, the rest of the day he'd go up in the trees and tug at the suckers with his pruner till you'd see the whole tree shake and hear a drone like a swarm of bees as he swore at it under his breath. He was a better climber than Rush, and it didn't take as much to get him mad. Rush was too tall to make a good climber, and where another man would walk right out on a leader to where he was going to make his cut, Rush would get down and wrap his arms and legs around it and shinny out on it like a caterpillar. That was why he burned so slow, so that all I could see was his face getting redder and redder and no sound at all, while in the next tree the branches was shaking and Whitey was swearing louder and louder as the afternoon went on.

When it come time to quit, we loaded the brush on the back of the truck, with Rush driving and Whitey standing on top and piling the branches we handed him. And even there Whitey was getting suspicious of Rush because Rush would jerk the truck ahead to the next pile before Whitey had finished loading it and then stop so fast it knocked Whitey off balance. "You wait and see," Whitey said to me. "He's gonna drive like a nut this afternoon just to get even with me."

Whitey was so full of resentment he could hardly talk. But he'd made a good prediction about Rush's driving, because that evening Rush drove faster than I'd ever seen him drive before. He drove so fast going over the dirt road to the dump that we almost lost the load of brush before we got there. And after we'd dumped it, it seemed almost as though he'd been holding back on account of it, because he picked up speed again, leaned on the horn and passed everything in front of him. It was so bad I kept telling myself how lucky I was to be sitting with my back against the cab where at least my head wasn't going to go through the windshield.

As for Whitey, he was convinced Rush was doing it all on purpose to get even with him. He hung on without a word and only nodded his head and muttered to himself, but I could see he was white as death. We had about twenty miles to go along the main road from where we was working back home, and it was twenty miles of heavy traffic, on a four-lane highway with no island in the middle. I could look back over the tail of the truck and see that center line right underneath us and feel the air when a car whizzed by my ear going in the other direction. And every time I looked up at Whitey his face was paler than before. Finally, just as we come to a red light and the brakes slammed on, I heard a yell, and there was Whitey jumping up and running toward the tail end of the truck.

"I've got enough of this," he was screaming. "I ain't gonna take no more."

Before I could stop him, he jumped off the back and was standing there at the crossroads, still ten miles out of town, with his coat over his arm and his face white and his legs shaking.

"How are you getting home?" I yelled.

"I'll take a bus. Or I'll walk or hitch a ride. But I ain't never ridin' with that guy again."

I was going to try to talk him out of it, but the light must have turned green, because the truck give a lurch and started up again. And there was Whitey, standing alone by the side of the road and getting smaller and smaller.

Rush probably didn't even know Whitey had jumped off. And the way he was driving, he wasn't feeling any better, either.

He drove back into town without slowing down, and when he finally got to the place where he always let Whitey off, he stopped and waited just as if Whitey was still on the truck.

By this time the traffic was really bad. I was riding all the way into the yard because I wanted to talk to the old man about my pay, and so I didn't get off at the usual spot. I just stayed on, thankful that the city traffic and the cops was making Rush slow down a little. I even was thinking this was a good chance to see where Rush went to run up all that mileage the old man was complaining about.

I don't know how long I sat looking at the car behind us before I realized who was in it. I don't even remember seeing when it first started following us. But after I'd been looking at the face of the guy behind the wheel for a while, just staring at it the way you do out of the back of a truck at the car behind you, all of a sudden it hit me and I knew who it was. It was the old man, and he was following us into town.

I wanted to turn and yell at Rush and warn him to slow down. But even if I'd made him hear me, the old man would have seen right away what I was trying to do. So all I could do was sit there and watch, pretending not to see him.

What the old man was doing was following to see where all that extra mileage came from. With another outfit after his contract, he had to keep his costs down. Looking over Rush's mileage that day, what he'd seen must have give him an awful jolt to bring him out in this traffic to follow Rush. Anyhow, he had some ride ahead of him today. We was driving down Main Street, the way you'd have to to get to the yard, when all of a sudden I felt a wrench and heard the tires scream as we turned down a side street. That was all right, I thought. Rush was just trying to avoid traffic. I remembered him doing that before because one thing he couldn't stand was waiting in traffic. Then I seen the old man's car make the same turn and follow at a safe distance. But this street wasn't so crowded, and now Rush put on the gas. I tried to hold on tight, but before I got a good grip the brakes slammed on and I was thrown sideways. We'd turned into another street.

It went on like that for a good ten minutes, with Rush turning from one street into another like a rat in a maze, looking for a clear way into town. Finally we got into a narrow street opening onto another one that led over a bridge. I looked ahead, and the cars were lined up for a distance of five hundred yards. There was no side streets this time, either, and so I figured Rush would just have to wait. I settled back and breathed a little easier.

That was the wrong thing to do, because just then I felt another lurch as the truck pulled out of line and up onto the opposite sidewalk, around a telephone pole and back down the way we'd come. I just had time to see the old man's face as we went past. His jaw was hanging open like he couldn't believe what he was seeing, his big new truck with his name painted on the side of it being run through traffic like it was out of control. But that didn't bother Rush. At least, the idea of waiting in line worked stronger against him than just breaking traffic laws. And before we got to the next turn I seen the old man's car do the same thing and follow along after us.

It went on like this for a good twenty minutes, with Rush screaming down every side street in the city and not seeming to get any nearer to where he wanted to go. When he finally did get near the yard, he was coming at it from the west, even though we'd been working east of town. There was a line of people that had been blowing their horns and shaking their fists at us when we passed them, and we'd burnt a lot of gas and chalked up I don't know how much more mileage just trying to get home. When we got the truck into the garage, Rush stepped out of the cab and I jumped off the back just as the old man pulled in. "There's the boss now," said Rush, just as pleasant and innocent as anything, "in case you want to talk to him."

"Rush," I said, "I think I better wait till tomorrow. He's gonna want to talk to you first. He's been following you all the way into town."

The look on Rush's face was surprised enough, but it wasn't a guilty look. "I wonder why he wants to talk to me," was all he said. He wasn't going to have to wait long to find out.

"Eight miles!" the old man was roaring before he even got to us. "Eight miles extra you drove just to bring that truck in, and I'm not even counting the red light and the stop signs. Will you tell me what you think you were doing?"

"Boss, I was just trying to avoid traffic," Rush said mildly.

"Avoid it? You weren't satisfied to run into the traffic on one side of town. You had to go around and run into what was on the other side too. And I suppose you never heard of speed limits."

Rush's face turned real solemn.

"Boss, I swear to you I wasn't speeding. I was just simply trying to get the truck back to the yard the quickest way I could."

"Get out!" the old man sputtered. "Pick up your pay tomorrow. You're fired!"

Rush left. He threw his jacket over his shoulder and walked out of the yard, slowly, without a word. The old man turned to me. "Now what do you want?"

I took a deep breath. "Look, boss, he don't realize he's driving too fast. He really don't. You shouldn't..."

"Is that all you want to talk about?" I guessed it was.

"Then save your breath. Be here tomorrow morning at seven-thirty." And he walked into his office.

I came in next day as usual. He didn't have to tell me.

But I was feeling pretty bad about the whole thing. I thought how good it was going to be to ride in a truck with someone else at the wheel, but every time I thought of that I started feeling sorry for Rush again. It got so I was feeling as guilty as Whitey.

At first I didn't notice the noise coming out of the old man's office. Someone was in there arguing with him, but then someone was always doing that. So I didn't think nothing of it till I heard the old man say, "Then who was it that made that phone call?" And another voice yelled back at him: "It don't make no difference who made the phone call. You fire Rush, I'm quittin' right now!"

That was Whitey's voice. Whitey didn't even know about what happened after he jumped off the truck last night and the boss started following us into town. All Whitey could think of was his phone call as the reason Rush had been fired. And that had made him feel guiltier than he could stand.

I started to walk casually up to the office, where I could hear better, and a couple of other guys did the same. But before we got there the old man come to the door, with his face and neck red as a tomato, and give us a dirty look. "What do you guys want?"

There was nothing to do but go back to the trucks and wait till we seen Whitey come stomping out. His face was red too, and you couldn't tell if he'd won or lost till the old man yelled after him: "You can pick Rush up at the corner of Main and Grand. Does that suit you?"

Whitey didn't answer him. He didn't even turn around. He just opened the door of the truck and stepped into the cab.

"What happened?" I asked him. "Is Rush getting hired again?"

"Yeah, he's hired again."

Whitey's voice was about as sour as I'd ever heard it. "Well, that's great then," I said. "That's what you wanted, ain't it?" Whitey looked at me, and there wasn't nothing happy in his look.

"Yeah, sure," he said. "Only from now on I'm the one that's got to drive this lousy truck."

And that's how Whitey and Rush switched jobs on our crew.

The Last Elm

"That ain't no tree," said Frenchy. "That's just bones."

"It was the biggest tree around here once," I said.

"Maybe so, but t'ain't nothin' but a tombstone to a tree now. Ought to've come down long ago."

The five of us was up on Cherry Street, looking at an old elm et dry by disease. It stood near the sidewalk, behind a rusted iron grill fence in the front yard of a house that looked like it went with the tree itself—a square gray wooden frame with square four-paned windows down to the floor and a flat roof and a square porch with square columns. The only part of the house that wasn't square was the carved wooden lacework trim. Behind the windows all you could see was heavy brown drapes with tassels, all hanging full length to the floor.

The garage in back was the same. You could tell it'd been a stable, with the hayloft door hung on iron runners and the pulley under the point of the roof. It was the only old house left on Cherry Street. All the rest was apartments and office buildings except for the used car lot opposite, which was one reason why we was there that morning.

"You ain't kidding it ought to've come down long ago," said Mac. "That tree's dangerous. Supposing it fell over on the cars in that lot, or out in the street when somebody was going by. It's a wonder somebody ain't been killed already." He walked down the sidewalk, his cap tipped back and his hands in his hip pockets, studying the tree from another angle.

"I ain't gonna like toppin' this one," Whitey said.

"I'm toppin' it," Frenchy said. "I ain't scared of it."

"You can have it," Whitey said. "I wanta stay on the ground—and alive."

Whitey was heavier and a head taller than Frenchy, and although he was a good climber, there was no one to touch Frenchy. Frenchy could shinny up any trunk or leader he could get his arms around and crotch in with his line in a place another man wouldn't even try to reach. This old elm, fanning up into a crest like it did but gray and brittle with age and the elm disease, was a perfect job for Frenchy.

"OK, let's get started," said Mac. "Bub, you run the extension ladder up against the trunk. You ready, Frenchy?"

"Soon's I get this here saddle on."

Bub was Frenchy's brother. He was ground man. He untangled ropes and sent up saws and paint pots and piled up branches for us, but he never climbed himself. He run the ladder up as far as it'd go, and Frenchy climbed to the top, his climbing line and a hand saw and the end of another line hooked to his belt.

"Think I'll take that there leader about halfway up," he said after a minute, pointing to a big one that grew out over the street. "No sense makin' more work for myself than I hafta."

He took the end of his line and tied it into a ball and threw it over the leader. Then, with the other end tied to the ring on his saddle, he made a knot and pulled himself hand over hand up from the ladder with his feet climbing the trunk. In a few seconds he was standing in the tree.

"Nice view up here," he said.

Even from the ground there was a view if you stood in the right spot. Cherry Street was up on Northside Hill in what used to he the fanciest part of town. I guess when this house was built you could look down over most of the city and and see the Green and the Mattapaug River and the mills on the south side. But standing in the street today you couldn't see much anymore on account of the the buildings opposite. From Frenchy's perch, though, there was nothing to block the view.

He was climbing higher now and doing it all with his arms. A minute later he was crotched in near the top. He undid the hand line and threw the end over another branch and flipped it to the ground.

"Ready for the power saw," he called.

On a job like this we used a chain saw small enough so one man in a tree could operate it with a rope tied to it and someone holding the weight from the ground. Bub got the saw, and I tied one end of the hand line to the handle, and Whitey pulled it up to Frenchy by the other end.

"You better move the truck," said Mac. "If he drops a stub from up there, it'll go right through the hood."

I climbed into the truck and let it roll down the street a bit. When I got back, Frenchy had pulled the cord and the saw was roaring and sputtering and smoking in his hands like an outboard motor. People stopped in the street to look up, and the guy in the used car lot come out of his hut to watch.

Up to now there hadn't been a sign of life in the house. The shades were down upstairs, and downstairs you couldn't see in. The garage door was shut, and there wasn't a dog or a cat in the yard. You might've thought the house was empty. But when Frenchy started the power saw and the scream of cut wood come over the sound of the motor, there was a reaction even from the house, and we had our first glimpse of the old lady.

She was only ordinary size, but she was bony and straight in a way that didn't seem to go with her age. Although she must've been past seventy, there was none of that caving in around the shoulders and in the back that you sometimes see in old people, as though they didn't have the strength to support their own weight. She stood up straight like a young woman, and only the flesh seemed dried up and gone from her body. She just stood there on her front porch with her arms crossed and a scowl on her face, watching Frenchy make his cut. Then when the motor was turned off and we was lowering the branch, she started talking to Mac. Her voice was high and sharp, and she talked through her nose like the old Yankees.

"Do you intend to use that saw on my tree all morning?"

Mac touched the peak of his cap. "Yes, ma'am. That's the way we take 'em down."

"Then why does your man have that saw on his belt?"

Mac flushed. "Well, that one's only for small branches, ma'am. We use the power saw on the big ones. Otherwise we'd be a week cutting down your tree for you."

"You're not doing it for me, young man," she answered. "As far as I'm concerned, you've been at it too long already."

Mac shrugged and grinned sheepishly. "We've got orders to take it down, ma'am. "We're only doing what they told us."

"I am aware of that. And I realize I am no longer able to prevent you from cutting down my tree. But it does seem you could do it without making so much noise."

I could almost see Mac breathe easier. "I'm sorry, ma'am," he smiled. "That's the way we have to do it."

She drew herself up even stiffer. "Then I have nothing further to say."

She turned and went back into the house without another word. There was no curtain raised or light turned on. Whatever rooms she lived in, you couldn't tell from the street."

Mac come back down the walk shaking his head. "Trust one of them to give you trouble. Do you know the city had to force her to let us cut this tree down? That's right. Had to threaten to fine her and put her in jail. And look at the tree, will you. It's a hazard. Stubborn as a mule. They're all like that."

A few minutes later the door opened and the old lady come out again, with a flowered hat pinned flat to her hair and a light summer coat and a black handbag over her forearm. She turned the key in the lock, put the key in her bag and walked through the iron gate and down the street without a glance at any of us.

We'd taken down one whole leader already, as far back as the trunk, and we'd started on the second. The logs lay in the gutter like dead bodies. They'd have to be cut up before we could lift them onto the truck. It was beginning to get hot.

When she returned an hour later, we'd all taken our shirts off. She'd been walking, but she wasn't affected by the heat.

"Has the man from the city been here yet?" she asked.

"What man's that, ma'am?"

"The one who is in charge of the trees, of course."

"You mean Mr. Devlin, the tree warden. No, ma'am, he ain't been around here."

"Well, he will be. And when he arrives, you will please tell him I wish to speak to him."

Mac and I watched her go into the house.

"Oh, brother!" Mac muttered under his breath. "Is Devlin gonna be in a bad mood when he gets here!"

The job of tree warden was a political one in the city. It wasn't well paid, but it wasn't hard work, and whoever had it kept it as long as he could. Mike Devlin had held the job for ten years, which was as long as the party had been in office, and it didn't seem to've hurt him a bit. But when he drove up in his car a little later, you could see he was mad.

"Look, Mac, I don't mind if you argue with her. I do that myself. But you don't hafta insult her."

"Who insulted her?" Mac protested. "All I did was tell her why we had to use the power saw."

"She says you talked back to her."

"I explained to her is all." He turned to me. "You was there. Tell him that's all I done."

Just then the old lady's sharp voice interrupted. "I'd like to have a word with you, sir, if you don't mind."

Devlin scrambled out of his car, letting the door swing open behind him. "Yes, Mrs. Wilcox, right away." He almost ran up the front walk, his jacket flapping open and his necktie draped over his shoulder. He took his hat off and stood in front of the old lady on the porch, wiping his forehead on his sleeve. "I wanted you to see with your own eyes what they are doing to my tree," she said.

Frenchy was sitting on a limb about thirty feet up and Whitey and Bub was holding the ropes for him. All of us had stopped what we was doing to watch Devlin and the old lady.

"They're doing a first-rate job, Mrs. Wilcox," Devlin said. "Look how nice they've took this limb off. They oughta have them all off by this afternoon, and tomorrow they'll finish the trunk and cart the wood away."

"And you don't think it's a crime to cut down a lovely old elm?"

"Oh, yes, ma'am, I do. But like I think I mentioned to you once before, and like the Board of Aldermen told you last week, this tree is diseased. Maybe a few years ago it could've been saved, but the way it is now it's got to come down."

The old lady didn't budge. She stood her ground on the top step, her arms folded and glaring up into the tree while Devlin worked his toe against the bottom step, turned his hat around in his hands and tried to explain the facts to her.

"If the tree is diseased," she said, "isn't that my concern?"

"Well, no, not exactly, Mrs. Wilcox. You see, it's your tree, but the branches hang all the way out into the street and over the used car lot. A branch could break off any time and hurt somebody, or even damage someone's property. Besides, a diseased elm oughta come down right away or it infects other trees."

"Do you see any other trees here on Cherry Street?"

"No-o," Devlin admitted slowly. He looked like he was cursing himself for letting her score a point, even if it didn't mean anything. But then he kinda gathered himself together and leaned forward and used his confidential tone. "Mrs. Wilcox," he said, "last week, after the city'd been trying for three or four years to get you to take this tree down, you told us you'd let us do it. You agreed to it. We made all the arrangements, hired the crew, and the tree's halfway down already. Now just between you and I, why don't we let them finish the job? What do you say, Mrs. Wilcox?"

Her jaw moved a little. Then she tightened her lips. "And you must use that infernal machine to cut the branches?"

Devlin straightened up triumphantly. "'Believe me, Mrs. Wilcox, it's the quickest and the easiest way. By tomorrow it'll be all over."

She glared at him for a minute, then took a deep breath. "Very well. You may cut down my tree however you wish. I have nothing more to say."

Devlin watched her go back into the house. Then he jammed his hat back on and walked fast out the gate. "Come on, you guys," he said through closed lips with the sound coming from somewhere in his stomach, "get busy and finish the job before she changes her mind again."

Up in the tree the chain saw started up. Whitey and Bub pulled their ropes taut, and a new shower of sawdust fell on the sidewalk. As Devlin slid across the front seat of his car and turned on the ignition, Mac leaned in his window and said, "You mean the city's gonna pay to take down her tree?"

"Don't worry, she'll get a bill," he grunted. "She can afford it better than the city can. Now you boys get back to work. I gotta have a drink after this."

We took off two more leaders before lunch. By now the branches furthest out were down, and the old elm didn't look much like an elm any more. By the time we stopped for lunch, it was getting real hot and there wasn't much shade under that tree. We put away our tools, rolled the logs off the sidewalk and drove to a gin mill downtown for beer and sandwiches.

"They'll always give you trouble," Mac was saying as we ate. "If you're doin' it one way, they want it the other way. Or else they change their mind when you're halfway finished and don't want it done at all. This one'd have us put the tree back together if we could."

"Yeah," Whitey said. "She likes it all right when the sun's out, but wait till a storm drops one of them leaders on a wire and knocks out her electricity. Then you'll hear her howl."

Frenchy didn't say a thing: He was the kind of guy that does more work than anybody else but never talks about it. He rubbed his hands and began to pick under his nails. Finally he said, "Well, an old tree like that one, she musta got used to it. I sorta hate to cut it down myself."

It took us the rest of the day to top that tree, even with the power saw. Frenchy worked downward, and he was careful not to go too far out from the center to make his cuts. He knew he was safe enough himself on account of his rope, but he didn't want to break a leader and have it crack the sidewalk or dig up the lawn. So by the end of the day the leaders were off, and the trunk was standing there gray and bare, with patches of bark torn off below the fresh cuts. It looked like somebody's arm reaching up out of the ground with half of the fingers cut off. Before we left, we sawed up the logs and stacked them so we could finish up quick next day.

"Maybe we can have it cut by noon," said Mac next morning. "Then we can get outa this heat."

We worked from the ladders now, with Frenchy still on the power saw. The trunk was thick, and the chain didn't dig deep enough to cut through the first time. So he worked first from one side and then from the other and cut the trunk into big chunks, with just the weight of the power saw to carry. When he'd finished, the trunk was laid out all over the lawn and the sidewalk in six-foot cylinders, like the pictures you see of old Greek ruins with busted columns of some temple laying in the sun. What was uncut was only about three foot of stump sticking up. It looked like an elephant had went off and left its foot there.

"That does it, I guess," said Whitey.

"Look at that wood," said Mac. "It's gonna take two truckloads at least to cart it off."

"Maybe we could leave it here and let her use it for firewood," Bub suggested. Bub was always looking for the easy way.

Frenchy just looked at him pitying-like. "Chunks that big? Who do you think's gonna lug 'em into the house for her and set the fire? You're gettin' lazier by the day."

"We maybe c'd split 'em up for her," Bub insisted. "No harm in askin'."

I guessed Bub wasn't looking to get out of work this time, so I said, "I'll ask her." I went up the steps and rang the bell. After a minute she come to the door.

"So it's down at last," she said. I couldn't tell whether she was happy or sad about it.

"Yes, ma'am, and we wondered if you wanted us to leave some of it here for firewood."

"Firewood! I should say not! Do you think I want anything left to remind me of that lovely old elm? Firewood, indeed!"

I guess I never should've asked her. I started down the walk, but I had the feeling she was still there.

"You men do intend to remove the stump too, I hope."

Mac took a deep breath. "No, ma'am. They told us to leave it."

"Well, I'm telling you to remove it. That's what I want done."

Mac scratched his head and looked at the stump. "'We can't do it today, ma'am. We got another job this afternoon. If you'd said so yesterday, we could've left enough there to pull it out with the winch. This way it'll take a couple days to get it out. Maybe next week sometime."

She was hopping mad now. "You mean you intend to leave that stump so that I'll be reminded of my beautiful tree every time I go out?"

"Tell you what you do, ma'am," says Frenchy. "You take a can of kerosene and let it soak into the stump. It'll eat out that wood faster than anythin' you ever seen. After that you can just knock it over."

She seemed doubtful, but then her eyes brightened. "Kerosene, you say? I have kerosene. One of you come with me."

I followed her around the house to the garage. From somewhere she took a key, opened the side door, found a cord and lit a bare light bulb hanging from the ceiling. We was in a small room with small windows clouded with dust and cobwebs. It looked like it had been an office once, but the air smelled like the door hadn't been opened in a year. Against one wall was an old rolltop desk covered with dust, and tacked to the wall over it was an old oval photograph. It was faded and flyspecked, but you could make out a guy with a brown beard and a fierce look, in a Civil War Union Army officer's uniform.

"There's kerosene in that can against the wall," she said. "Take what you want."

It was next to some paint and turpentine, a full gallon of it. The old lady was looking at the picture over the desk, but when I picked up the kerosene she led me out and locked the door, leaving the guy to stare out into the empty room.

Frenchy had just finished cutting the trunk as low as the power saw would cut it. He took the can and poured some of the kerosene into the wood and watched it soak in. "That oughta do it, ma'am," he said. "You won't need the rest of the can."

"Then put the can on the porch. I can use what's left."

Frenchy looked at her. "Too bad we had to take your tree down, ma'am," he said. "Musta been seventy, eighty year old, that ellum."

Her eyes narrowed. "It was older than that, young man. My grandfather planted that elm after the Civil War, the year he built this house." She started to go, and then turned back. "He planted four of them on this property, two in front and two in back along with the other trees. This one was the last."

She opened the door, noticed the kerosene can, came back to pick it up and carried it inside with her.

It took us longer than we thought to pile the logs on the truck, and when the truck was full we still had another load to go. We took the truck out past rows of three-family houses till we got to a dirt road leading past a swamp to the dump. There was piles of brush, and blackened treetrunks face down in the ashes, and big stumps with dirt-covered roots clawing the air. It was a bad year for the Dutch elm disease.

When we got back, we loaded up the rest of the logs and swept up the sawdust. We didn't see the old lady but there wasn't a trace of what we'd been doing for her to complain about. The tree was gone, and the house was a little more exposed to the street, and in a corner of the lawn, not even noticeable unless you looked for it, was the kerosene-soaked stump.

I lived not too far from Cherry Street myself. It was almost on my way home. So when I heard the fire engines later on, I followed the crowd to see what was burning. By the time I reached Cherry Street, two engines and at least fifty people was there already, and the guy in the used car lot was moving his cars away. But no one had set foot on the old lady's property. They was just standing in the street watching her pour kerosene on that blazing stump.

"Go ahead, arrest me," she was saying to the cop. "Do your duty. Put me in jail."

Donovan, the fire chief, was there, trying to reason with her and at the same time asking who'd turned in the alarm and brought out two fire engines to put out a tree stump.

Alderman Di Costanzo showed up too, and together they talked to her about the months and years they'd been trying to have her take down the tree, and asked her what made her go and deliberately break a city ordinance now.

"It was your idea to destroy my tree," she said. "Why didn't you remove it altogether? I merely finished your work for you."

They quieted her down and promised to take out what was left of the stump. But she wouldn't go back into her house until the crowd was gone and the engines had drove off. Then she went back and shut her door behind her, leaving the city officials wondering what to do with her.

"What *can* you do with her?" the alderman asked the fire chief. "I been getting gray hairs for months over this thing."

But the chief was an older guy with more experience.

"Listen," he said, "this has happened before, and it'll happen again. They always give you as much trouble as they can because they know that's all they can do. So all you can do is wait for them to die off. You'll see. When she's gone, the house'll come down because nobody else'd live in it or pay the taxes. Then maybe the property'll be put to some good use."

So that was all. Everything was the same as before except for the tree. It was getting dark when I left, and inside the old lady's house there wasn't a light to be seen.

THE GREAT COUNTRY DAY
SCHOOL SHOOTOUT

It was a memorable day in September 1935 when Eddie Dooley finally entered Somerset Country Day School. Eddie was Irish Catholic, which was bad enough, but the fact that his father Mickey was well known locally as the proprietor of a saloon on the wrong side of Main Street made it far worse. Had the father been a lawyer or, better, a judge or a doctor, the idea of Eddie entering the fifth grade with the Bancroft and Hurd and Beecher children might not have caused such a stir. But as the son of a saloon-keeper, well...

However, the Country Day School was desperate, and no one knew this better than Grace March, its founder and principal. Grace March and Mildred Waterman had come to Somerset five years earlier filled with the ideas of John Dewey and the dream of making progressive education a living reality. They had chosen Somerset because, in addition to being a quiet New England town, it lay just outside the gritty industrial city of Quassatuck and counted among its eight thousand inhabitants several of Quassatuck's leading manufacturers. The present generation of these families had begun to flee the city in the twenties and had built comfortable homes in the wooded hills around Somerset, leaving the city with a public school system they considered adequate for children of immigrant factory workers, but not for their own. And the Somerset public schools were not much better than Quassatuck's.

So Grace March was confident the town was ripe for a private country day school financed by the new families. She was also sure the better local families would be anxious to have their own children grow up with the scions of the Bancrofts and the Hurds and the Beechers.

Grace was right in principle. But her success in convincing the new generation of Quassatuck's Yankee aristocracy was due not so much to a felt need on their part as to the energy and influence of a few of their wives who like Grace had been exposed to the new ideas afoot in university circles.

Mabel Beecher in particular shared Grace's excitement and was convinced the school could make a go of it. It was Mabel who sold the idea to the wives of the second- and third-generation factory-owners many of whose fathers had gone to work in their teens but who now recognized the fact that a private school in Somerset would help their sons get into a good prep school and go on to Yale.

The school began with two dozen children in a large house a block from the Lawn Club and the Episcopal Church—familiar ground for the parents and far enough from the contamination of Main Street and its public and parochial schools. And at first it prospered. There was an art class and a theatrical group nurtured by Mildred Waterman and a music program led by Grace March herself. The children, from the tiniest tots in kindergarten to the handful of sixth-and seventh-graders, were encouraged to express themselves freely in a day when public school benches and desks were still bolted to the floor. Music was taught with illustrations from a wind-up victrola and a few scratchy records, such as Casals playing *The Swan* and Rosa and Carmela Ponselle singing *The Barcarolle*. The children were given triangles and tambourines to strike rhythmically as Grace played Schubert's *Marche Militaire* on an upright piano donated by one of the parents. Mildred Waterman's Christmas pageant brought out the specific talents of budding scene painters, costume designers, actors and even playwrights. Beaming parents sat on folding chairs to applaud a surprised Joseph returning with an armload of fire wood to ask his wife, "What's that you've got in the manger, Mary?" and to smile with respectful approval as more shepherds and Wise Men than needed gathered to kneel at the manger so that no child would be left out of the performance. In Science class older students read *The Earth for Sam* to learn about dinosaurs and Piltdown Man, and one boy even hung an entire solar system, more or less to scale, from the classroom ceiling. Even so, time was somehow found to learn the multiplication tables as well.

Yet, as the country sank deeper into the Great Depression, the Somerset Country Day School barely remained solvent. It lost its lease and had to move to a house almost outside town to which most of the children had to be driven. Parents who had helped with chauffeured station wagons in bringing children in from Quassatuck now delivered carloads of local pupils as well. Tuition rose, and more than one family, no longer able to afford keeping its child among the wealthiest, had to resign itself to a lower rung on the social ladder and turn to the public school.

But when it became clear that the youngest couples, those with kindergarten-age children, were fewer than before, and that those whose offspring had begun in kindergarten and were now in the fifth grade would have no replacements to offer when these were gone, Grace March ruefully began to admit that the well was running dry.

"I'm afraid we'll have to broaden our base," she told Mabel Beecher, "if we're to stay alive."

"You mean open our doors to...?"

"To those who can afford to send their children here."

"But not to just... anyone, I hope."

"No, only to a select few."

"But how to select them? We can't put an advertisement in the newspaper."

"There have been some inquiries," Grace said somewhat mysteriously.

"I should imagine so—from some of the pushier elements, no doubt."

"Not exclusively. The Dooleys, for instance..."

"The Dooleys?"

"You know. Local people, not from Quassatuck. They own real estate, and they're in manufacturing too, in a way. They have an interest in a coal company, and a brewery, and..."

"Not Mickey Dooley, the saloon-keeper!?"

"Well, I suppose he does own a tavern too."

"You mean that Irish clown has approached you to put his brats in our country day school?"

"It was his wife, in fact. She's a Fitzpatrick; you know, the funeral home. She's a very respectable woman, really."

"Yes, the daughter of an undertaker and the granddaughter of one of my great-aunt's housemaids. You're not serious, Grace!"

"I did turn her down last year but now I think it can be worked out. Apparently the boy is quite talented, and she sincerely wants him to have more opportunity to develop than he's had in the parochial school. Besides, it could prove to be a broadening influence on the other children culturally as well as artistically. And Mabel, what choice do we have?"

The question was put directly to Mabel Beecher in full knowledge that the Beecher Button Company, one of Quassatuck's oldest firms, had fallen on hard times and further that Mabel and Andrew Beecher had not produced another child to follow those already in the upper grades.

Mabel did not respond directly.

"Who else has made inquiries?"

"Well, there are the Kaplans. He does own the largest department store in Quassatuck ."

"Jews. Who else?"

"Really, Mabel, those are the best offers we've had. We just can't afford not to take at least one of them."

Mabel Beecher considered for a moment.

"Grace, it isn't like five years ago, when I could go to my friends with an exciting new idea. The school has been functioning well. I have shown what progressive education can do. But the fact is, the money just isn't there any more. Nor are the children. So if they don't really need the school for their own children, why should they subsidize it for the Dooleys and the Kaplans?"

"It's not a matter of subsidizing anyone," said Grace, flushing. "It's simply a matter of sharing the benefits."

Mabel looked away, then caught herself. "Grace, you know me well enough to know that I am not prejudiced *personally*. But you must also realize that I have to convince the others."

"I understand."

"I know you do. Now let's be practical. The Kaplans are out of the question, of course. But you say the Dooley boy has talent?"

"He draws very well and he can write. Mildred is truly excited at the thought of working with him."

"What grade would he enter?"

"He's eleven and ready to enter sixth grade. So we wouldn't have him for more than three years."

"I suppose that's good, from one point of view," said Mabel. "Well, perhaps in the meantime we can attract a few more of the right kind. I'm so sorry you're in such a hole, Grace. But I do trust your judgment. And you can count on me to convince the others."

So Eddie Dooley entered Somerset Country Day School that fall. He was only an average student, but he was a rambunctious boy, carefree and uninhibited, and a good playmate for the others his age and for the smaller children as well. For that Grace March was thankful. At least they accepted him and didn't avoid him. And because he was bigger than most of them and brought his own football to school, tirelessly practicing scrimmages with the younger ones, he was the object of hero worship. Even when the ball went through a school window, his mother paid up promptly and offered to contribute toward better sports facilities. She was a large, handsome woman. She dressed conservatively, and her hair was carefully marcelled. Some said it was dyed, but Grace was sure it wasn't, and Mabel finally concluded she was simply lace curtain and anxious for her son to rise above his father's status. If so, Eddie seemed unaffected and behaved as if social differences did not exist.

But it was Mildred Waterman who thought the most of Eddie Dooley, for here at last was a boy with real imagination and talent to be developed. He kept a battery of colored pencils and crayons in his pockets and decorated everything he could lay his hands on, including his homework.

And he was a cartoonist, as well. More than once during study period he was caught drawing the panels of an imitation Dick Tracy episode and was taken aside and lectured by Grace March, who confiscated a notebook filled with his cartoons. Eddie promised he wouldn't do it again, but the next day he showed up with another notebook and began to fill it with more picture stories. Mildred, who had begged Grace to see the first book, took it home and brought it back the next morning with her eyes shining.

"He's good, Grace. He's really good. The characters are cops and robbers, and borrowed at that. But the story line is clear and direct. Each episode has punch. I'm really excited about him."

"I didn't notice the story line," said Grace, "but I did notice the spelling. Did you?"

"He'll learn," Mildred insisted. "He learns fast when he's interested in something. I've watched him. "He only draws when he's bored."

"I'm glad of that, but first he needs an education."

"He'll get one. And you know what? I'll start a magazine and ask each child to contribute a story. We'll turn it out on the mimeograph machine and send copies to all the parents."

"And you'll correct everyone's spelling?"

"They'll correct their own mistakes with my suggestions. I'll mark their papers and teach them to use the dictionary. I'll tell them their stories will only be printed free of errors. Do I have your blessing?"

Grace March raised three fingers over Mildred's head and made a mock sign of the cross. "You do. And you'd better pass the blessing on to Eddie Dooley."

"To the others, you mean. Eddie won't need it."

The Somerset Country Day School Magazine became the most exciting new project of the school year. It eclipsed the Italian invasion of Ethiopia as a topic of interest, though more time was given to reading about Ethiopia now, and and to building grass huts in the school yard out of saplings and burlap. It survived the onset of the Spanish Civil war too, though there the issues were less clear-cut and Eddie was heard arguing with the other boys who said they were for the Loyalists. "I'm for the Rebels," he told them proudly. "They're defending the Church." The others jeered, but their embarrassment was plain to Grace, who guessed this was the first time they had heard a Catholic point of view.

But Mildred's eyes were fixed on the first issue of the magazine, and political considerations were foreign to her nature. She urged the children on, cajoling recalcitrants and even suggesting topics for those without imagination. With Eddie there was no need. He not only wrote a story but illustrated it. Then he wrote another and another, and by the end of a two week period he had turned out a half dozen wild and woolly tales of cops-and-robbers, cowboys-and-Indians and World War dogfights over the trenches.

Mildred was overwhelmed. She read each story carefully, marked each grammatical and spelling error and forced him to make his own corrections. But she didn't criticize or change a single piece of the action, as she was forced to do with some of the others. Finally she took Eddie aside and told him in confidence, "You know, Eddie, I can't publish *all* your stories and only one by each of the others. So you'll have to choose one and save the others for other issues. Why don't you pick the best one and tell me why it's the best?"

Eddie didn't hesitate for a moment. "This is the best one," he said, pulling out one story and handing it to her.

"Why?" she asked without looking at the story.

"Because there's real suspense. You want the bad guy to get killed, and when it's the good guy you're sad. But you know that's the way it had to be."

"All right, let's see." Mildred looked at the story, smiling inwardly because this one was her choice too. "Shootout in the Red Horse Saloon" was the title, with the illustration showing in rear view the lower half of the body of a tall cowboy with spurs and two Colts at his hips. He was facing the swinging doors of a saloon, which was seen with the tiny figure of the bad guy framed by his legs, opposite him at the bar inside.

"It looks fine, Eddie," she said. "I'm proud of you. Now forget about these stories and start thinking about the next one."

"That's easy," he said. "I've got it all worked out in my head. All I have to do is write it down. It's kinda like Flash Gordon, y'see..."

She stopped him and sent him back to his desk. Then she read the story again and held it to her breast. At the end of the day she took it to Grace March together with the half dozen other stories which would appear in later issues.

"I think you'll agree that this vindicates us in everything we've ever said about Eddie. It's that good. And for an eleven-year-old it's unbelievable."

"I'll look at it tonight," said Grace.

She did, comparing it with the others, to which it was obviously superior. Yet a sense of uneasiness crept over her, and she tried to formulate what she would say to Mildred.

"Don't you think there's a bit too much violence?" she began tentatively. "I mean, look at the titles of some of the others: 'Jack and His Animal Friends,' or ''My Summer Vacation.'"

"But they're nothing," Mildred protested. "I practically had to write them myself. Those kids' minds were a blank."

Grace sighed. "Then I wish you'd done the same with Eddie's. Anyway, I'll show it to Mabel. She approved of taking Eddie."

But Mabel Beecher's perusal never went beyond the title and the illustration. "'Shootout in the Red Horse Saloon'! And with a saloon actually pictured, down to the swinging doors! Grace, you can't publish this. Either it would be Eddie's last day in school or else half the parents would withdraw their children. 'The Red Horse Saloon,' indeed!"

"Mabel, it's only a Western," said Grace. "The children all follow them on the radio and read them in their Big Little Books. They're not intended to depict real life."

"That's just it, Grace. In Eddie Dooley's case everyone will say that's just what it does. Like father, like son. And when they start asking what Mickey Dooley the saloon keeper was doing during Prohibition, the game will be over. Parents will say Eddie just hasn't adapted at all. They'll say, 'We told you so. You tried to make a silk purse out of a sow's ear.'

"Besides, you don't allow any of the children to read such trash. I've seen you confiscate more than one of their comic books. Why, you even found one of those horrible 'pulp' magazines in my Johnny's desk. It had been passed from boy to boy for a week. You can't allow Eddie Dooley's story to be published by the school after doing that!"

"But what can we do? We promised him we'd publish it."

"Just tell him you've changed your minds. Surely he can write a story without a saloon in it. At least, I hope he can."

Grace returned to Mildred with the bad news.

"Why, that's ridiculous!" fumed Mildred. "The story is perfectly innocent. He made it up out of what he sees in the movies. It's pure American folklore."

"That's not what the parents will say, Mildred. And they hold the purse strings. Doesn't he have one without violence?"

"They're all violent, I told you, but the violence is just a game. As for the saloon, I hope you don't want me to tell him we can't publish it because it mentions the business his father is in."

"Well, we'll have to find a solution. We simply can't publish that story."

"We'll publish it, or I'll resign!" said Mabel Waterman.

"Now, Mabel dear," said Grace, "you know you can't do that. We've been together a long time. We believe in the same things. And I'm afraid you'd have a hard time finding another job."

Mabel's eyes filled with tears. "But this boy deserves to see his story in print. "He's the only one with real talent, and it may be the only talent he has. He'll need it to make his way in the world, while the others won't."

"Then let's sit down and see if we can't find a solution together."

They found one after many hours of agonizing. It was Grace, the perfect diplomat, who thought of a way to reconcile opposing parties ready to do battle. The answer was simple enough. The Somerset Country Day School Magazine, Volume I, Number 1, appeared on schedule after hours of typing stencils and still more hours of fitting them to the mimeograph machine and running off copies by hand. Much ink was spilled, much paper wasted, but the magazine included every story written for it, from the most amateurish by one of the Hurd children, who were among the wealthiest in Quassatuck and were related to the Bancrofts, to Eddie Dooley's "Shootout in the Red Horse Saloon." Eddie's story occupied last place—the place of honor, he was assured. The copies were collated by hand and carefully stapled together with the cover page listing the stories inside. Finally, each copy was placed in an envelope bearing a parent's name and address, sealed and handed to a child to take home as evidence of the creative work pupils in the right kind of progressive school could do— and incidentally to save the school the cost of a mailing.

There was only one difference between the copy sent to Mr. and Mrs. Michael Dooley and those sent to the

Beechers and the Bancrofts and the Hurds. A second cover stencil listing Eddie's story had been run off and substituted for the cover sheet sent to all the others so that Eddie's story, "Shootout in the Red Horse Saloon," appeared as the final piece and was proudly carried home to his parents by Eddie. Only if someone had weighed the envelopes individually would it be apparent that all the others were somewhat lighter than the Dooleys' copy because Eddie's story had not been included and the cover sheet made no mention of it whatsoever.

When it was all over Grace March heaved a long sigh and swore Mildred to secrecy. Eddie had not suspected that none of the other parents would be contaminated by reading "Shootout in the Red Horse Saloon," and Grace was sure in her own mind that none of the parents, including Mabel Beecher, would ever know. After all, the Dooleys didn't travel in the same circles as the Beechers and the Hurds and the Bancrofts.

Eddie was exultant over his literary success, but he couldn't understand why there would be no second issue of the magazine. He'd already written several more stories, any one of which he considered an advance over "Shootout." But Mildred explained to him that the costs had been too high and urged him to continue writing or return to comic strips such as *Prince Valiant in the Days of King Arthur*. But Eddie told her he was more interested in the future than in the past, something like *Flash Gordon*. Mildred didn't tell him she had run off one copy of his story for herself, which she hoped to show him years later after he had made a name for himself as a writer.

The school continued to lose money and despite the best efforts of Grace March and Mabel Beecher never found enough acceptable families to fill the gap left by the growing children of its first patrons. Progressive teaching methods, of course, were adopted later by public schools everywhere, but by 1939 the Somerset Country Day School had ceased to exist, and its devoted founders had moved on to teaching jobs elsewhere.

As for Eddie Dooley, he finished eighth grade at public school and, unable to pass the entrance exams for the prep schools, spent four years at Somerset High and then was drafted into the Army. He still planned to become a cartoonist or write stories for a living after the war, even though he never had an opportunity to be on the staff of *Yank* or *The Stars and Stripes* or any of the Army's other outlets for literary talent. Instead he went directly through infantry basic training and then overseas as a replacement in an infantry regiment, where his talent for leadership demonstrated at Somerset Country Day School earned him a promotion to sergeant. He was a squad leader when he was killed in action during street fighting in the Rhineland. The citation for his Bronze Star noted that, when pinned down by sniper fire from a bombed-out building, he had kicked in the door and, though mortally wounded, had killed the sniper.

The Bronze Star and the Purple Heart were of some consolation to his parents, but Mildred Waterman had lost touch with people in Somerset, and so it was many years later before she learned what had happened to Eddie Dooley.

Justice Be Done

1

The telephone on my desk seemed to reverberate long after I'd hung up the receiver and settled back to stare at it balefully.

The voice had been pleasant enough, almost familiar though I'd have given a lot to know whose it was, and the words it spoke were so simple and ordinary that they might have come from any one of the legmen who phoned in tips for my column.

"If you're interested in a little item on your bogey man," the voice had said, "why don't you come up to the old home town and have a talk with someone who knows something about him?"

"Who is this?" I'd asked with professional suspicion, though I half knew already it wasn't the kind of tipoff that bears a signature.

"Just a friend. So why don't we make it tomorrow, say about one o'clock? Go to the Blue Moon and have a beer in one of the booths. Make sure you go alone, but don't worry; it'll be worth your while. You may even get a free lunch out of it. And I can promise you it's just what you need to get yourself off that big hook in the editor's office."

And that was all. I was supposed to fly up to Connecticut by tomorrow noon, canceling out on an interview
with a congressman I'd been after for weeks, and all on
the basis of an anonymous tip.

Yet I knew I was going to do exactly what I'd been
told to do, because as things stood now I was in no position to refuse.

The hook in question was to be found in my editor's
office, and the bogey man responsible for my being on that
hook was none other than Senator Temple Phelps, the drug-
busting crusader from Yankeeland. It seems I'd been making accusations in print without proof, and my editor was
under pressure to drop my column. On my shoulders was
thereby to fall the mantle of scapegoat for a considerable
part of the opposition to Phelps, to his party and to the
investigation he was pursuing into the ties between the
drug traffic and certain politicians. It was a role for which
others may have felt me highly qualified, but it was one
which understandably I did not relish and which I was
about to go to great lengths to avoid playing.

Perhaps I should explain my special position in regard
to so famous a man as Temple Phelps. Almost everyone
was familiar with the image—the Latin-quoting Yankee
senator who came down to Washington like a clean north
wind, incorruptible and irresistable as the great glaciers that
once covered most of New England. They considered him
a latter-day Puritan here to clean up corruption in high
and low places and restore to us our ancient virtues. A
strange figure to be the idol of millions; but the voters'
mood was in favor of a house-cleaning, and he seemed
made to order for the job.

His background was impeccable: Yale College, Harvard
Law School, clerk to a Supreme Court justice, then a significant twist which had sent him, rather than into corpo-
ration law where the money was, back up to New England

to teach law, raise a family, and finally—he was thirty-six at the time—accept the presidency of a small college, one of the best. It was a position for which he was eminently suited, both socially and financially. He traced his ancestry back to a Mayflower Saint and a witch-burning divine, to say nothing of ship captains, soldiers and a colonial statesman. His wife Marjorie had brought him wealth and with it the freedom to pursue his goals without regard to salary; yet they lived unostentatiously in a Greek revival white-columned house on the shady main street of town. Their son, Warren, was a senior in at one of the better schools and seemed a perfectly normal preppy.

You couldn't attack such a man as Phelps frontally, or through ridicule or innuendo. It backfired every time. As a columnist for a paper controlled by the opposition I had been trying hard but it just wasn't our year. He broke every rule of campaigning and still won by a landslide. Being above suspicion, he got away with every unorthodoxy simply because he was a college professor and not a professional politician. We all know eggheads have to be careful how they talk to the voters. Some talk down to them, and some talk over their heads, and still others try to talk to ethnics in their own language, most of them losing more votes than they gain. Temple Phelps, on the other hand, spoke to them neither in French nor Italian nor Polish nor Spanish. He spoke in Latin, in a sort of dialogue with himself on the subject of civic virtue, and still they voted for him.

Quoting Latin aphorisms, in fact, was an old habit of his, and somewhere in his academic past it had earned him the nickname "Tempus". This may not have been the correct rendering of Temple in Latin, but it got the idea across, and it stuck. It seemed to humanize his austere image, because although he was a throwback to his Puritan ancestors even to a physical resemblance, his manner could be charming and his smile boyish and disarmingly sincere. This lent conviction to his pledges, though few realized that carrying them out would have meant a revolution. It was when he began to try that the real trouble began.

It was the first time in my memory that the party had found itself completely on the defensive. At a high point in his crusading career Tempus Phelps was investigating alleged connections between certain high-placed party members and elements of the Johnny Dorato mob, connections said to extend from the old home town to Washington and back, and to include heroin and cocaine.

This was embarrassing to us, to say the least. Our explanations and reasoned arguments were being brushed aside in favor of Phelps and his high moral purpose, and we were ready to use any weapon to defend ourselves, including me. I'd tried to help by devoting a series of columns to pooh-poohing the whole investigation as a desperate attempt to find corruption where none existed. I'd ridiculed Phelps as a professorial Don Quixote tilting at windmills, and very cleverly, I thought, I'd coined a catchword title for the series: "Tempus in a Teapot."

It didn't work. The mail flooded in not only from towns across the country where the column appeared but from places where no one would have thought they'd even heard of New England, let alone Tempus Phelps. I dropped the subject in my next column, but before the week was up I was eating my words.

"Larry," my editor told me as I stood on the carpet in his office, "you have been attacking a sacred cow, and the faithful don't like it. If you want to convert a man from a false religion, you don't make a joke of the idol he worships. You've got to string along with him, flatter him until you find a way to show him his idol isn't everything he thinks it is. In other words, you've got to find the flaw in that idol."

I shook my head. "Tempus Phelps hasn't got a flaw. That's the whole trouble with him." It was what put the fire in his eye. Another man would have hesitated to make the accusations he made, if not out of prudence then out of plain humility. But not Phelps. Humility wasn't in him. He knew he was right.

But the boss just looked back at me hard.

"He's a man, isn't he? He's human."

The question didn't require an answer. He just let it sink in. Then his voice returned to its normal tone as he picked up a sheaf of papers and started going through them.

"Let me know when you've found it, my boy. It might make a big difference in your life."

Well, I had a wife and kids to raise, and that was why, when the phone on my desk rang that afternoon, I was not going to refuse the offer that came with it, even if it meant walking all the way up to Connecticut to get it.

2

I didn't have to walk, though. I flew up on one of those clear, cool fall days that make you think of New England wherever you may be, the air filled with a pungent dryness and even in the city the odor of burning leaves. Quassatuck was one of the largest towns in the state though it wasn't the capital nor Phelps's home town. But it had attracted industry in the past, and during World War II it had been known as the Brass Capital of America. But the brass industry was gone, and even the mills were being torn down, giving way to malls as the city tried to rebuild its center and attract new industry. I walked along these streets now, observing the faces of people who had emptied half the houses in Georgetown and on Capitol Hill with their votes and had sent Phelps in to clean out what was left. No one recognized me; they simply continued on their way unaware of the fascination they held for politicians, like a princess in a castle tower, and unaware of the trap being set to nullify their will as expressed in the last election.

At the appointed hour I entered the tavern known as the Blue Moon and took a seat in a booth. And before five minutes were up a man I did not know had taken me out the back door into a waiting car and to a restaurant which we also entered by the back door, climbing a flight of stairs to a private dining room. There, alone at a small table, his napkin tucked under his chin and several strands of spaghetti joining his lips to his plate, was a personage whom I knew only too well.

"Why, Judge, what a surprise!"

"Larry, my boy, how good of you to come," answered Judge J. Clement Wells with a twinkle in his watery blue eyes. "And what a pleasure for us. It isn't every day that we small town folks are honored by visitors from our nation's capital."

Judge Wells was one of those individuals who embody so completely the role they play that you half suspect they make up for the part each morning before the mirror. In Wells's case the model was almost a caricature out of Herblock, even to the pince-nez on a black string; for no man without consciously making up could so look the soul of honor and integrity yet by his actions reveal himself so totally false. "Clement is my middle name," he liked to say, and clemency is what he obtained for clients like Johnny Dorato and his friends. I should have known it was Wells who was behind the phone call I'd received the day before.

"Yes, my boy," he finally began after numerous generalities while my meal was being served, "life plays strange tricks on all of us. Fortune takes us to the heights then casts us into the void. And what rhyme or reason is there in it, finally? The only thing we can count on, the only constant, is human frailty."

He dabbed with his napkin at the tomato sauce on his lips and poured himself a glass of wine. I sensed that he was coming to the point.

"Yes, human frailty. In the law we see all too much of it. That's what I could never understand about Temple Phelps. You'd think a man with his background and training would realize none of us is free from some frailty— none of us. But then, Phelps has always been a theoretician of the law, a professor, not an everyday, down-to-earth practitioner like myself. That has been his greatest failing. His fatal flaw, you might say."

"Then you've discovered some of Phelps's own human failings, Judge? If so, you know him better than I do."

"Certainly I know him better than you do. We're both at the bar. I see him at reunions, club luncheons and the like, to say nothing of professional associations. But that's not what I'm driving at. Here, perhaps these will enlighten you."

From under his chair he produced a sleek and impeccable leather briefcase, pulled the zipper carefully around three of its edges and withdrew several large photos which he handed to me across the linen tablecloth.

"Look these over and tell me what you see."

I saw scenes of considerable gaiety, with roulette tables, a plush bar and guests in evening dress with arms about each other and glasses raised on high. I recognized the place as one of Johnny Dorato's clubs which recently had been raided and closed as a result of revelations made before Tempus Phelps's subcommittee. A hidden camera had obviously been used, and what was of particular significance was the cast of characters. For there, grouped in convivial chumminess were not only Johnny and some of his henchmen but certain well-known faces in the local and state political picture. I could only whistle.

"This," said Wells, "is the situation which you have been trying to downgrade in your column as unimportant or even nonexistent. Unfortunately, these are only prints. The negatives are in the hands of the subcommittee and are to be presented at next week's hearings, as is a videotape. Now do you see why it would be wise to take this threat seriously?"

Ruefully, I admitted that I did.

"On the other hand, we are thankful now that we took a few precautions of our own. These," he handed me another set of prints, "were taken at the same place but on a different occasion. Now tell me if you recognize any of the players."

I compared them. Same bar, same mob. But this time, instead of political figures, I saw to my astonishment, there in a white dinner jacket and with the familiar high, domed forehead and solemn jaw of his father, though softer and weaker and in one shot bestowing a kiss upon a rather luscious blonde, none other than Warren R., only son of Senator Temple Phelps.

I whistled again, rather more loudly.

"This time," said J. Clement Wells, "you can well whistle at what you have seen. Not, mind you, that young Phelps's conduct was in any way more sinful or reprehensible than that of many of his well-heeled contemporaries—it was, in fact, a secret school outing including drugs with some of his classmates—but because of the effect such photos are bound to have on the current Senate investigation. And, oh yes, I almost neglected to show you this one."

What he handed me this time was a photocopy of an I.O.U. in the amount of several thousand dollars from Warren R. Phelps to John Dorato. The two names seemed to leer out at me like two guilty figures caught at night in the beam of a cop's flashlight. The date was months earlier, long before the current investigation and before Phelps had even been nominated by his party for the Senate.

"It's unfortunate none of this could be used in the campaign," remarked Wells. "But at that time the existence of the club was unknown to the subcommittee. And now that the club is closed we can at least avoid further attacks. So the wind was not so ill that it brought us no good at all."

"Let me get this straight," I said. "You mean young Phelps lost his shirt to Johnny Dorato at roulette and owes him that much money right now?"

"That, my boy, I have no way of telling. But even if the debt has been paid it would seem only prudent on Johnny's part to keep a photocopy. Besides, there is this one last item."

This time I found myself looking at a receipt for $25,000 "for services rendered" and dated a few weeks later.

"Good God! You mean he was on the payroll too?"

"Not at all. He may merely have run a few errands, brought some of his classmates to the club and introduced them to a source of cocaine."

"Cocaine?"

"Yes, didn't you know?" purred Wells. "Young Warren is hooked, as they say, and Johnny is his source of supply."

"So if the Senator pursues the case, you could threaten him not only with a family scandal but with a jail sentence for his son. Is that it?"

Wells's smile was almost a fatherly one now. "Not I, my boy. I want as little to do with this as possible. But we thought that Larry Gillis, being so to speak identified with the opposition to Phelps, might allude in his column to certain compromising material—documents, photos and the like—which might arouse the Senator's interest. Your editor could hardly object if you have the proof. Then you could write the crucial column and hold it, sending Phelps a copy with the understanding that it would not appear unless he allows it to. After all, *we're* not interested in destroying him. *We're* not the Puritans. *He is*."

The judge's hand was on his breast. He flushed slightly with indignation. "We're merely defending ourselves. There are plenty of other investigations his subcommittee could be making, and we're sure that even such a paragon of virtue as he would hesitate to sacrifice his own son to further his own political ambition."

I leaned back in my chair and drew a deep breath. "Just after I got out of the Army," I said, "I had crazy ideas about staying out of the rat race. I wanted to go to the islands and sell fish poles to the natives. But then I finished college and got married and started raising a family. Do you think I would have made out, Judge?"

Judge Wells frowned severely. His tone was the one he used on the bench, sternly pontificating before passing sentence on some ex-juvenile delinquent.

"You mustn't think of it that way, my boy. This is politics. Besides, I have a theory about Temple Phelps. He is a victim of human frailty like the rest of us, but his failing is ambition. He flies the banner of public morality because corruption is a popular issue. But no man succeeds as he has without ambition to drive him, and ambitious men are prudent, even opportunistic. He'll soon see he has nothing to gain by pushing this thing. He can afford to let one fish get away; there are plenty of others in the sea. Besides, this one is poisonous, and good fishermen always throw poisonous fish back."

Something had moved behind the Judge's benevolent smile and his pince-nez. It looked like the hardness of calculation brought on by fear, and it betrayed itself in his eyes. But it only lasted an instant, and then the mask slipped easily back into place.

"No, Larry," he said, sighing, "in this vale of tears all of us are frail and sinners. So let him who would cast the first stone beware. What this old world needs is a little more live and let live. You mark my words, Temple Phelps will see it that way in the end."

3

I've been called a hack more than once in the past, and I guess that's what I am. But I do have a knack for making revelations quietly or with thunder, and I do know my readers. In a few hundred words I can make them laugh or cry, and I can make them love or hate. Their reaction to my "Tempus in a Teapot" columns is an exception that proves the rule. Then I'd been whistling in the dark, and my tone showed it. Now, however, I had facts and I was going to make good use of them.

I fell in with the Judge's scheme and teased the readers along. "Big Surprises Promised at Hearings," I crowed without explanation in my first column. Next day I alluded to it while discussing something else: "...like the Dorato hearings, one of whose participants is due for a bigger surprise than any of the spectators." I managed to drive into the readers' skulls the date and hour of the hearings, a sense of their importance and the possibility that revelations might overturn the whole proceedings, drag names through the mud and discredit the process of Congressional investigations itself. Those who could add could draw the conclusion that Phelps was the man who might end up as defendant at his own hearings.

On the other hand, if he decided to soft-pedal the accusations, nothing is more quickly forgotten than a promised event which doesn't take place, provided other juicy items are offered to occupy the readers' minds.

When I had completed this elaborate tease, I wrote the crucial article, naming names and places, but ran off only a single copy, locking the disk in my safe with the originals given me by Wells, while the article and photocopies of the evidence, neatly stapled, went into an envelope bearing the Senator's name, which I placed in my inside pocket. I was sure of myself now. Pointing to the evidence, I'd ask the father whether he was interested only in destroying political enemies or whether he would apply the same law to all and destroy his son too. The final words were those I'd used in my headline: "Will Tempus Fugit?"

At the press conference the day before the hearings it was apparent I wasn't the only one who attached importance to the event. Every reporter present sensed a climactic struggle in the making, and Phelps himself seemed not averse to making a play for publicity. The crown of his high forehead seemed to shine at once with the sweat of his eagerness and the nobility of his purpose.

"Ladies and gentlemen," he said in his cold yet emotion-charged tones—and indicating that his remarks were off the record—"tomorrow will witness the beginning of the end of Johnny Dorato's evil power in this country. He will be asked specific questions concerning his gambling operations in New England—yes, in my own home state— and he will be unable to answer these questions without incriminating himself. The subcommittee will then turn the evidence over to the Department of Justice for prosecution. I can promise you that it won't be long before we shall have cut out at least a part of the rot which has been eating away at our society. Let us pray we are not too late in destroying it before it destroys us."

A typical high-minded declaration from Professor Tempus Phelps. And even while sharing some of his fervor, the rest of us were unused to sharing his high perch above the mass of humanity and were wondering why we too shouldn't be included in his scathing remarks. It had been said of Phelps that his holier-than-thou attitude gave no real offense to voters because they truly believed he was holier than they. If this was true, their reaction to his fall would be all the more violent.

We fired questions at him from all sides. What was the evidence? Couldn't he at least give them one item for the evening news?

Tempus smiled down imperturbably from his mountaintop. Deadlines meant nothing to him. All he wanted was good coverage for the climax of his investigation next day.

"If I were to tell you what kind of evidence we have, you know as well as I these hoodlums would find a way around it."

They nodded solemnly. It wasn't that he had the politician's knack for descending to the media's level. Rather he seemed to want to raise them to his own level, taking them into his confidence like a general at a staff meeting. And like the voters themselves, I could see that most of them felt uncomfortable though flattered.

Then he turned to me.

"As a matter of fact, it's almost as if they knew already what was about to happen. The veiled threats over the past week in your column, Larry, would indicate that, wouldn't they?"

I must have flushed at his words, but I tried to return as bland a smile as I had received.

"Why, I'm in no position to make threats, Senator. You know that. I'm only a reporter."

It may have sounded hollow, because the others gave me a look of hostility. So I dove in head first. "In our business, Senator," I said, "we hear a lot more than we are able to report. So unless we're sure someone else has got the item too, we naturally exercise a good deal of selection and restraint."

The silence may not have lasted more than a second or two, but punctuated by those steely blue New England eyes, it became more than a little oppressive.

"Larry," he said finally, pleasantly enough but without shifting his gaze, "why don't you drop into my office when this is over and let me tell you how exclusive your item really is?"

The press conference broke up with the same doubts and suspicions floating in the atmosphere of anticipation I had intended to create in my column. It was a sort of triumph for me in my campaign of hints, even though my colleagues in their Phelps-induced high-mindedness avoided me on the way out.

"Fine time of year," Tempus observed, looking out his big office window. "Almost as invigorating as the air back home."

Was it the professorial gift for small talk before a serious dressing down that made me feel like a freshman hauled into the dean's office on a charge of peeping Tomism, or did he know about my meeting with Judge Wells? Whichever it was, once I'd been waved into the easy chair facing his desk he became the hard-eyed judge once more, peering at me from above his bridged fingertips as he tipped back in his swivel chair.

"All right, Mr. Gillis, you and your friends have got something on me which you plan to use if I bring out my evidence against Johnny Dorato tomorrow. That's it, isn't it?"

I swallowed. "I guess that's one way to put it, Senator."

"Then suppose you tell me first what you think my evidence consists of."

"Well," I began, "maybe some of it consists of photographs."

"That's right," he said. "Some of it does indeed consist of photos. Go ahead. Your move."

For some reason the leather chair felt low and uncomfortable. "The point is, Senator, those aren't the only photos that could be used in this investigation."

"Aha!" His eyes narrowed. "Then if that's the case, if somebody in my own party is mixed up with this gang, then I say let the chips fall where they may. *Fiat justitia, ruat caelum,* as the saying goes. 'Let justice be done though the heavens fall.' Or as someone else said, 'Publish and be damned'."

"Then maybe you'd better read my column based on tomorrow's hearings," I said. I opened the envelope and took out the typewritten sheets, but not the prints or the photocopies.

"Say, I envy you your job," he smiled. "So you write your column before the event and take a long weekend." He glanced at the column, then took out his glasses and read it again with a hard-lipped frown. "'Will Tempus Fugit?'" he murmured approvingly without looking up. "I like that."

He returned to the beginning and scanned it again. At one point his jaw muscles hardened, but if there was the slightest change in his tone, I couldn't detect it. Then he looked up and said, "All right, let's see the evidence."

They seemed of a paltry insignificance as I handed him the sheets of paper which were supposed to face a man with the spectre of personal tragedy as a reward for pursuing his ideals. He held them up to the light singly and in pairs and then placed them side by side along his desk top and compared them minutely. When he was satisfied they were authentic, he carefully stacked them in their original order and joined them to the printed sheet. Then, with still no change in his tone or expression, he removed his glasses and looked hard at me across his desk.

"Is that all you have, Larry?"

"That's all, Senator. Isn't it enough?"

Not answering my question, he asked, "May I keep these, or are they by any chance your only copies?"

"Those are your copies, Senator."

"Thank you, I thought so," he said without a trace of irony, placing them back into the envelope and then into his own pocket. He stood up, his professorial urbanity returning as if the dressing down were over and I was being sent back to class. A smile and a handshake were even part of it.

"Well, Larry, I thank you for dropping in. I'm sorry to keep you and your friends waiting, but you understand that I can't give you my answer without taking certain things into consideration."

"Tomorrow is plenty soon enough, Senator."

"Tomorrow it will be, Larry. I give you my word."

4

That evening I had a visit in my office from a woman who came unannounced and entered without a word when I opened the door. I had seen enough pictures of Marjorie Phelps and had even seen her in person during the campaign; so my surprise was due more to the fact of her coming here at all than to the recognition of who she was.

She slipped past me and into a chair before I'd had a chance to speak. "No doubt you've guessed why I've come," she said.

"Will you have a drink, Mrs. Phelps?"

"Thank you." I poured out a jigger of Scotch for each of us. Marjorie Phelps was a handsomely elegant woman, quite distinguished and only slightly matronly. She was a hostess, a clubwoman and in every way the important man's important wife. But she seemed to sense the incongruity of her situation and was attempting to cover up the fact of her begging by adopting a tone of haughty superiority.

"If you think the Senator sent me, or knows that I am here, you are mistaken. He hasn't even told me what sort of threats you are holding over his head."

I sat down opposite her. "Mrs. Phelps, suppose you tell me what you would like me to do for you."

"I don't think you would understand my feelings," she went on, ignoring what I had said. "I've never seen him in a fouler mood than he is tonight, pacing his office with the door closed and mumbling something about you, and the hearing, and some photos... and our son Warren."

"Believe me, Mrs. Phelps," I said with an attempt at compassion, "I'm sorry for him, and I understand how you must feel. But politics is a dirty business. If you enter it, you've got to expect these things."

"Do you really think you understand anything about us?"

I was suddenly aware that I was a pawn in an affair of which I could control neither the opposing forces nor the end results. Whether I understood her feelings or not was of little importance.

"Let me try to explain it to you, Mr. Gillis," she continued. "Warren may resemble his father physically, but he is my son in other ways. If he lacks his father's legal brilliance, he has in its place a gentleness and a sensitivity of which my husband is totally unaware. Remember, I am not a New Englander, and I thank God that my son has something in him besides cold reason and moral superiority."

"Mrs. Phelps," I replied, "I'm confident that things will work out and that nothing will happen to your son."

She seemed not even to have heard my words, much less sense the hollowness in them. "I am only a mother," she went on, "But I have shielded Warren from his father's incomprehension and have tried to counteract and soften his rigid discipline. I have given him what I could of the love a child needs. If he has done something wrong..."

Her voice broke. Suddenly her haughtiness left her, and she was just a woman from whose eyes something like a veil had been torn. Then, just as suddenly, she regained control of herself and continued.

"If he has done something wrong, then I want to know about it and not have it used as a weapon with which to blackmail his father. I'll pay you what you want for it."

"I wish I could help you, Mrs. Phelps," I said, "but I'm afraid the ball is in the Senator's court."

She stiffened. "I see. You mean to say you are not your own master in this affair."

"I suppose not many people ever are, Mrs. Phelps."

She looked at me with that fine contempt which her breeding had taught her to apply in such cases. "The right sort of people are," she said.

She rose and started to leave. At the door she turned and faced me. Her eyes were moist. "If your choice is between my husband and my son," she said, "then I beg you to spare my son."

Then she was gone, and I was alone at the door, staring out into the half-lit hallway.

5

The proceedings of the next day's hearings are a matter of public record, both written and visual. Anyone interested could view the highlights on the evening news and the entire proceedings on C-Span. I can add nothing by describing the scene, how the committee room was jammed with people from outside the Beltway who had waited hours for a chance to get in. Or describe Phelps or the other members or the Dorato mob behind their microphones, this one wiping sweat from a bald head or that one chewing on a toothpick, or Johnny himself with that smirk on his face, pulling at his ear each time a question was directed at him. The TV cameras were better placed than I to see all that, as was the housewife in her kitchen. And if afterward she like thousands of others was asking herself why she had detected no trace beforehand in Senator Phelps's face of the actions he was about to take, then I am unable to enlighten her. For I myself, with all the knowledge I'd gained the day before of him and his family, had no inkling either of what decisions he had made until he was ready to announce them.

I can only say that in his manner and appearance Temple Phelps was completely unchanged from previous performances, and even from my view of him the day before. He simply gazed down on his prey like a hawk waiting for the moment to pounce, like an avenging angel holding a flaming sword with which he would cauterize the nation's wounds. There was no hesitation or doubt to mar that extraordinary forehead and purposeful jaw. But what purpose guided him I still was unable to fathom.

Then, looking around, I saw Marjorie Phelps seated inconspicuously, as elegantly distinguished as ever, with her face half hidden by a veil, as if the nakedness I had seen there the night before were still imprinted on it and had to be concealed. The cameras, I learned later, had picked her up too, and all America would see the loyal wife of the principal gladiator in this combat. But while they may have mentioned that this was her first appearance at one of her husband's performances, none could guess the real reason behind it.

At her side was young Warren Phelps, the future Ivy Leaguer, but with in addition the reluctant look of a small boy hauled into church on a Sunday morning. He was in his senior year at prep school, and some wondered why he had skipped classes to come down in the middle of the term to witness a hearing which was climactic in its way but which procedurally was expected to be no different from dozens of others.

Then Johnny Dorato himself entered, like a movie star the center of a swarm of minions, lawyers and all those whose association with him it was to their advantage to have known. Even Judge J. Clement Wells was down for the occasion, and at one point our glances met, his exuding a bland self-confidence and lending that aura of unquestioned respectability of which the Dorato organization had particular need.

I watched as the parade of witnesses began, the now-familiar procession of subterranean characters come to deny, procrastinate, explain away and finally sink back into the well-known hoary response: "...on the grounds that any answer I give may tend to incriminate me." I observed them all, the mother's strained silence, the son's academic urbanity and the scarcely concealed swagger and smug self-confidence each witness brought with him, knowing as well as Johnny and I that the damning photographs and videotape would not be brought forward.

And I remember the instant when the atmosphere changed, when the faint cold breeze of suspicion swept across the caucus room, and Johnny sensed, and Judge Wells sensed and Marjorie Phelps sensed that damning evidence might be brought forward after all. I remember it was in the middle of some offhand remarks by Phelps himself, which always took on the character of a speech, like the ones in which he referred to the mob as "that nest of secret rodents, gnawing by night at the very foundations of our society, until upon awakening we find the entire structure undermined and ready to crumble into dust."

It was this speech, so typical of Phelps the educator, Phelps the campaigner, even Phelps the senator, which nevertheless alerted the caucus room. Because this was not the time for it if the photographs were to be suppressed and the hearings kept in the realm of pious generalities.

This was not the time to hurl accusations which were not going to be backed up by facts.

So a vague but general shifting of positions and freezing of smiles was instantly noticeable among the mob and probably in myself as well. Nor did the feeling decrease with anything he said afterward. The figure we saw, rather tall and spare, with that narrow-shouldered New England cut of his dark suit and the habitual Phi Beta Kappa key strung across the buttoned waistcoat, lent no softening note to the harshness of his words and gave only a promise of greater rigidity, of increased sternness.

There was no longer any doubt now in the caucus room that Temple Phelps would not compromise, and I could only sit in awe as he spoke the final words, more glacially than ever before, quoting not only from Latin but from the Bible as well:

"...a time for us to stand and face this rot and eradicate it whatever the cost, whatever personal grief it may bring us. For though it be our own right eye which offends us, no choice is left but to pluck it out and cast it from us, lest the whole body of our nation be destroyed."

A silence followed as the cameras continued to grind, even casual observers with no knowledge of the case sensing that this was the crucial moment. Then Phelps nodded his head, and the photos were produced and the videotape played on a giant screen. And one by one the witnesses were recalled and confronted with the undeniable facts, for this time the Fifth Amendment was invoked in vain because the evidence was there.

And when it was all over and the committee had directed that the facts be turned over to the Department of Justice for action, a strange catharsis filled the caucus room, and the spectators sank back exhausted. Only the faces of the defendants reflected in their fury the remaining emotion, and as I caught their glances I saw through their trapped rage the hard flame of hatred and knew the signal had been given me to wreak their revenge by publishing the column I had written for the next day. Judge Wells's eyes said it to me through the loose-jawed dismay of his features; Johnny Dorato's eyes said it to me through the smirking shell of his self-confidence. Tempus Phelps had asked for it. Now he was going to get it.

But the hearing was not over yet. It was Phelps's turn, and there was almost apology in his tone as he excused himself for taking up more of the subcommittee's time on a matter which, if not merely personal, was nevertheless relatively unimportant by comparison with what had gone before.

A faint ripple of irritation crossed the spectators' faces. Why drag in more details after the issue had been decided? Why not simply adjourn and clear the room if the rest was unimportant? The show was over; it was time to go home.

But the words Temple Phelps now spoke were simple enough. A newspaper article was in his possession, an article not published or even printed yet but which would be next day, as a kind of payment to him for the exposure which the Dorato gang had just undergone. The article was backed by photographs of which he had copies as well. He dropped them on the desk before him, then frowning squared his shoulders as he drew breath and looked up again.

"I am not one to welcome personal publicity of any kind," he went on, "favorable or unfavorable. However, since the appearance of the article seems to be inevitable, I think it perhaps preferable to bring the facts to light here rather than through a so-called sensational revelation in the media. The article concerns relations between John Dorato and my son. Warren, will you come forward, please."

Murmurs of astonishment filled the room. Above them a woman's voice was heard: "No, darling, don't go!" as a pale figure rose, broke away from his mother's grasp and slowly approached the witness chair. He walked steadily, quietly, but weightlessly as in a dream. And as he took the chair the entire nation was able to watch the face-to-face meeting of father and son, each seated before a microphone so that for a moment I had an hallucinatory impression that one and the same man was looking in a mirror at his own face across thirty years of time, metamorphosed by life, however, into something more than the difference between youth and age. For at no time had the essential difference between two generations been more apparent, despite the similarity of features.

In fact, the physical proportions were the same, and Warren was actually taller and broader than his father. But something indefinable, an infirmity of purpose, a missing compulsion marked him as ease-loving, well-adjusted, precisely without and freed from that hag-ridden complex which drove his father. And when the senator began to speak, his voice remained as flat and emotionless as it had been while questioning the Dorato gang. Only the tone was lower, at times in fact hardly more than a whisper.

"Is it true that you know John Dorato, Warren?"

If the father's tone was low, the son's was even lower. "Yes, sir," he answered using the same form of address as the other witnesses, though with him it was the form his father had always required of him.

"And you have known him for more than two years?"

"Yes, sir."

"Then perhaps you can explain these photographs."

The prints were passed to young Phelps. He blanched as he looked at them. For a moment he was unable to speak. Then in a strained voice, hardly audible, he said: "That was a long time ago, at least a year."

The father frowned. "And this?" the copy of the I.O.U. was passed between them as from the right hand to the left hand of the same man.

The dismay on young Phelps's face seemed to reflect, as much as a sense of guilt, a surprise that his actions and associations should be taken amiss, that people should see anything wrong in his connections with Dorato.

"But I don't owe that any more," he protested. "I paid that back. He tore it up when I paid him."

The senator's features didn't move except for a slight rolling of the jaw muscles and a tightening of the lips. "How did you pay it back? With this?"

It was the receipt "for services rendered." The caucus room was tense as this last bit of evidence was added, weightless yet crushing, to all the others, resting on the table between the two faces of Phelps—the one frigid, incorruptible, lined only by fatigue; the other still soft and smooth in its accumulated guilt. From across the room I could hear the faint sobs of Marjorie Phelps, her face hidden in her hands.

Warren had not answered. "Would you care to tell me the exact nature of the services rendered?" asked Phelps.

The boy's mouth worked soundlessly for a moment. Then, barely audibly, he said, "Oh, various things. I ran errands. I brought people to his place and introduced them to him. Things like that..."

"Did you sell cocaine for him?" the father asked.

"No, Father. No, I didn't," the son protested. "I only distributed it. I didn't keep any money for myself."

Phelps's eyes were dry, but his voice contained something humble, almost pleading in its tone.

"Did you really have to do that, son?"

For a long minute we watched young Phelps's face for some sign of contrition, some sign that he would break down and ask his father's forgiveness. But the softness of his features remained fixed in mere surprise.

"But I had to have it, don't you see?" he finally replied. "And the stuff doesn't come free."

The senator's jaw hardened. He recoiled a fraction of an inch, almost invisibly to a television viewer. But then his shoulders squared, his brow lowered and his face returned to the flat lawyer-like dryness of before.

"Has it occurred to you, Warren, that you are as liable to prosecution as any other witness here today?"

Warren was incredulous and unable even to whisper an answer. His father continued.

"Do you really believe that the facts concerning your actions may properly be withheld while those concerning other witnesses are forwarded to the Department of Justice?"

"No, sir," the microphone whispered after a pause.

"Or that all the facts brought out today can now be withheld, including those concerning yourself?"

"No, sir."

"Then I have nothing more to add. I can only say that I have no doubt you will take your punishment like a man. Unless there are further questions on the part of this subcommittee, I move that these proceedings be adjourned."

6

Next morning my column appeared rewritten and updated, but in no way hiding the part it had played in the hearings. In fact, I built the connection up, recalling how I had promised surprises and generally crediting myself with omniscience. Whatever happened to Dorato or young Phelps, I was in the clear. I'd only done my job as a newspaperman, and the publicity for me might even help me survive the party's debacle.

Besides, within the space of a few hours public opinion was giving indications of making one of its unpredictable flipflops. While his own party had made Phelps the hero of the day, was jubilantly predicting election-day landslides and was even letting drop hints of Phelps as presidential timber in the not-too-distant future, the opposition had considerable balm for its wounds in what people were beginning to say not only inside the Beltway but at their television sets across the country. What kind of man, went the new line of thought, would send his only son to jail for any reason whatsoever? What kind of man would sacrifice his own flesh and blood on the altar of abstract principle, and with no more emotion than this one had shown in the caucus room that morning? No wonder the kid went off the deep end, with a father like that, a man who loved only Justice and quoted Latin, but had never heard of Mercy. Or was it Justice he loved? Wasn't it more likely that what he really loved was himself and his own career? Look at him now, the crusading gang-buster, and already being boomed for President! He wasn't a man; he was a monster!

This was the reasoning which the party was already preparing to use and which I myself was planning for my column before the hearing had even broken up and the domed forehead was seen leaving the caucus room with the other members of that eminent subcommittee. All that afternoon, as the air waves crackled with the name of Phelps and his personal history and his great victory against the forces of evil, a new picture was taking shape in the kaleidoscope of Washington politics, and the professionals were planning their strategy and placing their bets.

And although Phelps himself had ducked the reporters and was refusing all interviews, the horse-trading and the educated guessing went on around his name and in spite of his physical absence. There was a report that he had left town, had flown north to be in seclusion. There was a rumor, at least partially confirmed, that Marjorie and Warren Phelps had left for the family's winter home in Florida, without the senator. But none of this mattered; the jockeying went on without them.

Then at ten that evening I had a call. It was Casey, a leg man I used from time to time on stories I considered too sordid for my lily-white hands.

"I'm at Phelps's place in Georgetown. Get over here on the double. There's something screwy going on."

A half dozen people were already gathered in front of the comfortable nineteenth-century town house when I arrived. Casey ran up to meet me.

"He's in there alone with the lights on everywhere and the phone ringing. We got a glimpse of him behind his desk and not moving a muscle. Wait, here come the cops."

A minute of ringing the bell, a few knocks, a pass key; it wasn't hard to get in. We found him in his study, perfectly erect in the high-backed chair behind his desk. He was dressed comfortably but impeccably in an expensive bathrobe over a clean blue-striped shirt and a professorial bow tie. His eyes were open, and he stared across the desk at us as coldly as if he were questioning the witnesses at that morning's hearing.

The pistol was in his lap, clutched firmly in his right hand.

"Jesus!" somebody whispered, "a guy they've been talking about for President!"

No one else spoke. His presence, even in death, cowed us. It was as if we were waiting for him to begin some discourse on civic virtue, intoning in that peculiar voice of his, flat yet filled with fervor, with liberal quotations from the Latin. From the high dome of that august forehead a gleam of light reflected as if from a marble Roman bust in some Pantheon consecrated to civic virtue, where generations might come to pay respect to this and other greatnesses past and dead.

A man moved, and then all of us came to ourselves and crowded around the body, someone even suggesting that "maybe this was a put-up job," the work of the Dorato mob in a futile act of revenge. Or of the wife, or of the son. Where were they?

But when I saw the note he had left, the few words in Latin carefully and finely inscribed on his personal stationery, words which I understood only because I'd encountered them with him once before, I knew that no one but Phelps himself could have been responsible for this final act.

"*Fiat justitia, ruat caelum,*" I said. "Let justice be done, though the heavens fall."

"Jeez!" said Casey. "You speak Latin?"

"Sure, fluently," I said. "But I'm afraid I don't know much about justice."

THE OUTSIDE WORLD

Fellow Voyager

No one saw the tall man in the gray trenchcoat come aboard. He was just there when the ship left port—and asleep at that, sprawled on the afterdeck amid three or four pieces of battered luggage, which one of the swarm of porters must have carried for him, if he hadn't carried the man as well.

For he was still very drunk when they found him, and the captain himself had to be called to decide the issue.

"It's too late to throw him off now," lamented the purser. "And not another port before New York."

"So we've got no choice but to keep him," said the captain, not yet noticing the eyes, which had opened, nor the flickering smile which pulled at the corners of the mouth.

Then, somewhat thickly, the voice answered.

"I'll take the best stateroom you've got. Make it the bridal suite," he said, pulling all the while at something deeply buried in a pocket of the trenchcoat.

They laughed until they saw the roll, a great wad of dollars held up to his face as he peeled off the bills very deliberately, one by one.

But the captain was quick to make amends. "Unfortunately, sir, there are no first-class accommodations left. This is really a freighter, with very few cabins. But I'm sure we'll be able to find something to your liking...won't we?"

"Yes, of course," answered the purser, taking his cue. "As a matter of fact, there does happen to be one first-class cabin vacant. A last-minute cancellation, you know. Otherwise, the ship would be full, of course."

"Naturally," mumbled the man with a grand gesture.

The captain's face wore its most gracious smile. "Now that that's settled, I'm afraid you'll have to excuse me, sir. I'm needed on the bridge. The purser will take care of your needs. I wish you a most pleasant crossing."

And with a bow, which was correct and only slightly obsequious, he left them, muttering, "Bridal suite! On this tub?"

The man's name was Dunn, as it turned out, and the figure he cut was in its way so extraordinary that each passenger had only to see him once to retain a vivid memory of him. They guessed he was fortyish, though he looked at least fifteen years older. He was obviously an alcoholic, and so far gone that they considered their estimate of his age very conservative. There was something in the dead whiteness of his hair, in his enormously elongated and emaciated frame and in his eyes, which marked him as an individual unlike themselves. Especially the eyes, which when he was drunk had an opaque quality, like two pale blue china figurines.

"The guy's cockeyed," said Charlie Muldoon the following morning as Mr. Dunn took his seat in the dining saloon. "And at eight-thirty a.m. too." Then a few minutes later he watched the gangling figure rise again without having eaten, weave unsteadily toward the door, stumble against a chair, right himself, and continue woodenly out of the saloon mumbling an apology to the woman whose coffee he had spilt.

Charlie loved to talk, and so far the language barrier had stood in his way in every port. But now with days as empty as the ocean before him and only a dull stranger sharing his cabin, he saw an opportunity. She was obviously an American and a fairly attractive one, though several years his senior. Nevertheless, thought Charlie, beggars can't be choosers. So with a cry of outrage at Mr. Dunn's clumsiness he sprinted to the lady's side, napkin in hand.

"Watch out, there's some dripping on your skirt."

He sopped it up before the chief steward had even been alerted to the accident.

"Please don't bother. It's nothing."

Charlie slipped into the empty chair next to her, his face registering mock ecstasy.

"Gee, say that again, will you? You don't know how long it's been since I heard a real American speak English."

She laughed and seemed ready to answer the questions he fired at her. Claire was her name, and her husband Henry was seasick in their cabin below. He was an archeologist, and they had been visiting out-of-the-way digs and fighting off mosquitoes. They had boarded only the day before for the return voyage.

"Sounds fascinating for you," he remarked ironically.

"Yes, I was bored stiff," she admitted. "Never marry an archeologist unless you're one yourself."

"Not me. My old man thinks I'm a future investment banker, but we'll see about that when I get back to the bank."

"But for the moment you're just out to have fun. Right?"

"How did you guess?"

"Oh, I'm pretty good at guessing."

So things were looking up. Charlie was even grateful to Mr. Dunn for having brought them together.

*   *   *   *   *

Monsieur and Madame Delval also came to know Mr. Dunn, for he had been given the cabin opposite theirs and placed at their table. It was a long table in the corner of the dining saloon, and while the Delvals sat facing the mirrored wall, Mr. Dunn, opposite them, faced the entire room but had to squeeze past two other passengers to reach his seat. He was often late and had to be helped by a steward. Nevertheless, the first time Monsieur Delval noticed Dunn was sober he became very friendly.

"Monsieur is English, I believe."

"No, Monsieur is American." He said it shortly and almost rudely, leaving the next move up to the other.

"Ah, then you must be familiar with New York."

"I've lived there."

A strange thing happened to Mr. Dunn's eyes when he was sober. The veil which seemed almost to cut off his vision was lifted and the pupils took on the quality of sharpened knives. Delval could look him in the eye only fleetingly, but that did not prevent him from talking.

"My wife and I will be seeing New York for the first time. Some of my works will be exhibited there next month."

"Oh?"

"Yes, I am a painter."

"What do you paint?"

"Anything. Everything. That which has beauty. I am a lover of beauty in all its forms."

"I see."

There was a pause, broken by Madame Delval.

"Perhaps it is not too indiscreet to ask what Monsieur's profession may be?"

"No, it is not too indiscreet to ask. I used to write. It is perhaps what I wrote which was too indiscreet."

Delval was delighted. "Then we must show some of our work to each other. After all, literature and painting are allied arts. Both seek the beautiful. So in a sense we are kindred souls, are we not?"

But Mr. Dunn had already risen and was crowding past the passengers next to him. As he left, Delval heard him mutter, "No, I think we are not."

"Insulting, don't you think?" Madame Delval remarked.

"Perhaps. But we must be careful how we handle him. There was something uncanny about his eyes, as if they could see every secret in one's heart."

"I doubt they see anything at all," his wife commented, "which may be a good thing for us, my dear."

M. and Mme. Delval had little to say to Mr. Dunn from then on. During meals (when he came to meals), he ate in silence while they craned their necks to speak to other passengers. They soon found followers, however, and in the lounge small groups gathered around them to hear the painter expound his theories. One evening they even had the captain in conversation, asking his opinion of a small canvas.

"Oh, but I'm not qualified to judge a painting," the captain laughed. "After all, I'm only a sailor."

"Precisely," cried Delval. "As one of those untutored in the arts, if I may say so, Capitaine, it is your reaction to my work which is important to me."

"Then as a sailor I must tell what I seem to detect is a face, but a face under water. Beneath the waves, as it were."

"Very good, Capitain. Seen with the eyes of a sailor. Now what about Mr. Dunn? What does his poet's eye detect?"

"Yes, do give us your opinion, Monsieur," urged Mme. Delval, handing the small framed blur of blue and yellow to Mr. Dunn, whose eyes by now were perfectly opaque.

"The poet's eye," said the slurred voice, "may well detect something. Mine does not, since I'm not a poet. For that matter, I'm not a painter. The only thing I've ever painted is the side of a boat."

"Ah, so Mr. Dunn has been a sailor," the captain smiled. "Bravo. Then if you can't judge paintings, perhaps you can judge the running of this ship."

They all joined in a hearty laugh, to which Mr. Dunn replied, "As a matter of fact, and speaking only as a sailor, mind you, I'd say your ship is in danger of sinking, Captain."

The laughter became a roar. But the captain didn't laugh.

"Perhaps you expect it to break in two," he said quietly.

"Not exactly," said Mr. Dunn. "But have you noticed the condition of the hull below the water line? Rust. Great thick scales of rust, Captain, especially at the port bow. It seems to me in heavy weather those plates could buckle."

The laughter was fainter this time, and the captain's face had drained of its ruddy color.

"You should not have come aboard, Mr. Dunn, if you thought the ship was in danger of sinking."

Now it was Mr. Dunn who smiled. "Touché, Captain. But where's your sense of adventure? This way it's so much more exciting, don't you think?"

The captain had regained his color but not his good humor. "The thought of sinking is hardly what I would call exciting, sir," he said pointedly, then took his leave of the merry group, pulled his cap down over his bald head and stepped out on deck in the direction of the port bow.

This was Dr. Julian's fifth voyage aboard the ship. As ship's doctor he was by now used to the complaints of the widows and retired couples who made up a large part of the passenger list. Most came on board with a supply of their own medicines, but occasionally someone fell ill with something more than seasickness and required his attention. His worst fear was that eventually one of them would die under his care and bring him into the glare of official scrutiny. But until that happened, his role on board was not an unpleasant one. And beyond that there were certain other advantages.

On the third day out Dr. Julian emerged from the sanctuary of his cabin and entered his dispensary ready for a busy morning: a small man with a sallow, night-time face as if seen by candlelight and skeleton-like hands with which he now clapped long strands of black hair across his skull. Personally he was feeling in excellent health today, and at the first sign of any change there was his own private remedy in his cabin. With a practiced hand he bent back the head of a white-faced man and flipped a small capsule into his mouth. Nothing interesting here, he concluded. Now for those in their cabins.

Jauntily he walked down the passageway to his next case, an American professor too seasick to leave his cabin.

"My dear lady, what do I hear?" he inquired gaily of the woman who opened the door. "Our patient hasn't responded to our little remedy?"

"He hasn't stirred, Doctor, except to vomit."

Dr. Julian's air became professional at once. The dark brows descended over the hollow eye-sockets as he peered into the wan face on the pillow. "Hm-m-m. Well, we can't have that, can we? Has he taken anything to eat this morning?"

"Just tea, but he couldn't hold it down."

Dr. Julian withdrew a small envelope from his pocket. "Give him one of these now. He will sleep. Then at noon, if there is still nausea, one more. After that we will see. And as for you, my dear lady, go up on deck. There's nothing you can do for him, and it's too nice a day to be down here."

Brushing off her thanks gallantly, he left them. A charming creature, he thought. Too bad he couldn't allow pleasure to interfere with work just now. But that was all right. He had a greater pleasure than the company of women waiting safely concealed in his cabin.

He was walking toward his next case along the narrow, dimly lit corridor. He could see clearly to the end of it, and in spite of the roll of the ship he walked with a firm step. Even as the tall silhouette appeared far in front of him he was still thinking of how well he felt this morning. One injection, so very small and carefully dosed, had lifted him to exactly the pitch he desired, and his mind, far from entertaining hallucinations, was razor-sharp, professional. It was only when the shadow grew in size before him, enormous now, weaving from right to left with the ship's movement and striking the bulkhead with each roll, that he really noticed it.

He stopped, stared at it blankly, and his face turned dead white. His mouth hung open and he shook his head to clear his brain and drive the awful vision away.

Instead, it grew larger, loomed closer and in an instant was upon him—the same devilishly red face and opaque blue eyes.

Then, without taking any apparent notice of him, it rose to half again his height above him, brushed against him without so much as a glance downward, and as quickly was gone.

In stark terror Dr. Julian rushed headlong from the passageway and toward the sanctuary of his own cabin, there to renew the dosage and banish the vision from his mind.

"How is he today?" Charlie Muldoon asked as Claire emerged on deck. The sea was beginning to get rough.

"Worse than ever, poor thing," she answered. "I expect he'll be in his bunk for the rest of the crossing."

"You poor kid. I hope you don't have to stay with him."

"Oh, no. He sleeps most of the time. In fact, the doctor told me to come out on deck."

Charlie drew closer as they leaned on the rail. "I'm sorry for him, of course. But especially for you."

"The end of a perfect vacation," she said with surprising bitterness. "From a mosquito-infested jungle back to tea with the faculty wives in the groves of academe."

Charlie was ready with a strong arm around her shoulder. "Come on, things aren't that bad. Tell you what. Let's go have a drink and forget about it."

The bar seemed empty. But then, it was only ten-thirty in the morning. It was an ill-lighted room, and when the bartender stepped out of sight a few moments later Charlie shifted his position, drew her to him and kissed her on the lips. She responded, embracing him desperately. "Oh, Charlie, it's been so long."

They continued to embrace until they heard a slight sound from somewhere in the darkness opposite, something like a wheezing cough or the clearing of a throat.

"Charlie, there's someone over there!"

Slowly they were able to make him out as their eyes became accustomed to the darkness. He was staring glassily in their direction with an inane grin on his face. "Let's get out of here," said Claire, breaking away.

Charlie hurried her out, snarling, "Son of a bitch," in the direction of the dark corner.

But what worried Claire most was not knowing just how much, if anything, Mr. Dunn had been able to see.

That afternoon the sea became very heavy. The captain, hoping to avoid the storm, ordered speed reduced to twelve knots. The center of the storm, according to his reports, was still many miles to the southwest. At first he had hoped to avoid it altogether, running the risk of keeping up full speed in a fairly heavy sea rather than heading at reduced speed through the storm. But he realized the ship would never take it now.

He jammed his cap onto his head and descended from the bridge. When he reached the stern, he placed both hands on the railing and waited. Then as the ship lifted high above the trough, he leaned out and glanced quickly along the whole curve of the hull and its rusty plates.

Nothing. Only a great sucking sound and the whirr of the twin screws before the ship slammed down into the water again. At least it looked solid. And it might hold, at that. But one thing was certain: he would have to reduce speed again if this pounding kept up.

He turned and walked around the port side toward the bow, his fingers laced behind his back. He damned the company under his breath. It was the last time he would allow himself to be put in a position where he had to accept command of a rusty tub like this one sight unseen and under a flag of convenience. When they reached New York, he was through. He might still find another ship, but if he didn't, at least it would be better than losing his master's license through negligence. To say nothing of the ship and its passengers.

He reached the port bow. With every swell the vessel reared like a giant animal and came down with a smack, sending sheets of spray into his face. Then he saw something. As the bow hung for an instant in the air, a flake, a crust, a scab of the hull perhaps five feet across suddenly detached itself and fell into the sea. Close to it the rusty edges of a half dozen others seemed ready to come loose at any moment.

He whirled and made his way toward the ladder, at the same time ordering a guard rope stretched across the bow to prevent passengers from going too far forward. Then he slowed. He mustn't let them see him worried. A panic was the one thing that would be intolerable on this ship. Everything else had already happened.

From the bridge he gave the order to reduce speed again. He would have to wait it out, hoping the storm would miss them. He cursed himself. Once again he was at their mercy. If it wasn't the company, then it was the sea itself. Always he carried the burden of responsibility, and never was he its master.

But at least none of the passengers would know. Either it would happen or it wouldn't. He was taking every precaution. No man could do more than that.

It was then that he saw Mr. Dunn.

The long figure was standing unsteadily at the port bow, one hand grasping the rail and the face, a scarf around his neck, turned into the wind. The captain could see that no guard rope had yet been placed across the bow.

"Get that drunken fool out of there!" he cried apoplectically. "Who let him up there in the first place? And why isn't there a guard rope across the bow?"

Men scurried from the bridge. The captain continued to yell orders at them long after they had left. And even as the crew members reached the deck the captain, watching helplessly from his perch, could see the long, bescarfed figure lean far over the railing as he himself had done five minutes before.

And as one crew member led the figure away from the railing and the others hurriedly tied a rope across the bow, the captain thought he could detect a self-satisfied, I-told-you-so smile on the face of Mr. Dunn.

Lying in his berth, the door of his cabin doubly bolted, cool rings of smoke rising from his mouth, Dr. Julian grappled anew with the problem haunting him.

Was there such a man on board, or by some inconceivable error had his morning's dose contained a milligram too much? Impossible. But if it had, he needed only to be more careful in preparing it, and above all, never again to betray himself by turning and running.

But if, on the other hand, the figure had been real...

Frantically he rifled through his confused memories of the last port of call. He could see the narrow streets now, the room dense with smoke and the smokers almost invisible in the corners. He never should have stayed for the pipe, not when the entire purpose of his visit had been business. You couldn't mix them. But where had he seen him? Was it inside or was it in the street? In the narrow street perhaps. But if it was in the room itself, then here was his betrayer, sailing on the same ship with him now, waiting only for the appearance of the narcotics agents in New York.

There was one way to be sure. He rose to his feet and stepped boldly from his cabin and up on deck. The storm had veered off during the night, and a fresh breeze was sweeping against his face. He felt his skin responding to it and to the warmth of the sun. He was in touch with reality again.

In the purser's office he asked to see the passports. He had seemed to recognize a woman passenger from a previous voyage, he said, and wanted to avoid an indiscretion. The purser leered, made a joke about the doctor and his patient, and laughed hugely at his own wit. But already Dr. Julian was flipping through the passports. He was sure it wouldn't be there. These faces were too real, too ordinary, not like the hallucination in the passageway below deck. His mind was already at rest.

But even the sight of the face didn't register with him at first. It was more youthful, and the lighting had changed it and brought it to life. He tossed the passport aside, picked it up again, still not thinking of it, and studied the photo. His fingers began to shake. Then, oblivious of the purser's cries, he was out the door and staggering along the deck, sweat glistening on his forehead.

The face, he knew now, belonged to the man who had boarded the ship at the last port, the same man he had seen in the room where he had stayed for the pipe.

The last days on the water were calm. For Charlie Muldoon a party was the only fitting way to end the voyage, and so as passengers drifted into the lounge after the final dinner, he mingled freely among them looking for Claire and hoping her husband would not be there. The Delvals were among the first, followed by admirers anxious to hear more about famous subjects who had sat for him. Dr. Julian was seen ducking out and looking ill. Claire arrived looking radiant and answering solicitous queries about her husband's health while sending a signal to Charlie with eyes full of promise. Finally, the captain himself appeared in his dress uniform, his face strained but with a show of high spirits now that the voyage was coming to an end.

M. Delval, holding court at a table near the dance floor, was regaling his fans with gossip about celebrities he knew.

"I have a canvas—oh, a small portrait, nothing more—which I think illustrates my point," he was saying.

"But Jacques, I don't think these people have seen it," his wife said on cue.

"Really? Didn't I show it with the others?"

"Don't you remember? We put it in the wardrobe trunk for safe-keeping. You *must* go down and get it, Jacques."

It took very little encouragement, and when he was gone, Mme. Delval confided to the others that it was a work of great value, which they'd had to insure for quite a large sum.

The faithful showed appreciation and waited expectantly.

*   *   *   *   *

On the other side of the room Charlie had finally reached Claire. "Everybody seems to be here except our lush friend," he remarked.

"Haven't you heard?" she said. "He fell and hit his head. The doctor told me when he came to see Henry a minute ago."

"He didn't break his skull by any chance, did he?"

"Sh-h, don't say such things where people can hear you."

"I don't care. That guy deserves anything he gets. If I catch him spying on us again, I'll break his head myself."

"Well, it was an accident. Let's leave it at that. The doctor just went down to have another look at him."

But Dr. Julian didn't find Mr. Dunn in his cabin, nor in the dispensary. And after a rapid search he sat alone, cursing himself. He'd had his chance when they'd brought the man to him. One shot properly administered would have put him out of the way, and no one would have suspected. Now it was too late. He'd never come back now to have his bandage changed.

The doctor looked at his watch. He'd give him another fifteen minutes to make sure. But then what would he do? He couldn't go out and look for him on deck, not in the dark. In the bright light of the dispensary, yes. But not if he saw him again in the dark. Not that apparition...

When Jacques Delval reappeared in the lounge, his face bore an expression of deep concern.

"Solange, are you sure you *didn't* put it somewhere else?"

"Of course. It was in the wardrobe trunk when we boarded. We showed it to the captain. Don't you remember?"

"Well, it's not there now. Our painting is gone."

It was all very convincing. They'd planned it carefully. There would be a report to the captain and an announcement over the loudspeaker, with an appeal to the culprit to leave the painting in the cabin and no more would be said. The New York media would have the story, together with photos, and their American career would be launched.

But when they were alone at last, Delval grabbed his wife by the arm. His face was pale. "I was seen," he said.

"By whom?"

"By that disgusting drunk in the cabin opposite ours."

"How could he have seen you? You dropped it out the porthole, didn't you?"

"I tried to, but it was too big, and I couldn't break the frame. So I took it up on deck and dropped it over the side. He was standing a few feet behind me, and I didn't see him. He had a bandage on his head and that silly smirk on his face."

"Couldn't you have looked first?"

"I *did,* and there was no one. The next instant there he was, and do you know what he was saying? 'A face beneath the waves,' what the captain was saying the other evening! He may be a drunk, but he remembered that."

Mme. Delval's face hardened. "We've got to find him. Talk to him, bribe him. Anything."

"But how? He disappears when you look for him, and then he turns up like a ghost when you're not expecting him."

"Don't talk like a fool. Look for him. In the men's toilet, on the decks. But find him. I'll handle him after that."

But M. Delval did not find Mr. Dunn. Nor did Mme. Delval. Nor did Dr. Julian, waiting in his brightly-lit dispensary.

When Charlie Muldoon stepped out onto the deck, the night air made his cheeks burn. He walked rapidly along the rail and in the passageway found Claire waiting. She had thrown a sweater over her shoulders, but her skin was warm. He kissed her in the darkness. "I know where we can go. Back by the pool."

"But the pool is out in the open. We'll be seen."

"Don't worry, no one goes there at night. And there's a spot that's out of sight."

The pool was an excellent place, in fact. It had been drained that day, and the bath houses were closed and the deck chairs taken in. Part of the superstructure cut off the view, and Charlie was certain they'd be alone. It was a perfect night. The stars were out, and they had it all to themselves.

When they looked up again, a full moon was just rising from the sea. They promised to meet in New York as soon as Charlie found an apartment of his own. They kissed again.

Then they heard the sounds: half groans, half indistinct mumblings, a long succession of words like an incantation to the moon.

Claire's fingers dug into Charlie's arm. "What is it?"

"I don't know, but I'm gonna find out."

"No, Charlie. Let's get out of here!"

He took her around the pool and toward the passageway leading back to the cabins. Then, looking back once more, they saw in the moonlight that one of the bath house doors was open. Inside, in a compartment hardly larger than a coffin but with a full view of the secluded spot where they had just made love, they saw him and froze.

He was standing bolt upright, his arms at his sides. His eyes, not blurred now but knifelike and penetrating, were staring beyond their heads at the moon. He seemed to be in a trance.

Charlie ran, pushing and dragging Claire with him until they stood before a ladder. Then he stopped.

"Go below and stay there. Don't come out again tonight."

"What are you going to do, Charlie?"

"I'm gonna fix that bastard once and for all. It's the last time he'll spy on us." And he left her.

But he didn't find Mr. Dunn in the bath house. And he didn't see him near the pool, or anywhere astern or on the promenade deck or at the bow or even in his cabin. And as each place he searched proved to be vacant, his fury increased until he was running frantically and wild-eyed throughout the ship.

At the pier the customs and immigration officials had come aboard and finished their work before anyone realized that Mr. Dunn was missing. "Who saw him last?" the captain asked, and no one could say. He had been at dinner, but after that no passenger or crew member admitted to having seen a trace of him. Dr. Julian swore he had not appeared in the dispensary for treatment and that he had failed to locate him. The Delvals had their own worries, of course, with the theft of their painting, and it was all they could do to keep official attention focused on the publicity they deserved. Claire had been in her cabin with her husband, and Charlie, as everyone knew, had been in the lounge with the others.

They examined his baggage and found nothing of importance. There was almost a ream of paper partly torn and scribbled on. But the writing was unintelligible, and each page had been cancelled out by two diagonal lines. The address on the passport turned out to be that of a New York apartment in a building since torn down and rebuilt, with a new landlord and new tenants who knew nothing of a Mr. Dunn. He had left the country years before, it seemed.

The case gave the captain some paperwork, but he was cleared and the investigation passed on to others. He was just as happy he wasn't there with his comments about the seaworthiness of the vessel.

As for the Delvals, they were relieved for a different reason. Their embarrassment of the previous evening had become a non-event, and only two channels carried the item on the late news, though their pictures did appear in the morning papers. They hoped they would be interviewed on a morning talk show.

Dr. Julian, forgetting his addiction, swore he would never touch the stuff again on board ship. Even now there remained some confusion in his mind, and he had great difficulty separating reality from hallucination.

Claire, while her husband, wan and thinner, was occupied with customs, found a moment to speak with Charlie Muldoon.

"My God, how could you do a thing like that? I never dreamt you were serious."

"Are you crazy? I never even saw him."

"Oh, don't worry, I won't say anything. You were careful to make sure I was compromised too. But I don't think we'd better meet again, Charlie, ever."

So Charlie had one more reason to hate and fear Mr. Dunn. And yet he couldn't imagine how the man had just disappeared. It was the kind of tale he liked to tell back home, and now he knew he would never be able to mention it to anyone, ever.

It was the same with the others. In fact, there was no one who could explain, even to himself, what had happened to the drunken stranger who had accompanied them on the final lap of their voyage.

Except one man, and he didn't count. He was only a crew member, a dish washer and cabin boy named José. José had entered the United States illegally aboard a banana boat and since then had taken what berths he could get, glad to keep working and out of the way of the authorities.

Which was why José wanted to mind his own business now.

He had been clearing tables in the officers' mess that evening and had seen something as he stood on the after deck with a crate full of garbage scraped from the plates. What he had seen was only a glimpse, just as the full moon was rising off the stern. Looking up, he had seen a figure like an apparition standing just outside the railing. It was an incredibly long and spectral figure to José, with its arms at its sides and its head tilted upward, seeming to gaze out at the moon and beyond. For a moment it had stood there motionless, and then it had stepped out into the pale circle with a step so calm, so measured that José thought only a blind man or a sleepwalker could have taken it, the body disappearing in the moon-reflecting waters of the wake, a mass of angry froth behind the twin screw propellors.

José was certain of what he had seen as he stood there with his crate of garbage, and for several seconds he had remained frozen, watching the black waters slip out beneath the hull. And he would never talk either, for he too had his reasons for avoiding the police. But at that moment he had thought he had heard somebody coming, and he had panicked. In his confusion he had done what he knew he was never to do this close to land. He had thrown the whole crate of garbage over the stern. Then, crossing himself, he had hurried down the ladder, later wondering whether what he had seen had even been real or merely his imagination.

While behind the ship, spreading over the surface of the water, a wreath of orange peels and empty eggshells...

THE MERCHANT AND HIS BRIDE

In a distant land and in a distant time there lived a certain merchant who had become rich with the accumulated wealth of many years. Now this merchant, whose wife was dead and who had not remarried to avoid being distracted while gaining his great wealth, decided at last to retire and take to himself a young bride. Fearing loss of their inheritance, his sons at first tried to dissuade him, but the merchant persisted and agreed to leave them the proprietorship of his affairs and a large part of his wealth. Then, freed of cares but still in possession of great riches, he set out to purchase the fairest bride to be found in all the surrounding villages and towns.

The bride he found was fair indeed but so costly that none but he could even dream of having her. The merchant, however, seeing her graceful step and her eyes like black olives, gladly paid the price and told himself as he did so: "For this I have worked long years and foregone much pleasure. Now I shall have my due."

The wedding banquet was the most elaborate and costly in the memory of any living. The merchant observed with satisfaction the revels of his guests, but mostly he gazed at the black olive eyes of his bride watching him from above her veil. He noticed that each time he looked into them the eyes would be lowered in modesty, and at this sight his passion would rise to new heights and his imagination would fly ahead to the night before them. Gone was all thought of the sons who, wealthy themselves now, sat with wives and family and friends around the table; gone too was all thought of their dead mother, his wife of long years past. Only the present mattered now, and it extended into the infinite future in his mind like the body of his young bride.

Finally it was time to retire. The merchant closed the door of the bridal chamber and shut out the sounds of the revelry below. Then he turned to his bride and one by one divested her of her exquisite garments, leaving to the last the costly veil which had hidden all of her face below the black olives of her eyes. The time of his pleasure was come, and the merchant feasted eagerly upon the body of his young bride.

At length he fell asleep in her arms, a sleep from which it seemed only the light of morning would awaken him. Yet in the late hours of the night, when the moon was gone from the sky and the cock had not yet crowed, the merchant awoke with a start and sat stiffly upright in the bed.

"What is it, my master?" asked his bride fearfully.

"I smell the smell of death," said the merchant. "There is death in this house."

"But that cannot be, my master. All whom we have seen tonight are joyful and in good health."

"Yet death has come to sit among them, and one of them will surely die. Let us turn away and leave this place."

And so, despite the protestations of his bride, the merchant rose and dressed and ordered all his possessions removed from the bridal chamber. "We shall go to the great city," he said, "where death is swallowed up in life and pleasures of every description await the man of wealth."

As they left the house of his birth and of his earlier life, sounds of continuing revelry came to the merchant's ears. Yet he did not tarry to bid farewell to his sons or to their families, for in his heart he knew that death had come to sit among them. Instead he turned his gaze toward the new dawn and the great city which lay beyond it.

When they reached the huge metropolis, with its ten thousand lights and sounds and sights all there for them to enjoy, the merchant immediately secured for his bride and himself the finest lodgings in the broadest avenue, where polished attendants in rich costume awaited his pleasure. Then, looking out from his balcony upon the spectacle of pulsing life below, he took the hand of his bride and said to her, "Here shall we live for the present alone and for the pleasures each night will bring us."

That evening, as they moved from sumptuous table to lavish entertainment, where players and dancers with utmost art aroused the passions of his mind for the night ahead, he looked again at the veiled face and the black olive eyes of his bride and said to himself, "Better we had come here the first night, here where life bursts forth from every street, rather than tarry in a place where death had come to sit."

Behind her veil the young bride was seen once more to lower her gaze in modesty. But this time the merchant fancied he saw a flickering in her eyes as of new desire awakened by his caresses; and noting this he felt his pulse quicken with renewed anticipation.

Now, in the luxurious surroundings which he had chosen, he repeated each step of the love-making of the previous night, but subtly varying his approach, correcting small mistakes and gently initiating his bride in pleasures she had never known. Then, sated again, he fell into the deepest of slumbers.

But once more, in the late hours of the night, the merchant awakened suddenly with clammy brow and sat up stiffly.

"What is it now, my master?" asked his bride.

Somberly he answered, "Again I smell the smell of death."

"Here, in this city of life and pleasure, my master? How can that be?"

"In this city of life and pleasure the smell is even stronger in my nostrils. Beyond each light I see darkness, beyond each dancer's rippling movement stillness, beyond each pleasant melody nothing but the silence of death. Come, we shall leave this city."

And leave it they did, again before the crowing of the cock, setting out with the dawn for the seclusion of a secret resort known only to the wealthiest, existing only to serve their pleasure. Here no intrusion of the poor, the sick, the dying was tolerated. Here only that life which each man desired for himself, only those entertainments created for the wealthiest would be found, and the hated smell of death would be excluded. "Here I shall be among others like myself," thought the merchant. "Nothing shall be present except that which I myself desire."

Here again, in the refined atmosphere of this most exclusive pleasure resort, the merchant once more sought out the finest rooms, filled with objects of the highest artistry, where silence would be broken only by the music of his choice, and where darkness would be lit only by those lights which he himself decreed. For each of his senses, in fact, there was a void to he filled by his desire alone. Which he proceeded to do, calling forth a world imagined only in his dreams, until at length perfection lay before him to be displayed before his young bride.

He did this throughout the entire evening, summoning each element in its turn, setting before her a table of infinitely refined delights in preparation for their love-making. "Why did I not do this the first night?" he asked himself, "instead of lingering at a country banquet where death could come and sit nearby, or instead of journeying to a city where death could lurk behind the sights and sounds of life?"

Whereupon he cast aside the thought and gazed instead into the eyes like black olives of his bride. And this time, rather than finding them lowered in virginal modesty, he encountered a gaze which returned his own with urgent boldness, so that beneath her veil he could almost make out the wanton moistening of her ruby lip.

It required great effort for him to complete the planned spectacle before retiring to the nuptial chamber; and once there, even greater effort to repeat each preparatory step with calculated refinement before plunging into the final act with a partner as eager as himself.

But once again, as he lay sleeping in his young bride's arms, he was startled awake by the same horrid smell of death.

"Even here?" he cried in despair. "And even stronger than ever? How can it be?"

"It cannot be, my master," said his bride. "Surely you are mistaken."

"Oh, that I might be," he sighed. "But no, we must leave here too, and this time find the solitude of a place where no life but ours can exist and where therefore death cannot enter."

And so it came to pass that the merchant was able to find a place in the very desert where no life but theirs was present: no servants to wait upon them, no artists to sing or dance for them, only the sun, the moon, and the stars. Even food and drink they brought with them. And here in the darkness and the silence of the night the merchant and his bride were able to relive each word and gesture of their previous nights, embellishing on them out of their sole imagination in a world where wealth no longer mattered, having been spent to purchase a place where pleasures infinite could be called up out of the mind alone.

"This time," thought the merchant as he dropped off into sleep, "death cannot intrude, for I am here alone with my young bride. Together we shall live each day for itself and at night make love. How foolish of me not to have thought of this in the beginning."

Nevertheless, once more and to his renewed horror, in the smallest hours of the morning, when the stars had almost completed their circuit in the sky before being extinguished by the dawn, he awakened with the stench of death stronger than ever before.

"Not again, my master?" asked his bride from her place in the bed beside him.

"Yes. Again and stronger now than ever. The desert itself is filled with it, so that I fear another breath of it and I shall die."

"But how can this be, my master, since we are alone?"

"Yes, how? When only I who love life am here, and you...?" He stopped and peered through the darkness into the black olive eyes of his bride, and in the faintest lightening of dawn he seemed able to make out her features. Was she smiling at him? And there, between the rubies of her lips, what was that awful whiteness which seemed to fill the night? Was it merely the whiteness of her teeth? Or was it...?

"It is you!" he gasped. "At the banquet it was you. In the clamor of the city it was you. In the seclusion of the pleasure resort it was you again. And now, even here in the desert, it is you once more. You are death itself! Get away from me!"

But instead of leaving him the young bride drew even closer and placed her arms around the merchant's neck.

"I am your wife," she whispered with a smile. "You have bought me and paid for me and taught me an infinity of pleasure. All pleasures, in fact, but the final one, and that is the pleasure which I have been waiting to teach you. So come, my master. Come to me this one last time."

And in the emptiness of the desert dawn no further sound was heard.

Leila's Homecoming

Leila remembered many sights: the red of dawn, the green of the rice paddies, the white of day when the sun burned her face, and the red once more from across the great river when the sun fell silently to earth, and then of course the grayness of all about her when the full moon shone brightly.

She tried to recall each memory often because in reality she had seen nothing of them since early childhood. But now, with each color there was an associated sound: a whiteness in the cries of men by day, a greenness in the touch of tender rice stalks between her fingers, even a blueness when the breezes of winter rose from the river in the evening. She had no need to see them now, having seen them once and knowing their shapes and colors in her mind.

But what of the faces of Ahmed her brother and of Malika her sister, whose voices once had been as light as day? Ahmed's voice was heavy yet hesitant now, and Malika's was harsh and querulous. Leila knew they would no longer look the same as when they were children, but what they looked like now she could not even imagine.

And what had she herself become? Did her voice seem as old to them as theirs to her? Had her skin turned dry and wrinkled like their late mother's? And what of him who had taken her as his wife and given her two children, Brahim and Aisha, and then had grown sick and died? What did the children look like? She wondered each time she placed her hand upon the shoulder of Aisha as once she had on that of Brahim, following as she was led to market or to the well and then back home. These two were hers. She knew them through their voices and through their touch. But of the sight there was no memory, and though it was God's will, she missed it bitterly.

This was why, when the strange woman with the strange odor and the strange accent came one day and spoke the even stranger words to her, Leila's heart was filled with excitement as well as with fear. For the woman's hands were not unpleasant as they touched her face and bathed her eyes, and her strong voice was firm and encouraging as she spoke the incredible words.

"Leila, wouldn't you like to see again?"

She pulled away, and her answer was immediate.

"No, never. Of course not."

"Why do you say that? You don't want to remain blind all your life, do you?"

"But it is the will of God," was Leila's obvious answer.

Yet the woman's voice was soft and gentle. "Leila, if it was God's will that you lost your sight, couldn't it be His will that one day you'd see His world again and praise His name?"

Leila shook her head, desperately trying to drive out the unpardonable hope which had entered her mind.

"If God wished such a thing, then He would will it so, and the light would return to my eyes. He wouldn't need you to do it for Him."

The voice was silent for a moment, but when she heard it again, it was even more firm and hopeful than before. "Of course God has no need of me, Leila. But since He chooses so many of us as His instruments, if He wishes to use me for His purposes, you wouldn't resist His will, would you?"

"But why me?" she asked, desperately seeking still more objections. "I'm of no value to God."

This time the voice was firm. "Don't say that, Leila. What do you know of God's will? He may not wish you to see at all, but He certainly wants you to try to see, or He wouldn't have sent me here to try to help you. So we can only obey and await His answer."

Conflicting emotions filled Leila as her mind told her she would never see again and her heart insisted she would. Finally, however, she simply gave up and submitted to His will.

Now she was told of the journey she must make and the long separation from her children, and while her mind told her not to undertake such a journey, the reassurances convinced her, and her heart took courage. The children would be left to Malika, and the stranger's friends would see that they would be cared for. So Leila accepted this, and the long journey too.

Thus began a time in Leila's life when new impressions assaulted her remaining senses so violently that she was almost grateful she had no sight to be overcome by them too. The cries of the villagers and the braying of the donkeys were replaced by a nameless, faceless roar, and the screams were louder and angrier than any she had ever known. The dung-scented air of the village had given way to stifling fumes and the baked mud houses to walls of stone and glass. Harassed, irritable voices hurried her every movement. She lay on a bed she did not recognize; she shared a room with strangers whose voices were punctuated by moans and even cries of pain. Every action of her daily life was performed differently in this new place, and even the bathroom had to be explained to her.

Finally one day, as she lay on a bed not knowing whether it was day or night, strange fingers touched her eyes, and two voices, like the first one back at the village in accent but impersonal and unfeeling in manner, discussed her case as if she were not there. She understood none of the technical words, of course, and she knew she had no need to understand since they were not questioning her. But once more she submitted to the will of God, Who had chosen these instruments to try to restore her sight.

What followed happened so violently and inexplicably that afterwards the sequence of the pains and discomforts she suffered was lost. She only remembered awakening one day to feel the pressure of a huge bandage over both eyes and in her lightheadedness wondering why such effort should be made to keep light out of blind eyes, or if God had restored her sight why He now was preventing her from using it. But it was explained to her that the bandages were necessary to permit her eyes to heal from the actions taken by these agents of God.

At last the weight of the bandages was slowly lifted from her face. Fingers touched her eyes again, and voices around her spoke—strange voices in their accents and in their odors, but voices comforting and pleasant to hear. Then a smooth hand was drawn lightly across her brow, and one of the voices spoke to her and said: "Leila, now you may open your eyes."

Her eyelids were like stones. Fluttering, they resisted her efforts to raise them. She wanted to ask them: "Why do you resist? Don't you know it is the will of God?" But before she could complete her thought, a sudden impact like a fist seemed to strike her full in the face. The assault on her senses which she had first felt on arriving in this place was now reaching her not through her ears or her nose or her skin but from somewhere else, as if some stranger had intruded into her private thoughts and was forcing her to pay attention only to him. What, for instance, was that object moving back and forth in front of her? Was it a human figure? And those two other things on each side, much larger but moving only slightly? Could they be human faces, and if so, who were they and what were they doing? Whatever the truth, she was unable to make them out clearly, for all she received was the impression of lights and shadows moving but unfocused.

"Leila," asked the same voice now, "is there something before your eyes, or is there nothing?"

"There is something," she whispered.

"And what is it doing?"

"It is moving."

"Then follow it with your eyes, Leila. That's it. Now reach out with your hand and make it stop."

Her fingers went forward, awkwardly as in the dark, seeking to touch the thing which moved before her face. They touched a hand. She grasped it but felt something else, bright and smooth, in its palm. Both were moving. She wanted to stop and hold them, but something inside her made her pull back.

"What is it, Leila?"

"I touched something. I'm afraid."

"Touch it again, Leila. Don't be afraid. Stop its motion and hold it in front of your eyes."

She did as she was told. The bright thing stopped moving. "Now cover it with your hand. Make it disappear."

She released the object and placed her hand over her eyes.

"Not your eyes, Leila. Cover the thing that makes the light."

She tried again, found the hand and with her own hand was able to cover and blot out the light.

"It's gone," she said, almost with relief at the disappearance of this fearful new thing.

"Are you sure? Take your hand away. Now where is it?"

"It's come back. I'm afraid."

"Then put out your hand and make it go away."

"I'm afraid it will burn my hand."

"There's no heat, Leila. It's a cold light. Put back your hand."

She did so several times, the brightness coming and going each time, until at last the realization came to her that she controlled the light with her hand and saw it with her eyes.

"Do you understand what has happened, Leila?"

"I think so."

"Then tell us."

She summoned all her courage, fearful that it might not be so or that the saying of it might remove it forever, yet downing her fears with the sudden incredible joy which leapt in her breast.

"I can see again," she whispered, tears streaming down her face, then cried aloud, "God has given me back His light!"

In the days that followed objects of different kinds were placed before Leila's face—objects large and small, hard and soft, round and angular. She learned to associate the image of each with its touch or with its odor or with the sound it emitted. But when the faces of those who spoke to her appeared, she found it impossible to distinguish one from another. How was it, she wondered, that the faces of her brother and her sister could be etched so vividly in her memory while these remained nothing but featureless disks? The answer came when she was told that she would be given objects round and smooth to wear before her eyes and that through these, by God's will, she would be able to see clearly. Accordingly, one day an apparatus was placed over her nose and behind her ears, and she was told once more to open her eyes.

The sight this time—for it was a sight at last—was so beautiful that it was blurred by her tears. How fair, she thought, were the faces smiling into hers, and yet how natural that they should be fair, since their beauty reflected the sound of the voices and the touch of the hands which had served as God's instrument!

Soon the faces were multiplied as others, learning of the success of the operation, came to welcome her back into the world of the seeing. She was taken to visit other patients and finally onto a terrace from which she could see the whole city in all its magnificence. She saw the blue of the sky and the red of the sunset and even the brilliance of the stars at night.

But all of these were as nothing when set alongside the beauty of the faces of that first day by her bedside. If the faces of Ahmed and Malika and the faces of her children were in any way like these, then all the long and painful weeks of waiting would be justified, and with all her heart she would sing out the praises of God.

The day arrived when Leila was to return to her village. With her to guide her to her home was one of the nurses assigned to her case. They drove through the clamor of the city to the huge railroad station where they would board the night train. Leila noticed that behind the fine buildings there was ugliness and dirt she had not seen from the height of the hospital terrace. Then as the train drew away from the station the squalor of the outer edges of the city became apparent. But when the green fields came into view, along with the great river and the villages in the distance, once more the world was beautiful and as she remembered it. Her own village, she was sure, would be the most beautiful of all.

It was still dark when they reached her village. Leila was taken to a building much smaller than the huge hospital in the city but which smelled the same. There they rested, and in the morning they set out for Leila's house. Her body and her clothes were clean, for at the hospital she had learned the rules of hygiene. But sensing the familiar sounds and smells she was ready to forget what she had learned and to close her eyes and feel her way barefoot, as she had done so often before, to her house. Nevertheless, the desire to actually see at last the faces she had never seen was stronger, and as the door of the infirmary opened she peered out into the street for a glimpse of her home.

It was true, of course, that the sight confronting her was vastly different from that of the city she had left the day before. There were no paved streets or shining new buildings or frightening traffic, but only the dusty huts and the sundried, empty streets of a remote village. Here she saw a figure slip noiselessly by and a man on a donkey on his way to market. A group of dirty children in rags watched them and then scurried down an alley. Vaguely, Leila now recalled seeing such sights as a child, but somehow in her memory only the beautiful ones had been retained, and the ugliness, which now swept into her view, had been overlooked.

So it was with fear and anxiety that she approached the street whose touch and odor had always been a part of her life. And seeing it now, she remembered that not everything about it had been beautiful. The street itself was nothing but two rows of squalid huts built of packed mud and straw and discarded sheets of metal. Surely this wasn't the street where she had lived her entire life.

"Don't you recognize your street, Leila?"

"No, and I don't understand why it's so dirty."

"Then close your eyes and see it with your other senses."

She did, and the ugliness was transformed into the comforting reality she had always known.

"Do you recognize it now?"

She did not answer. Instead, with growing dread she began to walk unaided toward what she knew must be the house of her sister Malika. She recognized it from the odors and from the number of steps she would have to take to reach it, but the sight of it made her want to stop and turn back. Crouched at the end of even this street, like an unwanted dog at a banquet, Malika's house seemed to lean against the other shacks as if drawing sustenance from them. Was this really the place where her sister's children were being raised? And if so, where was her sister, and how could she allow that old beggar to sit before her very door?

Leila's breath came in short gasps as she crossed the threshold with the nurse. Inside, in the almost total darkness the sounds and the smells were familiar. But why were strangers gathered there instead of her own family? Who was the toothless crone stirring soup over the fire? And whose children were these filthy ragamuffins scampering around her legs? And finally, unkempt as they may have been, why had they allowed that disgusting old beggar on their doorstep to enter the house?

"Leila! So you've come home!"

The voices began to speak all at once. The sounds were coming from all of them. The old woman at the soup kettle was approaching her now, smiling her toothless smile and holding out her arms to embrace her, saying "Leila! You know me, don't you? I'm Malika!"

And in truth it was Malika's voice that spoke the words.

Then, as she returned the familiar embrace, she heard the voice of her brother Ahmed, saying, "Leila, my dear sister. Praise God who has let you see again!"

She broke away from Malika and turned to her dismay to see that the voice was that of the beggar on the doorstep. "You ... are Ahmed?" she gasped.

"Older and wiser than when your eyes last saw me, my sister." He reached out and drew her to him. "We are no longer the children you used to play with."

Leila turned to the nurse, who took her hand and said, "In such ways, Leila, life changes us all."

"That's right, my sister," said Malika in a voice edged with malice. "Even you, despite your beauty, are older."

"My beauty? You mean I am thought to be beautiful?"

"Men have said so," laughed the beggar, "though the white clouds over your eyes usually kept them away. But now," he leered, "perhaps they'll tell you so themselves."

"You talk nonsense," Leila retorted. "How could I be beautiful when both of you..."

Malika answered with a hint of scorn. "While both of us are ugly? Perhaps, my sister, the blindness which prevented you from seeing the truth helped preserve in you the beauty we all had as children."

"More nonsense. I won't hear it," cried Leila. "Nothing is beautiful to me but the thought of my children. Where are they?"

Instinctively, Leila had discarded the present and was thinking only of the future as already present in her children.

Malika cackled. "Look around you, my sister. Your children are here among my own. Pick them out if you can."

Leila looked in terror at the ragged urchins, all of whom had stopped to stare at her shyly in wonder at her new-found sight. Surely that thin one with the shaved head and the sores on his face was not Brahim? No, Brahim was bigger. And that ugly little girl with the runny nose and her finger in her mouth? Could that be Aisha? Of course not. Then Brahim must be the tall boy with the air of pride and haughty intelligence. And the sweet little girl next to him would be Aisha.

Timidly, hesitatingly, Leila pointed at them. "These two? Are these mine?"

Malika's laughter sounded harshly in her ears. "I thought you'd say that, my sister. The handsomest ones would have to be yours, wouldn't they? No, God is just, and the prettiest woman doesn't always have the handsomest children. Come, Aisha, say hello to your mother."

With a fascination turning to horror Leila watched the small, misshapen creature leave the group and limp toward her, a sickly hunchback.

"This is Aisha? My Aisha?" stammered Leila as the frail little girl rushed into her arms. And despite the disbelief in her eyes, immediately on feeling the child's body she knew that this was indeed her daughter, who for three years now had led her through the streets of the village. But how had she not realized that the child was crippled? How had she not even noticed its hump?

"Don't be so dismayed, my sister," pursued Malika. "She may never get a husband, but she's an obedient child. She'll wait on you and run errands for you. Watch." And Malika turned toward the girl. "Go get your brother. Your mother wants to see her son Brahim."

The child scurried outside, and Leila staggered back in growing dread of the sight which was being prepared for her. Brahim, the elder, had not guided her steps now for three years. He avoided her touch. She supposed that with male pride he had insisted on keeping more and more to himself as his voice had deepened. Yet in her blindness she had imagined him tall and handsome now, just as Aisha had seemed in the darkness of her eyes a lovely young girl.

"Here is Brahim, Mother."

The silhouette of Aisha had reappeared in the doorway and behind it the tall figure of her son. Now she would see him at last, the young man who would be the joy and consolation of her old age. Already she could see that he was tall and straight, just as she had imagined. But as the two figures entered the room and Leila stepped forward to meet them, she quickly realized to her horror that something was wrong, for her eyes now told her that the hand of her son was placed not in the hand of Aisha but squarely on his sister's shoulder.

"Brahim, no!" cried Leila. "Not you too!"

"Yes, Brahim too," cackled Malika. "It must run in the family!"

"Yet there are those who say he too is handsome," observed Ahmed sadly. "That is, until they see his eyes."

Later, when Leila had recovered sufficiently to speak coherently with the nurse, she asked this question:

"Why did the agents of God choose me and not my son for the operation? Why me and not my Brahim, whose life still lies before him?"

"Because," the nurse told her, "Brahim's eyes unfortunately cannot be cured. His blindness is permanent."

"Then why did God restore my sight at all, if it was only to see all the pain and ugliness in the world? Why didn't He leave me with the consolation of my memories and my illusions?"

"Because," the nurse answered, "God has need of you, Leila, to care for both of your children."

"But it is they who should be growing up to care for me in my old age, if God's world is what we are taught it must be."

The nurse placed her hand gently on Leila's. "What God's world must be, Leila, is what we are given by Him to see in it. He gave you back your sight so that you could serve His will."

"With a son who is blind and a daughter perhaps too sickly to live? Is this the future of God's world?"

"Who knows, Leila, what God intends for His world? We can only obey His commands and hope for better things."

And so Leila, her vision restored, rose and walked woodenly through the door of the shack where she had always lived and out into the blazing sun of God's new world.

TIMOCLEA
(After Plutarch)

He lay beside her now, muscles spent in flaccid repose and skin glistening with sweat beneath the hairs on his shoulders. On the floor lay the scattered pieces of his armor and his leather uniform. He stank of unwashed male and the stink had permeated the house, the bed, and the body which were hers. Outside, the city of Thebes was burning...

Thebes the ancient, the rich, the bountiful, its tawny fields of grain stretching far out across the Boeotian plain, ripening in the sun to nourish all of Greece. Thebes—raped, plundered, set to the torch, its men slain and its women and children enslaved for defying the barbarians from the north.

He raised himself onto one elbow and gazed on the whiteness of her skin as she lay on her back, naked and bruised, her eyes fixed on the ceiling of her violated home.

"I like a woman of spirit," he said. "Not the kind that squeals and cringes in a corner, but one like you that fights back. Look what you did to my face ... and my shoulder!"

She didn't have to look. She'd seen the red scratches as her nails had gouged his skin, and she'd seen the blood oozing through afterward; her body was smeared with it. Too bad her nails couldn't have been knives...

"Yes, if more women were like you, warfare would be a lot more fun than it is. By the gods, I didn't know they made your kind in a decadent place like Thebes."

Of course he didn't know. How could he, a Thracian, not even a Macedonian, the sub-barbarian mercenary of a barbarian boy-king named Alexander? What was the tutoring of an Aristotle to a savage prince, much less one of his hirelings? What could any of them know of Thebes or its women, the Thebes of Antigone and Ismene, yes of Jocasta and the Sphinx herself?

His fingers, thick and calloused from holding his sword and his dagger and his shield, rubbed coarsely down her body from shoulder to thigh.

"For a woman like you I'd fight the Persians themselves. Think of that! The Macedonians and the Thracians taking on the Persians, and beating them! And with a general like Alexander we could do it too, especially if we knew we'd get women like you for our pains—women like you and our share of the gold and jewels, of course."

Naturally. Women are used and thrown aside, but gold and jewels remain untarnished. They keep their value, and they can be traded for women or weapons or boys or anything else the manly heart may desire. Wouldn't this one love to know where her jewels lay hidden!

"That's something I haven't mentioned yet, sweetheart," he was saying, "the jewelry. In a house like this there's bound to be plenty. Look at the money it must take to own this place. Look at the houses even down in the city...."

Yes, look at them, they're burning! Thebes is burning, and not a man is left to avenge it. The husbands are dead, and the wives and children are ready for the slave market. Even the Sphinx couldn't be taken by brute force. But then, the Sphinx wasn't a Theban, was she? In fact, it was she who held Thebes in thrall with a riddle until Jocasta's son outsmarted her. Outsmarted her...

Her body had stiffened though her limbs had not moved and her eyes had remained fixed on the ceiling. But the Thracian had sensed the change and was patting her roughly in appreciation.

"So the thought of losing your jewels bothers you, does it? I'll bet it does—a lot more than a little loving from a man who knows how to please a lady."

He grabbed her wrist, and his voice took on a hardened edge.

"Listen, sweet, the two of us, just you and me, would make a lovely pair if you're willing. I don't have to put you up on the block to be bought by some idiot with money and no appreciation of class. I took you, and you're mine to do what I want with. I can sell you if I want, or I can can keep you and cover you with jewels, and nobody can say a word. So which will it be? I honestly don't want to have to sell you; I like you too much. But my men have been hunting all over this house and haven't found a single piece of silverware or jewelry. So tell me where it's hidden, and you can keep any dozen of the best pieces. Better than that, I'll buy you the clothes to go with them and dress you like a queen."

She tried not to react and instead remained frozen in outrage at the violation of her person. But her skin tingled and her body quivered in spite of her best efforts.

He had noticed the change. "Don't tell me this cuddling has warmed you up again. Come on, be serious and answer my question."

She twisted her hand free, and her head turned to the side so that her eyes, though expressionless, fell on the heavy, dirt- and blood-streaked features of his face.

"How about it?" he pursued. "You'll knock their eyes out. Isn't that what every woman wants? To belong to the top man and wear his jewels and be envied and admired by other women? Come on, tell me where they are."

"The well."

She mouthed the word with her lips not to speak it aloud. The image of the well had been in her mind, with its dark depths and its cold dampness and the oblivion it offered when she could stand no more. Her husband had dug it himself, locating the source of water through some secret method of his own, then setting his workmen to digging until the flow, cool and fresh, had welled up to irrigate the garden and bring forth life from the rocky hillside. He had designed the stone walls too and the stone parapet around the opening to serve as a resting place beside the windlass, and had planted trees to give it shade. It was a fine well, with walls as smooth as only her husband could make them, and its water was the sweetest of any in the city. Where else would a woman hide her most precious belongings from a savage horde of invaders but in this well?

"The well? What well?"

Her gaze never wavered. Her body never budged. "I'll show you."

"That's more like it," he grinned. "So what shall we do now, go to the well or have a little more loving first?"

"You don't want someone else to find it, do you?"

The fingers which had been moving against her flesh stopped and remained still as if in hesitation. Then they rose and fell on her in a slap of soldierly tenderness.

"You win. Let's go."

He sprang to the floor and began to dress while she rose from the other side of the bed and walked naked toward the sanctuary of her bath.

"Where are you going?"

"I'll wash first."

"You're clean enough."

"I'll wash and then we'll go."

The curtain fell behind her as she passed into the bathroom, cutting off for the first time since her nightmare had begun the hot gaze of the savage who had entered her home, tied up her children and violated her body. Deliberately she ran the water and with warm cloths attempted to wash away the stains and the odor which seemed to have entered every pore. Clean enough? If only he knew!

When she had finished (she hadn't finished; she would never finish washing away the stink of him), she dried herself and donned her finest robe, immaculately fresh and of the cut and material only the noblest of Theban women wore. Then she stepped from behind the curtain, observing coldly the admiration in his eyes. Not a bad catch for a Thracian barbarian, was it, this daughter of one of the oldest families in Thebes? A wildcat too, but he'd been the man to tame her.

"Come," she said, stretching out her hand to him, her chin high and a distant promise in her eyes.

"By the gods, there's no jewel to equal you, though I'd give you any of them your heart desires."

Dressed again for battle, eyes aflame, he grasped her hand and let her lead him out and into the garden.

It was to the garden that she had always given particular care, with grape arbors and rows of flowers from other lands and formal walks leading toward the rocky hillside; though now, with her husband dead and one of his killers at her side, she wondered why she had cared for it and what her having cared could mean for others, in years to come.

But time was short and the well was close by already, its hollow stone cylinder, the stone parapet and the shade tree and the rock garden nearby. Could he tell? Would he suspect?

"So that's it, eh? Pretty smart. Away from the house where no one would even think of looking."

Down below the city was still burning. Occasionally a shout or a scream could still be heard, borne aloft on the wind. But for the most part Thebes was already silent, the sounds of human life gone from its body, with only prowling bands of foreign soldiers roaming the streets like jackals tearing at a corpse. Thebes! Beloved, ancient Thebes!

Now they stood at the rim so finely shaped by her husband's hand. It was neither terribly deep nor terribly wide, but it was her husband's, and the flowers that bloomed in her garden owed their existence to it.

"Down there, you mean? At the bottom? What did you do, just throw them in?"

"The rope," she said, indicating the windlass.

"Then let's pull them up."

He grasped the handle and began to lower the bucket.

"You can't do it that way. It won't work."

"Then how do we get them up?"

"There's a hook on the bucket. You have to know how to guide it down to where the box lies. There, I can see something even from where I'm standing—something bright and shiny."

To point she had moved around slowly to the side opposite where he was standing.

"How can you see?" he scoffed. "The sun doesn't reach down that far."

"Oh, but it does, because I do see something shining. Come see for yourself."

"I don't believe it."

Nevertheless, he walked around to where she stood looking over the edge of the parapet. He was beside her now, looking down. The edge of the parapet reached the middle of his thighs, but the stone seat attached to it was at knee-level and forced him to lean forward.

"I don't see it. You're imagining things."

"No, I'm not. Lean over and you'll see it."

He pulled back abruptly and turned to face her. "Sure, so you can push me over the edge."

His body loomed over hers by a full head. How could any woman defend herself against such a brute? Best to let him have his way and just try to accommodate oneself.

She looked into his eyes, and a smile formed on her lips. "Can you see me pushing a man like you anywhere?"

He laughed. He thought he saw the awakening of renewed desire in her eyes and pulled her to him, his hands pushing deeply along her body through the gorgeous material of her robe. "Wait till I get you back in the house."

Her gaze remained level.

"Which do you want, me or the jewels?"

"I've got you already, but I want the jewels too. And I'll have you both."

"You're a very greedy man."

"Just a hungry man. I'm hungry to see a necklace of gold and jewels around that lovely neck of yours."

"I think my gold necklace was the last thing I put in the box," she said uncertainly.

"Then it will be the first thing I'll take out. Show me again where you see it, and we'll lower the bucket."

"It's right there where I'm pointing."

"Where?"

"You're not leaning forward far enough. If I can see it, you should be able to."

Both his knees were against the edge of the stone seat when she pushed. It was a mechanical action as of a lever which her husband had never tired of showing her, wherein a small force properly applied could move a far larger force. She enjoyed what was called a mechanical advantage, the fruit of thought and planning representing the triumph of mind over matter, of weakness over strength, of civilization over barbarism.

The man's body, caught off balance, pivoted over the edge of the parapet and plummeted into the well, his arms grasping the rope of the windless as he fell. She was unable to prevent the unraveling of the cord, which fell slack as he splashed into the water. And when his cries were heard again as he bobbed to the surface, grasping the rope with both hands and beginning to pull himself hand over hand, she could only wish in vain for a knife to cut the rope. Instead, however, she ran wildly to the rock garden for stones to cast down upon him. Roars of pain and rage followed, but finally there was only silence from the depths of the well. Exhausted, she fell onto the ground and into the arms of her tormentor's cohorts, alerted by his cries for help. But even finding herself once more a captive, she had the satisfaction of a debt repaid, a score settled.

Later that day, when young Alexander of Macedon, soon to be called "the Great" and now at the beginning of his career of world conquest, heard of what this woman had done in the name of Thebes and for the freedom of Greece, he had no choice in his heart but to award her her freedom and the restitution of all her property.

Her name was Timoclea.

A Suspended Sentence

The gray *deux-chevaux* Citroën lurched through the empty streets and out onto the country road. In the beam of its headlights the sugarbeet fields were a wintry brown, and patches of snow still clung to the paths leading off the highway. There were no other lights, either from passing cars or from houses, and the village lay more than ten kilometers distant.

"Doctor, come quick," the voice had said, calling from the one café in the village with the usual urgency of calls at two in the morning. "It's worse this time. She's out of her head. She'll do some harm if she isn't stopped."

"Hold her by force if you have to," he'd snarled, maneuvering his right foot into the shoe by his bedside. "I'm coming, and whatever you do, keep her away from the child."

Excellent advice, as usual. Dr. Coste always knew what to do. "I'd go to him for advice before I'd go to *Monsieur le Curé*," women would tell each other. "And no matter what he said to do, I'd know it was the right thing. Look at all he's done for others."

It was an enviable reputation, being thought of as a man who existed only for the purpose of helping others, and so he accepted being roused at night as one of the inevitable aspects of his profession. As a childless widower he lived alone, unkempt and perhaps a bit eccentric. He would pass acquaintances in the street without greeting them; occasionally he simply forgot a social engagement; there were food stains on his vest. But in his professional capacity he was scrupulous to a fault. When not out on a call, he almost always could be found in his study, which with his office was in the same house where he and his wife had spent fifteen years together.

"Where else would I be?" he would answer those who called timidly after office hours. "Bring him over right now if he's not too sick. Otherwise I'll come."

His tone was rude only because he was weary. They knew that and accepted him as one of their own, for long ago he had chosen them. Others in his class at medical school had opted for Paris or the Mediterranean, where opportunities were greater, practices more lucrative, life more pleasant. Few if any had taken as their first and lifelong choice the dreary expanses of northeastern France. But Coste had chosen this place knowing its need for doctors and its lack of outside distractions, and in making his choice he had felt a sort of preliminary fulfillment. Years later, when his wife had died, he had been surprised to note behind his honest grief a sense of satisfaction that now at last he would be able to devote himself whole-heartedly to his profession. No longer had he a private life; he was one with his vocation. It was a self-denial which was recognized by many in town as a kind of secular sainthood. After all, look at what he had done for Germaine Vaillant.

The little car chugged placidly along the country road like an old horse unhurried but sure of its way. He would be there in another ten minutes, and if it was too late, well, he couldn't be at every bedside all the time. He had more than one patient, after all. In fact, he'd had thousands over the years. But because most of them had been and still were aware of the case of Germaine Vaillant, and because a few of them still had the indelicacy to mention it to him, he knew that he would never be free of her and that as a result he would never hesitate to drive ten kilometers on a night call in winter. For as long as the final reckoning was not in on Germaine's life, no more could it be on his own. And who could tell which one of these calls might be the crucial one, the one which might balance the ledger in the end?

Germaine Vaillant. Her story was known as only the stories of lifetime inhabitants of provincial towns in France can be known. But in her case a blinding flash of notoriety had burned her image forever into the minds of her neighbors, so that each subsequent trial or disappointment in her life had been measured against that one indelible memory.

"Didn't I predict it?" one woman had cried that very morning in the market on hearing the latest turn of events. I knew it would happen. She's a cold, domineering woman."

"Yes, but how sad for her, after what she's been through."

"Well, if she's a martyr, she brought it all on herself."

Germaine Vaillant, in fact, was not universally liked. Too much separated her from other woman, both in her present life and in the past which had formed her. And now when her youngest son, who had been her favorite and the only one to show promise, had abandoned his studies and left home after a dispute with her, the reaction among the women was less one of sympathy than one of grim satisfaction.

"I knew he'd do it one day," she'd told Coste that very morning. "I could see it in his eyes each time I had to be firm with him." Then a note of pleading had crept into her voice. "But I didn't believe God would do this to me again. Hasn't He punished me enough already?"

"Are you asking me to describe the pathology of God for you?" he had said. "Am I supposed to know what was ailing God when He made the world? I'm no theologian."

But a theologian was what he was taken for in town, and nothing could remove that label from him.

"You warned me, of course," she had pursued. "You told me it would lead to this, and you said it as if it would be my fault when it happened."

"Germaine, listen to me..."

And again he found himself explaining what should have been as clear to her as it was to him. There were only three Vaillant children—he insisted on the number each time—a girl and two boys. The girl was all right; she was plain and obedient and hard-working; she would find someone to marry her. Of the boys, the first—named René after his father—seemed to have inherited his father's weakness of character. For whereas René Vaillant senior was known as an ineffectual husband and a drunkard, his son's weakness had already led him into bad company, occasional week-long disappearances and once into court for car theft. Nothing could induce him to strike out on his own and make an independent life for himself away from the scorn and contempt of his mother. Instead it was Philippe, her youngest, the serious student and idealist, who now at the threshold of manhood was abandoning his education and leaving home. The iron character which had cowed her husband, her mother-in-law, and her two eldest children, had driven away the only one who would not be dominated, the only one she really loved.

"I knew this too," she had answered. "You speak of character as if a person's nature were something to be turned on or off like a faucet. Do you think I enjoy carrying the entire burden? Don't you think I'd like to have a husband who would take a little responsibility? Of course it rubs off on the children if I'm that way. Don't forget who helped me gain this so-called strength. Don't forget who showed me how..."

Low buildings sprang into the headlights' beam, huddled together as if against the cold. The little car swung into the single paved street, around the frozen fountain and toward the far edge of the village. He knew the house; he had visited it twice before, not counting the night of the delivery at the hospital. And he dreaded the visit because he knew he would be asked, here and again, to give a woman the strength no woman should have. And all in the name of Germaine Vaillant.

Perhaps he was putting too much blame onto himself, after all. What he had given Germaine was not so much the strength as the means to do what she had already determined to do, one way or another. The reversal of the family roles which had followed her decision, with the harridan of a mother-in-law reduced to querulous impotency and the master of the household revealed as a spineless onlooker opposed to yet acquiescing in his wife's lonely act, might have occurred later in another family crisis. The strengths and weaknesses were there to begin with. Sooner or later the dutiful wife would have taken the reins of leadership from the faltering hands of her husband. Nevertheless, it was at this time, and in these circumstances, that the reversal had taken place, with Dr. Coste in attendance, so to speak, for the occasion. This much of the responsibility he could not deny.

"Welcome, Doctor!" He could hear the voice clearly even though the event was already years in the past. The man had been hidden behind the other patrons of the café as he had entered, and the sight of his face—flushed from drink already this early in the morning—had made him

want to retreat into the street. But the others had all turned
now in his direction, and he would have to stand there
and hear the indictment from the mouth of the husband
himself.

"Come join the company of ordinary mortals, Doctor.
This, Messieurs, is the man who not only cures the sick
but does away with those who can't be cured. And if
anyone should object—the husband, for instance—well,
that's just too bad for the husband. Messieurs, the world
is full of cuckolds. For all I know, this bar is full of cuckolds. But I, René Vaillant, claim the distinction of being
the only man here cuckolded by the family doctor, and
cuckolded in a way I hope none of you will ever be. Come
on, Doctor, have a drink, just to show I don't hold a
grudge!"

No one had laughed. No voice but that of René Vaillant
had followed him into the street that day. But the unspo-
ken indictment had come out at last, had entered the public domain. And wherever the sympathy of the others had
lain, the accusation was clear that he, Coste, had intruded
into a family conflict and destroyed the authority of the
husband by supporting the wife.

Would this same accusation be leveled at him some day
by the dull-faced peasant who was opening the front door
of his house to him now? Would this man, now so obviously at a loss to calm the hysterics of his wife, one day
accuse him of taking his place if not in bed then at the
head of his table?

"She's quieter now, Doctor. At least she isn't trying to
break things. But I don't like the way she's talking to herself. She's planning something as soon as I turn my back.
I can tell."

He entered the bedroom, where a single light bulb hung
from the ceiling over an old double bed piled high with

quilts and a night table with a basin of water and a glass. On the edge of the bed, wearing a styleless robe over a cotton nightgown, a young woman with red-rimmed eyes and haggard features was sitting.

"Well, Madame Bernard, still having trouble sleeping? You've got to try harder. This man of yours has to get up early." It was as if they had been speaking on another subject and she were merely pursuing her train of thought.

"It's no use, Doctor. This can't go on."

"Of course it can. Everything goes on, much longer than we think it possible."

"Not this. A while ago it started to cry. I found the blanket over its face. It couldn't even move the blanket."

Ever since the birth she had referred to her son as if he were an object rather than a human being.

"You must pin the blanket down. You know children that age can't move blankets anyway."

She dismissed his words. "If it weren't that, it would be something else. Come, I want to show you."

"Let's not bother him if he's asleep," he said, hoping to keep her away from the child.

Her eyes flashed suspiciously. "You don't want to have to look at him, do you? You don't like the sight either."

It was true. He knew it even as he denied it, even as he accepted her challenge by following her into the adjoining room. He didn't want to see it; he'd seen it at birth, and that was enough. The end result of a normal pregnancy, with all its attendant anxieties and pains overcome in a triumphantly banal delivery, was a creature which never in its life could dress or feed or wash itself, much less take on the hundred-odd farming chores for which its parents had intended it and needed it.

"I'll kill it," she had said at once, far earlier than Germaine Vaillant and without the urging of any shame-ridden mother-in-law. "No one must know what it looks like."

The husband was as final in his way as the wife, though more flexible as to the means.

"Give it away. Anything. What good is it to me, a son that can't work?" Besides, they had two sons already. This was the third, and in its condition it only stood to nullify the advantages of having the other two.

The solution, of course, was an institution where it could be taught some useful occupation. It could hardly be left with a father who already saw no use for it and a mother who was ashamed of its very existence. The problem was to convince the mother of the child's right to live.

Was he getting soft in his middle age? Was his vision, so much more acute, it seemed, than that of others, becoming blurred at last? If not, then why was this child any different from the firstborn child of Germaine Vaillant, that infant who today would be a grown man had he not handed the mother the means of killing it?

There was a difference. He could demonstrate it in the degree of malformation which would have left one child helpless for life while offering the other the possibility of at least partial independence. There was a difference between adding one more burden to a family used to toil and saddling newlyweds with a sickly nightmare just when they should have been founding a normal family. But most of all, there was a difference in parental attitudes. While one mother preferred killing her child to avoid having it known she had given birth to a monster, the other had killed hers to spare it—the child, not herself—a life without hope. Both René and Germaine had loved the tiny torso which was their firstborn; but under the goadings of her mother-in-law she had agreed it could not be allowed to live. Yet when the time had come, it was Germaine who had assumed responsibility for killing it, while the husband had been unable to oppose it. He, Coste, had watched the father take the tiny bundle from its crib that last day and speak to it out of his wife's hearing.

"Little sweetheart, they're going to kill you. They'll put you to sleep, and you'll never wake up. But you won't blame Papa, will you? He tried, and he loves you. Papa won't forget you."

Then Coste had left, and the mother had done the rest.

At the trial, which had been a sensation in its day, the fact of homicide had been established and guilt assigned. But an upsurge of public sentiment in favor of the accused had resulted in suspended sentences for all.

Suspended sentences. Coste's sentence was still in suspense. His entire life since then had been lived in suspense, as if waiting for the time when the sentence would finally be carried out. Yet he didn't regret his action. He would do it again in similar circumstances. But these circumstances here in this farmhouse, in this village at two o'clock in the morning of this day, these circumstances were not similar.

Yet wasn't there also a nagging fear of the consequences? With Germaine he had accepted his own guilt. But how could he have guessed that by helping her he would turn her into a creature hounded by the furies, reaching frantically to assume the burden of other lives in compensation for her lost child and in so doing destroying or driving away those she sought to protect? What would be the consequences, twenty or thirty years from now, for the peasant woman who stood here looking so strangely into the crib of her deformed son?

"It's sleeping now," she mused. "The others always woke up when I came into the room."

"Of course he's sleeping. He's a healthy boy."

"Don't mock me, Doctor."

"Madame Bernard, I'm not mocking you. If I say your child is healthy, it's because it's true. He won't do everything the others do, that's all. But he will walk, and many can't do that. He will hear and speak and see the sky and all the beauty of the world. And he will learn a trade and be able to support himself."

"You missed your calling, Doctor. You should have been a priest."

Her expression was sullen as she spoke. He'd hoped he might be convincing her, but now a hard line seemed to trace itself in her jaw. Where had he seen such a line before? Where indeed but in the face of Germaine Vaillant.

"You talk like a priest," she said. "No family of your own, and yet you tell others how to run theirs. If you were honest, you'd admit the child has no chance for a normal life."

He felt himself rising to the bait. He was playing her game.

"What makes you think so? What right have you to decide?" A sly peasant smile came to her lips. She was nobody's fool. She'd heard a few things.

"The same right, Doctor," she said triumphantly, "that you had when you decided the Vaillant child couldn't live."

There. He'd expected it. After all, everyone knew, even the peasants in the villages. And he deserved no better. He'd played at being God, and now he'd have to hear the accusations of those who lose their faith and throw the injustices of their lives up to God. Like God, he was accused of playing favorites.

Bitterly, he found himself commiserating with the Almighty.

But she had one advantage now, and she pressed it.

"How many others have you let kill their babies, Doctor?"

"None, of course."

"And how many others have you told to be patient and suffer, like me, with a monster for a child?"

Strangely, the answer to this question was the same. Handicapped children, children blinded or maimed he had seen, as well as congenital defects in some delivered by others. But never until now had he officiated at the entry of another deformed child into the world. Fate had somehow spared him that.

"Then I'm the first," she smiled. "All right, the Vaillant woman has had more children and a normal life in spite of what she did. "Tell me why I can't do the same."

He wanted to tell her everything about Germaine, everything professional ethics forbade him to say. Instead, he only asked, "What makes you think her life has been normal?"

"I'd settle for it. All these fine ladies in town think they have a hard life. She can come here if she thinks she has troubles. I'd be glad to trade my life for hers."

The woman's resentment at the other's social position had blinded her to the tie which should have bound them. More understanding had been blocked by that barrier than by any ocean or mountain range, and he was weaponless against it.

"How about yourself, Doctor?" she pursued, self-justified now and nearing her triumph. "You've lived all these years with a death on your conscience, and it doesn't seem to have hurt you any. You're free and respected. In fact, the whole town swears by you. I don't see you doing penance for any sin."

This was enough. He had not come over ten kilometers into the countryside in the dead of night to listen to accusations against himself.

"Monsieur Bernard," he said to the husband, "you called me because your wife was having hysterics. I am ready to give her an injection to help her sleep. Do you want me to do it or not?"

Bernard glanced apologetically at his wife and then looked away, He shrugged his shoulders. "If that's what she needs. She's got to sleep, doesn't she? So do I."

Her lip curled at the words. "Of course, do what you like, Doctor. We wouldn't have you drive out here for nothing."

He spoke calmly, almost absently, as he prepared the hypodermic. "Madame, I know I can't convince you if your mind is made up. I just want you to know I won't support you in your plan. Furthermore," he added as he withdrew the needle, "if anything happens to the child, I won't hesitate to say so."

The serum was in her, but its action would be delayed long enough for her to rise to her feet with blazing eyes.

"Hypocrite! You stand there without a care in the world and tell me to suffer the shame of a monster for a son. You've killed once. Why not twice? What's the difference? And if you can get away with it, then so can I!"

The child was awake now and crying. Its sounds seemed to infuriate her all the more.

"I'll tell them that too. Don't think I won't. If a doctor can kill and be venerated for it like a saint, then I think a mother can do the same without going to jail. Prove me wrong!"

He bade them good night, and the husband took him to the door raising his hands in a gesture of abdication.

"You've got to excuse her, Doctor. With women, what can you expect? They make everything into a tragedy."

"Would you let her do it?" he asked pointedly.

Bernard shrugged helplessly. "I couldn't very well stop her if she had her mind set on it."

"In other words, you think she's right."

The man shifted and looked away. "No, but you'll have to admit she has a point. After all, you haven't been punished...." And in the background, above the crying of the child, he could still hear the woman, her voice beginning to cloud with drowsiness, saying: "Prove I'm wrong, Doctor! Prove it!"

He turned toward his small gray auto, parked in the darkness of the street.

"Good night, Monsieur Bernard."

Darkness has its advantages, he was thinking. The darkness of village streets, of country roads, of an empty doctor's office now in the early hours of the morning. Darkness eliminated the non-essentials, made sounds more acute, helped thoughts range broad and deep. Darkness was what was needed now after the scene at the house of the peasant Bernard.

There was no point in sleeping. It was late, and daylight would be here by seven. There was very little time, really, to use the darkness.

He had never used it, he realized, nor the daylight either, to form thoughts without anticipating some necessary preconceived action as the result of them. Instead, he had filled his days and nights with appointments and pills and visits and advice, filled them with the ills of others. It was a sufficient occupation for many; some even considered it a noble one, and as such it had been for him too. But there was no denying it prevented thought, preoccupation with self; and while some maintained this was good, he was no longer sure. Why for a quarter century had he thrown himself headlong into good works, or at least into work? Was it to buy back with lives saved the one he had forfeited? Or was it simply to avoid a confrontation with his own deepest intuition, that a life once forfeited cannot be repurchased?

His memory ranged back over the ills he had treated. They were the ordinary routine of any small-town doctor, from births to deaths. And while he was fairly sure he had not lost a patient unnecessarily, he could not remember having saved one who might have been lost by any of his classmates in medical school.

He wondered now what the sum total of it all might be. Had the books been balanced at last, or was the same deficit being carried over still? How to know? Whichever way, however, he did know it was now about to reappear so that the weight of it, even if it had been lifted, would be felt again, and if not lifted would be doubled by a second act which he could not prevent even though it was being committed in his name.

"Prove I'm wrong, Doctor. Prove it!"

He heard the words again and again in the silence before dawn. The Bernard woman would kill her child, fortified by his example. Regardless of his warnings, living unpunished for the crime of the past he validated the crime of the future.

Unpunished! He wished he could tell her the truth. But did he know himself what might have been if he had never met Germaine Vaillant? Was it merely the death of her child that had driven him through all these years of expiation, or was it some deeper, more remote need hidden in his very nature which had made him manufacture guilt purely for the joy of doing penance? Perhaps what he really feared was freedom.

A profound weariness crept through him. His reason was serving him badly. In another few minutes his mind would convince him his whole existence had been an evasion, an accumulation of invented responsibility and guilt for the sole purpose of avoiding the unknown pleasures of freedom.

No, he would not let his mind take him there. At the end of that road he could already sense a land of pastel shades and perfumes, a riviera playground where duty and drab responsibility had no place and the deepest emotion was regret that the present could not be eternal. Reasonable this might be in its Mediterranean clarity, it was not for him.

For him the answer was clear enough, though shrouded till now in northern mists. It was a simple answer, with a single action which would at once atone for a past crime and prevent a future one. It was so simple that he realized he had known it all along, unconsciously, hiding it beneath the convolutions of his thought and the pressure of his daily rounds. And like a child playing a game, he had forced himself to follow the single strand of it through the labyrinth of thought and find what prize awaited him at the other end. And now that he had seen it at last he was able to ignore it and concentrate instead on the prize he really wanted, the one which lay already in his grasp, waiting only to be claimed.

He didn't have much time. Daylight would not wait. He went to his desk, turned on the small lamp and examined his appointment book. Banalities, nothing more. There was no one who would die from having missed one appointment.

He took a prescription pad and wrote a few instructions for the nurse who would let herself in with her own key. She was his age and hardened to the sight of illness. She would know what to do.

The rest of his affairs were in order. He was a model of tidiness in his profession if not in his personal life, despite long years as a widower. He was a very uninteresting type, really.

He was walking about the house purposefully now, turning on lights in each room just long enough for a look around, to make sure everything was in its place, then quickly extinguishing the lights to save electricity. In the cellar he found a length of cord used by the cleaning woman to dry laundry on her weekly visit. There was a pipe under the ceiling of the cellar, and even hooks on the walls, but he had no desire to create a mystery. Instead he took the cord up to the ground floor opposite the front door and looked for pipes or hooks there. Finding none and walking toward his office, he noticed the staircase against one wall, with its wrought iron bannister. This would do.

And so here he was, standing on a chair and tying the knot around the iron post, testing it with his weight and getting ready to tie the other knot, when he noticed the light was still on. So down again he climbed and went to the other side of the room, smiling at his own fastidiousness, to turn it off. Then carefully he made his way back in the darkness until he felt the chair, the cord, and the cold security of the bannister. This was better. The room was silent now and dark, as dark as he wanted it, though there was in the darkness a hint that before long there would be light. But not yet. He was in time.

And in those last instants of darkness his reason was able to form the final link in his chain of thought, find the prize at the end of the strand, that what he most truly had sought was not after all a conscienceless riviera of depthless color but only that which he already had in the cold dreariness of these northern fields, where faces are closed and appearances are unbearable and the truth can be glimpsed only fleetingly through mist.

It seemed to him now that he had found his own truth at last. It had needed but an adequate pretext, and now even this had been furnished.

Germaine Vaillant was not a woman to show grief, nor any other emotion, for that matter. As a local celebrity, so to speak, she had learned to wear a mask and avoid the baring of her private joys and sorrows to the gaze of the curious.

Here, now, at the funeral of Dr. Coste, its ceremony limited to what is accorded to those who take their own lives, she was not even sure that what she felt was truly grief. There was a sense of loss; but she already and still was feeling loss from the departure of her son, and this was not the same. With the boy it had been a cherished responsibility—for were not all her responsibilities cherished ones?—which had disappeared and left a sense of emptiness. The death of Coste, however, seemed to have deprived her of a prop rather than a responsibility. For she had been, she realized now with astonishment, his responsibility rather than he hers. More than an accomplice, more than a sharer of guilt, he had become through hearing her woes the bearer of her burdens. She wondered if he had realized it himself.

She knew, of course, the stated reason for his act; the nurse had given her a note with her name on it, in which he had been at pains to absolve her of blame. Yet the very act of addressing a note to her had shown his awareness of her probable reaction, however much he might have denied its validity.

Leaving the cortege now, Germaine was conscious of the whispers and the glances of the women. They were the same ones who whispered in the marketplace as she passed. For all she knew, she and Coste were being spoken of as lovers and his suicide ascribed to her jealousy. But the opinions of others no longer interested her. Following the one blaze of publicity in her life, she had learned to live apart and do what she had to do without concern for her reputation.

Perhaps that was her trouble. Had she been more like other women, perhaps she would have had more success with her children. As she looked around her house that evening, though, she knew it was too late to change. The daughter who had made the beds without a smile, the querulous old woman who raved of a past none of them had known, the husband who stopped at a bar every night and returned there after dinner, the son who was gone for a day or a week at a time, the memory of the other son gone now for good, this was what she had killed her first-born to protect. This was what was left to her after all else, including Coste, had disappeared.

She was seen to make several visits the next morning, including one to her bank and one to a lawyer, and they of course were commented upon. So was the fact that later in the day she got into her car and drove out of town. But not even she had known precisely where she was going until she had sought out and obtained from the nurse a name and an address—from the nurse who was one of the few in town who told no tales, though Germaine hardly cared if she did.

The road and the fields were dry, but the sky was heavily overcast as she started out, and fog was beginning to settle in the hollows. And when she reached the village, it was hardly brighter by daylight than it had been under the doctor's headlights. The house bore a street number but no name plate; yet she knew it was the right address, and she rightly suspected the husband would not be there during the day.

"I'm Germaine Vaillant," she told the drawn and list-less woman who opened the door.

"I know. I recognize you."

It was easy, as if the whole thing had been arranged after lengthy correspondence, and when she left the village an hour later, she had a sensation as if a gap in her life had been filled. All she had lived for had turned slowly to ashes. But what she had not been able to accept in her youth, not knowing what else might come in its place, now in middle age she was more than happy to assume as a burden, even as a joy.

Let the gossips talk; she would name it after Coste. Her family would accept it as they accepted everything, for the burden would be hers. And who could tell? They might even grow fond of it. At this thought the harsh line of her jaw softened, and for the first time in years her heart felt lighter.

Then, suddenly, thinking of Coste and sharing instinctively by now in his thoughts, she became aware that what she was doing had probably never entered his mind. He had sought only to balance his own ledger, and the final gesture had been hers to make, with Coste to thank for it. She smiled and wondered whether he could see her now, whether he knew now that sometimes things really did work out in the end.

Eyes to See You With

They say dead men tell no tales. But this one does, and I think you'll believe me when you've heard what happened after I "passed away."

"Since my husband passed away..." That's the expression she's been using. It's so much more refined than saying, "Since he died," and infinitely more refined than saying, "Since I murdered him."

So let's look the facts in the eye. My wife murdered me; it's as simple as that. Oh, not with a knife or a gun; nothing so crude, and not with her pretensions to gentility. But just as effectively nevertheless. She did it simply by hiding my pills and then taunting me when I needed them.

That's the truth of it, even if she couldn't be convicted for it in a court of law. But she overlooked one thing when she decided to rid herself of her husband and enjoy his house on the Intracoastal all by herself—she and her "yachtsman" friend, that is.

She forgot about my portrait.

You see, I'd stipulated in my will that while I was leaving the house to my son, I gave her the exclusive use of it during her lifetime—on the condition that everything inside the house be left exactly as it was at the time of my death.

Who would be able to check? My son, of course, since he would have the right to visit and examine the house whenever he pleased. I took dozens of photos of every room and added them to my will to show how it all looked. The snapshots from our European honeymoon were everywhere: on the tables in the living room, under the glass top of our dresser in the bedroom, on the coffee table in the den and even over the breakfast table in the kitchen. There was also the formal portrait of me on her dresser, taken when I was still in business and long before I retired to Florida and met her.

So everything was recorded on film for my son to compare with what he found when he dropped in on short notice from time to time, as he planned to do. This was how I kept control of things after my death. I knew he wanted the house for himself, and this gave him an incentive to inspect it often. As for her, if she so much as moved a picture of me from one table to another he would have a legal right to throw her out and move in himself. In this way I'd keep them both in line and, through the pictures, keep my memory fresh in their minds.

But I haven't mentioned the most important picture of all, the oil painting of me that hung over the mantel. You see, vanity aside, I'd been quite handsome as a young man, and growing older I became rather distinguished. It wasn't my fault, of course, but everyone told me so, and I had no reason not to believe them. Besides, I took advantage of it in my business, and I know for a fact that it was my looks as well as my money which attracted Phyllis to me. So naturally I didn't want her to forget where the house and the money came from, especially after our marriage turned sour. The portrait over the mantel was a way to accomplish that purpose and keep me alive in the eyes of everyone who visited the house.

It was also a way to help me keep an eye on her.

This is how I did it. In our European travels we'd visited the usual museums and galleries and chateaux and seen the portraits of kings and popes and lords of the manor. One portrait in particular had caught my interest. I forget who it was but the guide had made a point of walking us past it from one end of the room to the other to show us how the eyes followed us from the moment we came in until the moment we left the room. It was an optical illusion, of course, but when we got back to Florida I happened to run into an old painter friend of mine who had always wanted to do my portrait. I described what I'd seen in Europe and asked him if he could perform the same trick.

"Of course," he said. "I know that painting, and I know how the artist did it. I'll do the same for you, and if you're not satisfied, I won't charge a cent."

"Fair enough," I told him, and over the next few weeks I sat for him while my wife went to what she called her bridge parties but which I later found out included men, in particular the one she took up with.

He was a slick customer, one of those gigolos you find preying on well-off widows in retirement communities. A yachtsman, no less, and fifteen years younger than she was, which made him thirty years younger than me. By coincidence, he had a boat and was looking for a dock, and we had a dock and no boat. It wasn't a large boat, but the cabin was big enough for two, which made it very convenient. He'd take her out on the Intracoastal instead of to her bridge club, meeting her somewhere out of range of the neighbors' prying eyes while I was sitting for my portrait, and have her back by the time I got home.

Until the day I got home early and sat waiting for her.

"I didn't know you went to your bridge parties by boat."

"Oh, you saw me?" she said airily, not batting an eye as she put her lipstick back on and rearranged her dress where it had gotten wrinkled. "Chuck was on his way there and offered to take me. I couldn't very well refuse."

"Why not? Look at the back of your dress. I didn't know ladies played bridge in wrinkled dresses."

"Well, I won't do it again. I didn't realize the boat was so small. Next time I'll have him tie up at the dock and come with me in my car."

Then she changed the subject. "How's the portrait coming, darling? I'm dying to see it."

"You'll see it soon enough," I reassured her.

When it was finished, we hung it directly over the mantel, with a lamp attached to the frame shining directly down onto the face and leaving the body in relative darkness.

"Oh, it's absolutely *you*, darling!" she marveled. "Just look at those piercing eyes!"

"I see them," I said, adding to myself, "...and they see you."

The living room was a big one, with the kitchen at one end and the sun room at the other and the bedroom across the patio and the swimming pool. By day, with the curtains open, the portrait would be visible from almost every room in the house, with its eyes on whoever was there. But if you entered the living room from the kitchen and walked toward the sun room or vice versa, the eyes literally followed you all the way. That was what I liked most about it. There was no escaping it. And with the lamp set on the frame just over my head, the eyes actually glowed as they followed you. Wherever you might be, if you saw it, you could be sure it saw you too.

I never mentioned this aspect to Phyllis, but she noticed it herself after a few days.

"There's something about those eyes, darling," she said with a shiver. "They seem to follow me about the house."

"What do you mean?" I asked blandly.

"Well, just that they're looking at me when I come into the room, and they never stop looking at me."

"Nonsense. They look straight out into the room. When you see them from an angle, they're still looking straight ahead."

"No, they're not. It's like that painting we saw in Europe. Don't you remember?"

"I don't remember anything of the kind. No painting has eyes that move. You're imagining things."

I left her troubled. If I denied it and she was the only one who saw it, then soon she'd believe she was seeing things. Which was exactly what I wanted. My original purpose, you see, had been to keep her from forgetting whose house she was living in. But unfortunately, her yachtsman appeared on the scene just as I was sitting for the portrait, and that changed things for her, as well as for me. For her it made her realize she'd have to find a way to get rid of me sooner rather than later, and without risking being tried for murder.

My heart pills, it turned out, provided her with the perfect way.

A man with a weak heart should know better than to marry a firecracker like Phyllis. But I was fool enough to fall for her, and I lived to regret it. In fact, I died regretting it.

At first, like any newlyweds we were lovers. But that wore off, which was a relief to me and simply made her irritable. She'd pace the floor night after night in a negligee and high heels, with her arms folded and her fingers gripping her elbows as if she were rocking a baby and not her libido, while I read the financial pages and told her how our stocks had done that day. But did she show any appreciation for my ability to get in and out of the market at the right time? Not a bit. "Look at that moon on the water," she'd say. "I'm going for a walk."

"Not dressed like that, you're not. Do you want to be arrested?"

"But I'm just going to walk around the block."

"Then at least put on a dressing gown. My first wife was a respectable woman. Try to live up to her memory if you can."

"Oh, all right!" And she'd stomp into the bedroom and return in her dressing gown and walk out the front door. "At least *he* won't be staring at me outside," she'd say, spitting the words out at my portrait.

But "he" would always be there when she came back inside, and that was a thought she couldn't stand. She realized then that to enjoy my house she'd have to get rid not only of me but of my portrait too.

That was where I made my mistake. If I'd told her what was in my will beforehand, she might have realized killing me would do her no good, and I might still be alive today.

But that's water over the dam. I'm dead and have been for almost a year. I haven't been able to influence events in any way since she killed me, which, believe me, is the worst thing about being dead. But at least I've been able to predict the results of the precautions I took before I died. It's a small satisfaction, but it's a satisfaction nevertheless.

First, there was the sight of her face when my will was read. You could see her relief when she heard that exclusive lifetime use of my house was to be hers. The tension in her body eased visibly and a faint smile came to her lips as she stole a glance at my son, who'd rushed down at the news. He of course didn't like her and had hoped I'd leave the house to him. So his disappointment at the words was as great as her pleasure. But then as the clause beginning "...on condition that no object inside the house be moved..." was read, and that he would have the right to inspect the premises whenever he wished, the situation was suddenly reversed. Her jaw dropped, her eyes opened wide and she started up in her chair as if I'd jabbed her with a needle. Then, regaining her composure, she sat back with her face frozen and just stared straight ahead. She never glanced at my son, but I knew she sensed the satisfaction he felt in keeping this control over her actions.

He intended to use it, too. He'd be dropping in on her more frequently than he'd ever done with me, and always in the hope of finding any object disturbed which would permit him to have her evicted. Let him try, I thought. This would pay him back for the years of neglect when the old man had only been good for bailing him out. As for her, she'd get the house, but only so long as she behaved like a grieving widow. Oh, it was a great scene. I enjoyed every minute of it.

When the reading was over, they split up and left the building by different doors. Phyllis drove home alone and, as she'd expected, found her sailor boy tinkering with his boat. He hadn't come to the reading, of course. They didn't want to raise questions about my death. They didn't even plan to marry for a year. But as she parked in the car port he emerged from his cabin wiping grease from his hands and with a triumphant smile on his face.

"Now, baby," he said, "at last you can invite me into our new house."

"Not yet," she whispered, looking around anxiously. "Later tonight. Let's go for a ride in the boat first. I'll explain."

So the furtive meetings they'd hoped were over would have to continue while they tried to figure out what to do. She'd murdered me to free herself, and now that she was a widow she still wasn't free. And her yachtsman, who'd helped her do it to get into my house and fill my shoes, realized he still couldn't get inside.

My will be done! I thought as I watched them agonize. Each had something on the other, yet they could never enjoy what they'd killed for. Instead, they were up some backwater canal or in a motel secretly trysting just as they'd had to before they'd killed me.

She came home alone, promising to let him in after the neighbors had gone to bed. There were no late-night hijinks on our block. We were all respectable retirees, and so she wouldn't dare play the merry widow for a while. I intended to see that she'd never play that role.

So back she came into the empty house, with the mourners gone, no friends to comfort her and my son staying clear of her until he felt like conducting his first inspection with a stack of photos I'd left him of the entire interior. All afternoon and evening she walked from room to room under the steady gaze of the eyes in my portrait. They followed her to the patio where she read one of her trashy romances and to the sun room where she watched the evening news and to the kitchen where she ate her TV dinner alone. It was ten o'clock before the neighbors turned out their lights, and almost eleven before she *dared* let sailor boy in through the kitchen door. She couldn't turn on the lights, of course, and so she had to welcome him in the dark.

That was when she got her second surprise of the day.

Let me explain. During our married life I was the one who went around the house locking doors and turning off lights while she sat in bed reading or watching TV. She'd never been in the living room in the dark—not until this first night when she'd welcomed her lover into my house.

"Oh, Chuck darling, at last we're alone in our own house," she said to him as she locked the kitchen door. "Let's go into the living room. There's more room there."

He followed her, holding her hand, then stopped.

"Good God! What's that?"

"What's what?"

"Over there, against the wall!"

She turned and let out a small scream. "Oh my God, it's those eyes!"

And so it was.

In fact, I'd never told her that I'd asked my painter friend to paint the irises with a particularly concentrated mixture of luminous paint, more potent than the kind you find on the face of your watch. So after an evening with the lamp shining down on them from the frame the eyes radiated light so brilliantly in the darkness that you could see them wherever they were visible by day. Not the features, not the face. Just the eyes. But to someone like Phyllis, who knew the face intimately, the sight of those two greenish spots following her like a laser beam about the room was enough.

"He's watching us!" she whispered.

"Who?"

"My husband, of course! I told you his portrait follows me everywhere. Let's get out of here!"

"What for? It's only a painting. Turn on the lights, and we'll have a look."

He reached for the switch, but she held his hand.

"No, don't! The neighbors will see us!"

"The neighbors are in bed. And what do we care?""

"Do you want the old woman with insomnia to see us together and draw conclusions?"

"OK, then let's go into the bedroom."

But even there I'd arranged for a series of mirrors carefully placed to reflect the portrait from one room to another and finally into the mirror on my wife's vanity dresser. If she left the bedroom door open, the eyes would shine directly into her face as she lay in bed. She might close the door every night out of habit, but eventually she'd forget and leave it open. When she did, the shock of seeing my eyes would remain with her no matter how many doors she shut to keep them out. I hardly expected this to happen the very first time she took her lover into my bedroom. But it did, and it spoiled their little celebration. Hysterical sobbing followed, which our insomniac neighbor probably mistook for grief, and young Chuck kept his own voice down while he calmed her. But their hopes for the night had gone unfulfilled.

The following day our neighbor noticed the circles under my wife's eyes and said, "I heard you crying last night, poor dear. Why don't you take some of my sleeping pills? They'll do wonders for you. Here, I have an extra bottle. Try them. You'll see."

Phyllis had never had trouble sleeping and was doubtful. "I thought you still had insomnia, even with the pills."

"I do, but I've been taking them so long my body is used to them. They have no effect on me any more, and my doctor won't let me take a double dose. But with you they should work without any problem. Try them. Take one tonight before you go to bed."

And so it was that a well-meaning neighbor introduced my wife to drugs. Phyllis had laughed at the battery of pills I'd had to take every day for my heart. No coddling the body for her. She was a health nut. But now with pills of her own and my eyes on her day and night, I was satisfied she'd soon be on sedatives regularly.

I was right. What's more, the pills left her groggy during the day, and before long she required a stimulant to counteract them when her boyfriend wanted to play. So each afternoon she'd take a pill and meet him somewhere out of our neighbor's sight and go with him in his boat, abandoning the house she'd always coveted for herself. But each evening she returned, each night she closed the inside doors to block out my eyes and each morning she awoke wondering how she would ever find a way to enjoy her new life. She tried hanging a cloth over the portrait, but the first one was too thin, and the eyes shone through. She experimented with other cloths and finally used a blanket. But she had to be ready to remove it at a moment's notice when visitors arrived, since I was still her "dear departed husband" to all.

Three months later my son made his first visit, giving her only an hour's notice by telephone. Frantically, she pulled the blanket off the portrait and dashed from room to room restoring every other picture and every piece of furniture to its exact position in the photos. When my son and his wife arrived they all had a drink in the living room and acted out the charade under my portrait as each item was silently checked. And when he was satisfied, they left, but not before he inquired about her health. For by this time Phyllis was not looking well at all. Her eyes were vague and evasive. She avoided eye-contact. Her movements were jerky and erratic, and in every way she now looked like a woman caught in a net and unable to escape.

"I'm afraid I'm not sleeping well," she admitted. "I suppose it's just being alone for the first time in this house. I miss your poor father so much."

Well, my son is no fool. I'd told him about the fights, and so he knew things hadn't been what they should have been between us. But if he suspected that she had caused my death by hiding my pills, he was smart enough not to accuse her. Instead, he kept her on edge by making frequent inspections. What's more, he was fully capable of taking advantage of her weakness.

"You really should see a doctor, Phyllis," he told her. "You look terrible. I'm worried about you."

She laughed it off, of course. But his words troubled her because she knew the only cure was for her to get off the pills altogether, and that she couldn't do.

Then there was sailor boy Chuck. He didn't like what he saw in her face either. He'd helped a beautiful, fun-loving woman get rid of her husband so that he could move into her house on the Intracoastal. And now, three months later, he not only couldn't move in for fear of arousing suspicion but she wasn't even beautiful any more, and she certainly wasn't fun-loving. Their trysts were just as furtive and secret as when I was living, and now they'd become merely perfunctory. The novelty was gone and he was stuck with a woman fifteen years older than he was who was letting drugs and alcohol turn her into a middle-aged derelict. And all this while he sat in his boat looking at the house he'd helped kill for and couldn't even enter until late at night with the lights out.

Small wonder then that one day six months after my death Chuck the yachtsman simply disappeared. She woke up one morning and noticed the boat wasn't tied up at the dock. She thought nothing of it at first, but when he didn't show up that afternoon at their regular meeting place, she began to worry. She waited until dark, then went home and called the seedy hotel where he'd lived since she'd known him. He'd checked out early that morning and had driven off with his boat in tow.

That was enough for Phyllis. She went home and drank herself into a stupor, even forgetting to take her sleeping pills. When she woke up, it was three a.m., and she was lying half-dressed on her bed. She checked her watch and got up to undress. That was when she saw the eyes. In her drunken state she'd neglected to close the doors or cover my portrait, and the "piercing eyes" she so hated and feared were watching her now from the mirror on her vanity dresser. They'd been watching her from the minute she'd collapsed on the bed.

The following day the phone had to ring a half dozen times before she could find the receiver and bring it to her ear. "Chuck, is that you?" she asked.

It was my son. He'd be there in an hour. "What time is it anyway?" she asked, her voice slurred.

"One p.m. I hope I didn't interrupt your lunch."

"Lunch? No, I was taking a nap."

"Then I'll be there in half an hour, if you don't mind. I'm in something of a hurry today. Have to catch a plane. Is that all right with you?"

She only hesitated for a second. "Of course. I'll be waiting for you."

She staggered to her feet, dressed, plastered her face with make-up and rearranged her hair. When my son arrived, alone this time, she'd had only ten minutes to restore things to their rightful place.

He noticed it right away. "I'm afraid some of Dad's pictures are missing," he said.

"No, no, I had to move them when I dusted. Let me put them back."

She shuffled through various drawers and pulled out several snapshots. But in her hurry she didn't get them all.

"Look, Phyllis," he said, "this is a violation of the terms of Dad's will, and legally I could take the house. I won't do it this time because I can see you're a sick woman. But you'd better get to a doctor and find out what's wrong. I mean it."

She burst into tears, something she never would have done except when she was playing the grieving widow. "It's just that ... it's just that..." she sobbed. "I'll be all right."

It was just that everything had gone wrong for her. But she couldn't admit that. So all she could say was, "Thank you. I promise I'll put everything back. You'll see. Next time it will look perfect."

"Next time I want *you* to look perfect," he told her. "I'm serious. Get yourself examined right away. I don't want to fail in my duty to Dad again. I'll bring witnesses, and if I find the place like it is today, I'll have to take legal action. So I'd advise you to snap out of whatever it is that's bothering you or get into a hospital if you're really ill."

When he left, it was clear his warnings did nothing to help her, but merely faced her with an uncertain deadline which she knew she could never meet.

She became a recluse. She locked every door and window and stayed in her bedroom with her eyes fixed on daytime soap operas. If she ventured out, it was to the liquor store for booze, to the drug store for pills and only incidentally to the supermarket for a few TV dinners. By the time my son phoned again to say he was in town and would be there with witnesses in an hour, she was unable to say whether it had been a week or a month since his previous visit, much less whether it was day or night when he called.

She didn't even bother to dress but remained in the old dressing gown she'd worn those evenings when she'd stormed out of the house to look at the moon. She knew she wouldn't have time to put each item in its proper place. She readjusted what she saw in the living room—an ashtray one inch to the left, a lamp two inches to the right, all the while swearing under her breath that he'd never get her out of the house she'd sacrificed everything to own.

Then she looked at my portrait, confronting my gaze for the first time in months, and hissed, "It's all your fault, you dirty old man. You never should have married a young woman in the first place. And when you wore yourself out, you thought you could make an old woman out of me. Well, you can't. I'm young, do you hear me? Young! I've got years of life ahead of me in this house, and I'm not going to let you spoil it all with your nasty, leering looks!"

When my son and his witnesses arrived, he had to use his own key to get in. They found her sitting cross-legged on the floor opposite my portrait, looking up into my face and laughing silently to herself. She gave no sign of recognition or even of having heard the doorbell ring. It was as if she were all alone with me in our living room having a conversation. Except that she was doing all the talking.

"Now I'm the one with the eyes, darling," she was saying very calmly and smiling. "I can see you, but you can't see me. I can look at you all day and all night, but you can't look back at me now or ever again. Because I've got eyes to see you with and you've got nothing."

The fruit knife was still in her hand, and the chair was still standing under the portrait where she'd climbed up to reach my face. And when my son and the others turned to see what she was looking at, what they saw was my face under the lamp as my friend had painted it—strong and handsome and dignified as always, but with the radiant pupils and irises neatly cut out and nothing but holes in the canvas where they should have been.

That was when my son picked up the phone and called not only for my lawyer but first for an ambulance with a strait jacket.

My son and his family have since moved into and are occupying my house without interference from my wife, as was my intention.

This tale was recorded by a client of mine on a mini-cassette. He left it with me in a sealed envelope not to be played while his widow still lived in his house.

The story is uncannily accurate in many of its details. Phyllis did in fact lose her mind and is now in a psychiatric hospital, completely withdrawn and with a poor prognosis for recovery. And, at the peak of her unraveling, she did cut the eyes out of my client's portrait.

But there were a few inaccuracies. He did not die in a frantic search for the pills his wife had hidden. Rather, he simply dropped dead while pushing a cart down a supermarket aisle. He was alone, and the pills were in his pocket at the time. The authorities found no indication of foul play.

And by the way, my client's son did not move into the house. Instead, he sold it and has left the area. As for the house, it has since been torn down and replaced by a condominium.

BEETHOVEN AND THE CHUCK-CHUCK BIRD

In far-off Madagascar, behind the African continent and halfway to the polar sea, there lives a bird known as the *totocaf*, or Malagasy cuckoo. This may or may not be his correct name ornithologically, for his song is only somewhat like that of our own cuckoo bird. In fact, it sounds rather more like "chuck-chuck," so that when he sings, it goes something like this:

"Chuck-chuck-chuck-chaw-w-w

Chuck-chuck-chuck-chaw-w-w."

The same notes, over and over, sad and forlorn, are all this poor bird can sing—if singing is what you hear when he does it. Actually, the song is so sad that in Madagascar they say he sings it only when it is going to rain. And rain it does in Madagascar, and during every rainy season the sound you hear is "Chuck-chuck-chuck-chaw-w-w; chuck-chuck-chuck-chaw-w," so much so that we will simply call him the chuck-chuck bird.

Now two things must have occurred to you already about this song: first, that there has to be a reason why just one bird would have such a sad song in a land where other birds sing beautifully and greet each day with joy;

and second, that the sounds I have described seem strangely familiar and in fact resemble the opening notes of the fifth symphony of Beethoven.

If these two things have occurred to you, then you are on the right track. The song does sound like Beethoven, and there is a reason.

You should know, then, that once when the world was younger the chuck-chuck bird (who was not called that at all in those days) sang a song so beautiful that people everywhere, and other birds as well, stopped whatever they were doing to hear its lovely notes. This was true not only in Madagascar but throughout the world, for in those days the whole world was blessed with nature's sweetest songs, all issuing from the throat of what we now call our poor lonesome chuck-chuck bird. But sadly, the fact is that a single thoughtless transgression brought a dark curse on the happiest creature on earth.

How did it happen? Well, one day many years ago in another land a strange man was seated at a piano playing and making marks on a piece of paper. Throughout the long night he had been busy recording the sounds which were beating in his brain, the sounds of a new music in which man would rise up against the forces crushing him and take the power of the gods into his own hands. The man was Ludwig van Beethoven, and it was his fate to create new sounds in his head while losing the ability to hear the sounds of the world outside. He had reached manhood in an age of revolution, and though he himself was going deaf he would make others hear and feel the joy of brotherhood and the liberation of all men from the yoke of the past. With pen and paper he was setting down for all eternity the four hammer-blows of fate, the notes he would weave into the symphony of man's triumph over destiny.

Now for such a task uninterrupted silence was of course the first necessity. The great man's mind needed calm and solitude and the utmost concentration to forge the notes which would inspire future generations, and it was thanks to these conditions that so much of the work had already been sketched out. Only a few more sessions of agonized effort and the symphony would take its final form. Only a little more silence and the world would know!

But how could a little bird perched on a windowsill to sing the joy of a new day know that such a song, at this particular moment, would be most unwelcome?

The window was thrown open, an angry voice was heard and a hand reached out to drive him away.

"Poor soul!" thought the bird as he sprang to safety. "I'll just fly around and then come back and try to calm his anger with my song."

But far from calming the titan's fury, the song only made it worse.

"Get away and let me finish my work," stormed Beethoven. "Can't even my cursed deafness protect me from these idiot sounds?"

The bird could hardly believe its ears. "Idiot sounds? Why, the poor man is ill. He needs my song to restore his love of life."

So saying, he flew back again to perch on the sill, this time to sing even more beautifully than before.

This was too much for Beethoven. Flinging the window open again, the Prometheus of music leveled a finger at the tiny fellow and thundered: "Go, bird! And take my curse! Take my four notes of fate and sing them in the farthest corners of the world. Sing them there till the Day of Judgment, so thy maker may know the weight He has placed on mankind. Then for man's response let Him hear my symphony. That is my curse on thee. Go!"

And slamming the window shut, the god-demon returned to the composition of his fifth symphony.

So imagine the effect of such a curse on a little bird whose only sin was the praise of life. "What did it mean? Did mankind no longer wish to hear of joy? Could this be? Why, how could he even sing those four silly notes, much less take them to the ends of the earth? He gave them a try. "Chuck-chuck-chuck... Chuck-chuck-chuck-chaw-w-w."

"*That* is fate knocking at the door?" he exclaimed. "Why, I'll be the laughing stock of every ornithological club in creation. I can't do it. I'll sing my own song, and let Beethoven sing his ... if he can."

With that, the little bird opened his beak to warble once more the blessed notes of joy. But what was this? Had he forgotten them? Where were they? Try it again. Yes. No! Not "Chuck-chuck-chuck-chaw-w-w." That's not my song. Where is my song? Have I really been cursed?

Again and again he tried to sing, but it was no use. Nothing issued from the poor bird's beak—nothing would ever issue from it—but the four silly notes put there by a man in anger.

Unbelieving, the poor bird returned to his friends, singing the silliest song any bird was ever given to sing. And of course, the other birds laughed and laughed—that is, until they realized that they too had fallen victim to the same curse, the whole species of *totocafs*, and were doomed like him to sing only Beethoven's notes, and badly at that, from then on.

It would be pleasant to be able to report that the other species of birds were horrified at their companion's loss of his voice. Unfortunately, bird nature is little better than human nature, and more than a few of them were secretly glad that a sweeter voice than theirs had been stilled. It was one rival less, after all, and no doubt it served him right. He must have done something very wicked to have received such a curse. Well, that's what happens to those who fly too high—or sing too well. Better to be a steady, hard-working warbler and know where your next meal is coming from than be a prima donna or an arrogant genius imitating God. So the mighty have fallen. "Well, so be it!" they said before shrugging their wings and resuming their song.

But not all. A few there were who would miss the glorious song and despair of ever replacing it. Gathering together, they asked each other what could be done to restore their little friend's voice. Therapy, perhaps? Could they teach him to sing again? How could they, since not one of them could sing himself? Then find a bird who could? Alas, there were none. Finally, in sad resolution, they chose a delegation to go to Beethoven's house and beg him to restore their brother's song, and putting on their finest feathers, they solemnly set out.

They arrived at the great man's house in the afternoon, when he lay exhausted after the efforts of the night before and had not yet found the strength to go out for his daily walk. Lighting on the windowsill, they peeked in and saw the frightening countenance in repose, eyes closed and chin upon his chest, with sheets of music lying all about on the floor. The window being open, they entered and perched here and there in the room. Then together they recited their prepared speech.

At the sound the master stirred. The creases in his brow smoothed out, and a smile began to form on his mouth. Presently he opened his eyes.

"Oh, Mr. Beethoven," began the leader of the delegation, "excuse us for disturbing you, but we're here to ask a favor."

Beethoven, whose growing deafness made it even more difficult to understand them, heard only the chirping of little birds, and in his exhausted state he smiled and tried to imitate the sounds.

Seizing the moment, the leader exclaimed, "Surely, Mr. Beethoven, it can't be you who cursed our little brother and took his song away. Such a kind man as you would never do a thing like that."

"What little brother?" asked Beethoven, making out the words with difficulty. "When did I ever curse a bird?"

"Why, just this morning, Mr. Beethoven, when he came to your windowsill to sing."

"Oh, that one," said the composer, scowling darkly. "Well, he should have known better. It was a critical point in my work. I'd just discovered how to grapple with fate, and a birdsong was not the way."

"But he couldn't have known that, sir. And now our most beautiful voice is gone forever ... unless you'll lift the curse."

"Lift it? I can't even lift the curse on myself. You birds don't realize I'm possessed by demons sometimes, and what I say then can't be unsaid. If I've cursed your friend, he'll stay cursed. Besides, what's wrong with the song I gave him? It's one of my greatest. He should be proud to sing it."

At that the birds began to cry. But being birds, their lamentations sounded to Beethoven like a concert of the angels, and he lay back and closed his eyes to listen.

After a while the chirping stopped, and the leader of the birds made one more desperate try.

"Please, Mr. Beethoven, if you don't restore his voice, the world will never hear his song again. I thought it was your destiny to bring music into the world, not to take it away."

The titan frowned. His hand went to his brow. He shook himself and rose to a sitting position.

"I, Beethoven, take music out of the world? I'll tell you what I'll do. I can't give your friend his voice back, but I can do better than that. I'll write another symphony, and in it all the birds on earth will sing, and the sunshine and the rain and all the joy of life will be heard. I'll put your voices in it and the voices of all the people I wish I could be like, and through it the voice of your friend will be singing, making it the sweetest music ever heard."

The master's eyes glowed, his fists were clenched and the muscles of his neck were taut. And the birds could see that the demon was in him and that what he said would come to pass.

And thus it was that on the twenty-second of December in the year 1808 in the city of Vienna a concert was given with the eccentric master, wild-eyed and half deaf, conducting two new symphonies from his own pen, one in which fate knocks at the door and the other a pastoral symphony in which nature triumphs over man and leads him through joy into eternity.

So the other birds returned and tried to console their little friend that his song would be heard in the sublime music of Beethoven. But our *totocaf* was unconvinced, knowing that nothing, not even Beethoven, would ever sing better than he.

Which is why in far-off Madagascar the poor chuck-chuck bird—ludicrous, quizzical, forlorn—continues to announce the rain with his own version of Beethoven's knock of fate, somewhat out of tune and something like this:

"Chuck-chuck-chuck-chaw-w-w,
Chuck-chuck-chuck-chaw-w-w."

You may believe this story or not, but to hear the song you'll have to go all the way to Madagascar. As for the bird, you'll have a hard time finding him, for he hides in the bushes out of shame for the song he has to sing. You see, a curse is a curse, and not even a concert of the angels can erase it.

THE COLD WAR REMEMBERED
(*Excerpts from a novel to be published*)

How Chilly was Liberated from Obscurity and Had its Rendezvous with Destiny at Last

In the town of Chilly, on the river Chize in northeastern France, nothing of historical note had ever occurred. Ignored by Caesar, overlooked by Attila, rejected by Charlemagne as the seat of a county and by the Church as the see of a diocese, Chilly had neither been occupied by the English nor visited by Joan of Arc. In the Wars of Religion it had scarcely been touched, and both Richelieu and Louis XIV had taken it for granted.

"Happy countries have no history," say the French to console themselves for their own. But Chilly had never accepted its good fortune. With the Revolution it had sent its sons to man the frontiers and swell the Grande Armée, though the Emperor had never stopped, let alone eaten or slept or held council there. The Industrial Revolution, for its part, had left Chilly looking in 1900 almost as it had a century before. And while during the first World War the area had suffered its share of destruction and loss, even in misfortune its lot had been outshone by that of other towns. Not one battle in all those four years bore its name.

By the time of the second World War, drearily occupied by a minor German garrison, Chilly had long abandoned hope of achieving greatness and dreamed only of its liberation from the hated occupier and especially from the accumulated rancor of its own frustration.

So when the Allied armies approached during the summer of 1944, joy at last entered the hearts of the Chiléans, as the town's Gallo-Roman origins had dictated that its inhabitants be called. Officials uncertain of their political survival polished speeches of welcome, cooks prepared ovens, girls primped, boys readied long-hidden weapons for use against a departing enemy and all dug from attics faded tricolors to hang from Chilly's windows.

But a full day and a night of far-away rumblings and cannon fire were to pass without sight of a single liberator, and it was only when the sun rose again that two reports turned joy into gloom and seemed to confirm the mediocrity of Chilly's destiny. First, the town of La Flaque, Chilly's great rival and the *préfecture* of the *Département de la Chize,* had just welcomed the spearhead of one of Patton's armored divisions; and second, Chilly's German garrison had departed stealthily by night, and without firing a shot, abandoning the place to the enemy as not even worth the effort to defend it. The town was left free but empty, without an object for its rage or its joy.

Yet Chilly did find a liberator at last, though it found him only three days later and in a way all too characteristic of the destiny it had always known. He arrived tall and steel-helmeted in an open jeep, a lone ranger from across the seas, a plumed knight every bit the hero of their dreams. Stopping him in the main square, the population fell upon him and bestowed on his cheeks the kisses of its daughters and the joyful tears of its mothers. Then the town fathers unseated him from his iron steed, carried him into the Hôtel de Ville and opened the Golden Book for him to sign, knowing this to be an honor normally reserved for prefects, senators, and even greater dignitaries.

In doing so, however, they made the mistake of freeing him momentarily from their grasp, at which the shy liberator broke and ran from the building, sprang astride his waiting charger and sped off into the sunset, leaving the town fathers in disarray and the Golden Book unsigned.

Puzzled, the fathers, who had already decided to rename the town square in his honor, began to berate one another for frightening him away. They did not ask why he had liberated Chilly alone, nor why he had arrived from the east rather than from the west, nor even why his jeep was later found a mile outside town, its gas tank dry, with no sign of their hero. Instead, they accused one another of lapses in the rules of protocol surrounding such visits, lapses grave enough to have offended and driven away the eminent personage they had intended to honor.

In desperation they appointed Octave Brouillard, a local schoolmaster and therefore an English scholar, to question future American visitors until their hero's name could be learned and properly entered in the Golden Book. Brouillard, less confident than they of his command of English, accepted reluctantly. Yet within a day his mission had been accomplished, for their liberator reappeared the very next morning, this time from the west and this time accompanied by what must have been a two-man Guard of Honor, since their uniforms were relatively clean and they wore armbands bearing the mysterious letters "MP."

Seeing them, Brouillard rushed up with notebook and pencil in hand and addressed to the sergeant of this Honor Guard the English phrase he had been practicing all morning.

"Pardon, Monsieur, 'ow do you call 'eem?"

"How do I do *what*?" frowned the chevroned warrior, and would have driven on had the street not been blocked by Brouillard's fellow citizens. Observing the schoolmaster with the suspicion reserved for indigenous populations unable to communicate in English and probably seeking cigarettes anyway, the sergeant asked his companion, "You know what this guy wants?" "Nope," answered the other. "Then give him a fag, and let's get outta here."

Brouillard did not catch the exchange but, being prepared, thrust the pencil and the notebook into the sergeant's hand and pointed respectfully at Chilly's liberator. "If you please," he said. "'Ees name."

The sergeant guffawed. "His *name*? *This* guy's *name*? What does he think he is, a *general*?"

"You mean a general f— up," laughed the other.

So while Brouillard, his eyes popping, snapped to attention at the one word he had understood, whispering, "*Un général!*" The sergeant wrote the words in the notebook, handed the schoolmaster a cigarette and forced a passage with the jeep through the crowd, disappearing from Chilly and from their lives.

Brouillard examined the sheet and scratched his head as the others pressed around him. "It is an unusual name," he hazarded. "But then, *les Américains*, I am told, are of diverse origins, and it is possible that a phonetic orthography has been employed to transliterate from an unknown etymological root. But imagine, a *général*! And so young!"

Disregarding Brouillard's arcane speculations, the townspeople had a hero at last and were determined to honor him. And thus it was that the unfortunate words were inscribed in the Golden Book and soon after appeared, with the date, on four plaques in the town's main square, in honor of that memorable day when Chilly-sur-Chize had its rendezvous with Destiny.

The words on the plaque, which can only be suggested in English, read, PLACE DU GENERAL F—UP.

The offending name, it should be noted, was soon erased from the Golden Book and the square rebaptised PLACE DE LA LIBÉRATION. But had the Chiléans known, they might have overcome their chagrin and waited a few more years for a truer rendezvous. For this one, when it came, was to be more than an accidental encounter with a GI deserter. Chilly may well have been a town of minor importance throughout its history, but in American Cold War planning it would become a link in a vital chain of depots supplying the Seventh Army in Germany. It would also become a home away from home for thousands of Americans who had never heard of it before. And while some of them would come to love it, others would hope they might never set foot there again.

Fifty-One Days in June,
or How World War III was Narrowly Averted in Chilly on the Chize

1

In the darkness of the War Room, lights blinked madly. Blips, like exploding rockets, burst across the radar screens. On a giant wall map of Europe, an airman placed in position the tiny oncoming planes, moving them relentlessly forward toward the French border as new reports came in.

"Scramble!"

The order had been passed with the first blip, and already word had been received in the War Room that our planes were taking off.

"Are we in time?"

A wristwatch emerged from the stern-faced officer's blue sleeve as the oncoming enemy planes moved west of the Rhine. "We'll know in a minute, sir."

"Unidentified plane sighted!" came the report from the lead fighter.

"Good. He's intercepted him."

"Fire one."

Silence fell across the War Room. Tension was at the breaking point.

"Got him!"

Every pair of lungs in the room emptied in unison. The room itself seemed to contract and regain its normal proportions. The stern-faced officer rose to his feet.

"All right, bring them back."

Men heretofore invisible in the darkness began to call orders. Lights flashed on. The alert was over.

In a seat next to the blue-suited officer a bulky figure shifted, withdrew a large red handkerchief from his pocket and began to mop his brow.

"Well, Colonel, what do you think of that?" the blue-suited officer asked.

The bulky figure rose and returned the handkerchief to the hip pocket of his green uniform. "Frankly, Colonel, I could have sworn it was for real."

"If it had been, we'd still have intercepted them. We're ready for them here at Eurpes Air Force Base."

"I can see that. Colonel, I'm truly impressed."

Colonel Mervin Throwbach had good reason to be impressed. It was the first time he had sat in the War Room at an air base and watched an air defense exercise. In fact, it was the first time he had set foot on an American air base overseas in any other capacity than as a passenger in a troop transport or as a visitor to the base exchange.

But Colonel Throwbach's reasons for being at Eurpes Air Force Base today were anything but personal. They were highly official, and they had to do with his newly-assumed functions as Commanding Officer of The U.S. Army Quartermaster Depot at Chilly-sur-Chize, thirty miles away in the farmlands of French Lorraine. As a courtesy to the new commander of a neighboring installation he was being given a special orientation. And although Chilly QM Depot might not have the strategic value in the eyes of the Pentagon that Eurpes Air Force Base had, it was plenty important to Colonel Throwbach. It stocked GI boots and mess kits and items of issue from tent pegs to toilet paper. What army could fight without its tent pegs or its toilet paper?

As he took leave of his hosts, a weight of responsibility settled on Colonel Throwbach's broad shoulders. He had seen photographs of conditions during the Battle of the Bulge, though at the time he himself unfortunately had been located in a rear area near Paris—where things had been bad enough, what with black-marketeering in Quartermaster items which had forced him to deploy considerable efforts to apprehend the malefactors, including midnight forays into their lairs near Place Pigalle, where danger lurked on every street corner. And having been recalled to active duty now a dozen years later as a reserve officer, he was determined to play at least as significant a role this time as before. He might not wear the combat infantryman's badge, but he nevertheless knew a thing or two about warfare. Mervin Throwbach was nobody's fool. He might not have an alert system as elaborate as that of the Strategic Air Command or even as that of Eurpes Air Force Base, but if war came, he would be ready.

It was a sobering thought, even a terrifying thought, because he knew as well as any other officer that all the Army asked of him, now or ever, was to obey orders. If war came, he would receive his instructions. But what they would consist of, nobody but the Commanding General and his G3 knew. And to Throwbach's outrage and disgust, they had been unwilling to tell him in detail what these instructions were. It was as if they felt he couldn't be trusted with classified information—he who had soldiered for years in the Army Reserve, maintaining his status by attending weekly drill and summer camp through the Korean War. His unit had not been recalled for duty in Korea. Nevertheless, he considered himself worthy of something higher than the command of a supply depot lost in the French countryside. In fact, he considered himself qualified to serve as G2 or G3 on any general staff in the army. Stock levels and inventories were no challenge for a mind which ranged widely in the field of global strategy.

He brooded over this injustice as the staff car covered the last miles back into Chilly. The briefing had aroused him. Somewhere in the service dedicated men were thinking deep thoughts and dealing with life-and-death situations. It was nothing less than tragic that he, one of the few equipped to dwell in such realms, had been denied the expression of his talents and relegated to a backwater.

Need he tolerate it? No! he decided, bringing his fist down into his palm as the staff car clattered over the temporary bridge across the Chize river and down the rutted and pot-holed road into Chilly QM Depot. No, by God! QM Depot or not, Chilly would learn a few lessons from Eurpes about readiness. And perhaps, with a little luck, the army might even hear some day about Chilly and Mervin Throwbach.

"O'Toole," he asked his driver suddenly, "are you ready?"

"Ready for what, sir?"

"Ready for combat, O'Toole? I mean, when the balloon goes up?"

"I guess so, sir."

"Then tell me what you expect to do when the word comes."

"Sir, I guess I'll just do what they tell me to do."

"No, O'Toole," said Throwbach as the vehicle pulled up before his office, "that answer isn't good enough. But don't worry. Before I'm through here, you'll know. You and everyone else at Chilly QM Depot will have full instructions."

And pulling his weight from the staff car as O'Toole held the door open for him, Throwbach strode head down into his office, hung his gold-braided cap on a hook and barked at his secretary, "Get me Major Blivens."

Homer Blivens had been Intelligence Officer, or S2, of Chilly QM Depot for over a year, and until recently he had found it a highly gratifying assignment. It had the double advantage of clandestinity and irrelevancy—clandestinity in that the documents he received were rarely classified even Confidential and so were of little interest to the Depot Commander, and irrelevancy in that nothing in them mattered anyway as far as the daily business of storing and forwarding Quartermaster items was concerned. This had suited Homer Blivens perfectly, since his sole ambition at this point in his career was to complete twenty years of service and retire, which would happen in exactly fifty-eight days.

Homer Blivens's dream world, however, had been shattered by the arrival of Mervin Throwbach as Depot Commander. Unlike his predecessor, Throwbach was already taking a vital interest in both Intelligence and Plans. All classified material of any nature was now being hand-carried in a specially prepared Green Book for presentation by the major to the colonel—not at the start of business each day but within fifteen minutes of its arrival, day or night. And though it was three days now since any such document had arrived, Homer Blivens dutifully unlocked his combination safe, withdrew the Green Book and bore it stoically under his arm to Colonel Throwbach's office, where he appeared suitably out of breath, his brow furrowed in thought.

"Close the door, Major," came the Colonel's funereal tones.

When Blivens had done so, Throwbach rose, went to the door, opened it, peered out and closed it again.

"Major," he said, "this conversation will be classified Secret. Secret Noforn. You are to treat it accordingly."

"Yes, sir," Blivens sighed inwardly. Outwardly he was of stone.

Colonel Throwbach returned to his desk, stared long and hard at Blivens and finally, in a dark voice, spoke.

"I wonder, Major, if you are aware of The Threat?"

"The Threat, sir? What threat?" Blivens had wanted to say. But he had not survived almost twenty years in the Army and attained his present rank by saying things his superiors did not wish to hear. So he answered instead: "I think, Colonel, that every man here is aware of The Threat. Even, if I may say so, those without our access to the most sensitive classified information."

As it happened, this was not exactly the answer Throwbach had been seeking, and this may also explain why Blivens's career, while a safe one, had not been characterized by rapid promotion. So it was with some asperity that Throwbach now said, "I have my doubts about that, Major. Would it surprise you if I were to tell you that even I, until my visit today to Eurpes Air Force Base, was not fully aware of the extent of The Threat?"

Nothing more could surprise Homer Blivens about Mervin Throwbach, whose every action since his first days at the depot had been a surprise. So he said, "Then it's true, sir? It's really that bad?"

"Worse, I'm afraid," said the Colonel, content that the Major was finally talking his language. "I just wonder how much time we have left."

"Fifty-eight days," thought Blivens. "Anything after that is your worry, not mine." What he said aloud, however—and reassuringly—was, "At any rate, sir, we'll give a good account of ourselves."

"I'd expect nothing less, Major. But it's not enough."

"Sir, I'm working on a new estimate right now," said Blivens brightly, reminding himself to cover some sheets with scribbling when he got back to his office and stamp them WORKING PAPER: SECRET NOFORN. "I just hope I'll have time enough to finish it."

"That," Throwbach smiled grimly, "is what you are going to find out."

"Sir?" For once, Blivens was not ahead of him. Desperately he now sought a stance from which he could spring into the path of the Colonel's thought, whatever it might be. He was not prepared, however, for Throwbach's next words.

"The time, Major. I want you to find out how much *time* we have left."

"Sir, you mean before...?"

"Exactly. To the day. Even to the hour."

Beneath his immobile exterior Blivens felt every organ in his body squirm. There must be an answer even to this insanity, a way to anticipate the idiot and block his path.

"Of course, sir, the indications we receive at this level are hardly adequate to base an estimate on...."

"Indications?" the Colonel cried scornfully. "Who needs indications? Don't you read history, Major? Don't you read Lenin?"

Blivens sighed. It was too late now. Let him talk.

"History," intoned Throwbach, "is the source of all wisdom. It holds no secret for those who understand it, for the past is key to the future. So with Lenin's intentions in mind, I ask you, do you read history?"

Homer Blivens, of course, did not read history, let alone Lenin. However, Mrs. Blivens was an avid reader of historical romances and often told him the plots of the novels she read. So Blivens felt at least partially justified in his answer.

"Colonel, how could I do my job as S2 of Chilly QM Depot if I didn't read history?"

"Good boy!" said Throwbach. "Then I want you to go to your history books and, as S2, come back to me in one week with an answer to this question. It's a simple question, and I'll state it simply. When does it begin? On what day? At what hour? Have you got that?"

I can tell him one thing already, thought Blivens. It won't begin in anything under fifty-eight days. But, like the old soldier he was, he stiffened to attention and saluted smartly.

"I'm on my way to the post library now, sir."

Throwbach returned the salute, his jaw hardening. Army life was not an easy life, and he felt keenly the severity of the orders he sometimes had to give. But lives depended on the answers Homer Blivens would bring back to him.

"Oh ... and Major..."

Blivens wheeled, seeking in the older man's face some sign of hesitancy. Was there a glint of moisture in his eye?

"Yes, sir?"

But the jaw hardened, and the glint was gone. "Nothing, Major. As you were. That's all."

"Thank you, sir."

But Homer Blivens did not spend the next week at the post library. He spent the next half hour there, time enough to ascertain the number of historical works available and to assure himself that a year would not suffice to read them all.

His next stop was the bar at the Officers' Club. Beyond that, he had no firm plans.

Mervin Throwbach, however, had more plans than he would ever be able to put into effect. And now that he had a command of his own nothing would prevent him from implementing them.

So before Blivens could have reached the library even at double time, another officer, Major Harley Shirk, was standing at attention before him with a thick document under his arm in a red-bordered cover envelope marked SECRET.

"Major," began Throwbach, "what would you do if I told you that enemy planes were heading toward this depot right now?"

"Sir, I'd put Plan B into effect immediately."

"And what is Plan B?"

"Plan B, sir, calls for the orderly evacuation of all personnel, including dependents and civilians."

"Evacuation? What about the stocks, the uniforms? What about Chilly Quartermaster Depot?"

"I'm afraid, sir, the depot would have to be abandoned."

"Ridiculous!" cried Throwbach, highly incensed. "How do you think I'd look, fleeing before the enemy?"

Major Shirk held up the bundle he was carrying.

"Sir, Plan B calls for evacuation. It comes from G3."

"I don't care where it comes from. Plan B is personally unacceptable to me. Now show me your own defense plan."

"I'm afraid, sir, there is no defense plan. G3 considers every depot in France to be indefensible."

The veins in Throwbach's forehead swelled with rage. "They do, do they? Well, if they think I'm going to accept their opinion on that, they don't know me. Major, I want you to write me up a defense plan."

"Yes, sir. But Colonel..."

"And I don't want any hedging. This depot is going to be defended, and I want a plan telling me how. Do you understand?"

With quiet resignation, Major Shirk saluted, did an about face and left without even stopping to gather up the shards of his career from the floor before the Colonel's desk.

Harley Shirk had heretofore maintained a precise and active schedule at Chilly QM Depot as befits any ambitious young officer. But he now headed, as had Blivens before him, to the bar of the Officers' Club, where, like Blivens, he had no further plans.

2

It happened that the bartender on duty that day was a certain Nicolas, or Nick, as he was generally called. No one, no doubt, except the Provost Marshal, the Counterintelligence Corps and the French police knew what Nick's nationality was, though it was assumed he had one. But whatever it might be, it was considered irrelevant since Nick was thought by all others, including himself, to be a citizen of the world.

Now Nick rightly felt, as he told one and all, that the principal qualification for a barman, in addition to skill at mixing drinks, was the ability to remain a model of discretion. The conversations of officers who enjoyed his hospitality were, however unwise and in violation of security rules, to Nick a sacred trust. Frequent inquiries made about him by the French and American police had convinced him that unlawful disclosure of information gained in the course of his duties would be ill thought of; and so, as a man of absolute honor and integrity, it would take an item of far more than usual interest to make him run the risk of losing his pleasant occupation.

So Nick paid no attention whatever to the first part of the conversation between two despondent majors at the bar.

"What's gotcha down, boy?" Blivens had asked from behind his second gin-on-the-rocks at the sight of Harley Shirk.

"Old man's got another wild hair up, I guess."

"It's chronic. Tomorrow he won't even remember what he asked you."

"Yes, he will. Today he wants nothing less than a war plan."

"That's all? From me he wants to know when the war starts."

At the last words a mental tape recorder inside the head of Nick the bartender began to roll.

"How are you supposed to find that out?" Shirk pursued.

"By reading history, stupid. How else?"

"Well, when does it start?"

"On Tuesday the 24th of June, at 0400 hours."

"How did you arrive at that?"

"That, my friend, is the day after I depart this command on my way to retirement."

"He'll catch on."

"If he does, it'll be the first time since he got here."

In fact, whether or not Colonel Throwbach would understand the significance of Blivens's projected date for the commencement of World War III, Nick the bartender did not. Nick's English was excellent in the field of bartending; his memory was phonographic, so that later he could recite the dialogue of others with a high degree of accuracy. But his understanding of the subtle ironies in the two officers' conversation was weak, so that when the words were played back by him to others still less aware of the inherent ironies, the words would carry a meaning totally contrary to that intended.

This, however, was no concern of Nick's. He was paid to report conversations, not to analyze and interpret them.

As for the two majors, they ended their talk on a hopeful note, agreeing it would be safer to proceed as ordered, since neither of their products would ever be acted upon.

3

They could hardly have been more wrong. Mervin Throwbach was at that moment writing his own estimate as well as his own defense plan. Like many commanders, he felt himself as competent as any member of his staff in that person's specialty. Unlike most commanders, however, he had nothing more urgent to do than to carry out on his own the tasks he gave his staff. Others might have been tempted to use their spare time to satisfy personal interests, or even to foster friendly relations with the local French community. But not Mervin Throwbach. For him, command of Chilly QM Depot was a challenge, and he intended to use it to make a name for himself. Besides, he didn't trust the French.

So it came to pass that when Homer Blivens and Harley Shirk appeared to present the fruits of their labors Throwbach, unbeknownst to them, was ready for them.

"Well, Shirk, how do you propose to defend the depot?"

"Sir, I have my plan right here."

It was a good plan except for its basic assumptions. It utilized the tactical principles taught at Fort Benning. With a position defense rather than a mobile defense, dictated by the requirement to hold the depot at all costs, it foresaw the necessity of holding the ridge line beyond the Chize River also. If the aggressor could be denied the key terrain overlooking the town and the depot, it might be possible to hold the depot. Even so, the roads leading westward would have to be kept open to bring in supplies.

Throwbach listened without comment as Shirk placed the last defender and stepped back grimly satisfied that he had foreseen every eventuality. Then he settled back and fixed the gaze of his narrowed eyes on the younger officer without a word.

Finally, Shirk could stand the silence no longer.

"Well, sir, what do you think of it?"

Throwbach shrugged. "Oh, I suppose it's not too bad...."

"Sir, it's the only plan that stands a chance!"

"Except that you've left out a few essentials. First of all, we can't defend the ridge line or keep the roads open without tactical reinforcements."

"I assumed we'd get them, sir. The depot is indefensible if we don't control the key terrain."

"Now don't get excited," Throwbach smiled benignly. Not often had he had an opportunity to hear a plan and systematically reduce it to rubble. "It's simple," he explained. "We'll defend the depot by digging in."

"Digging in, sir?"

"That's right. We'll go underground. The Headquarters of the Strategic Air Command is underground, isn't it?"

Before the bewildered major could answer, he went on. "Besides, you didn't say how you plan to defend us from an attack from the west."

"But that's Chilly, sir. The French are our allies."

"Are they?" His steady gaze told of his deadly earnest.

"I assume they are, sir. It's what we're taught."

The colonel smiled thinly. There was pity in his smile. "Let's just say this: We don't turn our back on anyone."

"But sir, how will we get supplies?"

"Supplies? Why, what else have we got at the depot? Now look here, we're going to dig in. We'll close the gates and post guards along the walls. Have you ever seen a fort the way they used to build them here?"

"But sir, that was in the Middle Ages!"

"The terrain is the same, isn't it?"

Shirk's mind whirled as he sought objections to this folly.

"What about the dependents, sir? How do we evacuate them?"

"We don't. They'll be cared for here. A man's family can be a great comfort during a siege. Any objections? No? Then get out there, and start executing the plan."

Homer Blivens gazed in consternation as Shirk's haggard figure emerged from the Colonel's office. His own self-confidence, however, would not outlast the presentation of his fatal date.

"Your date is wrong, Major," Throwbach said simply.

"I don't think so, sir. Let me show you my reasoning."
Bluff it out. Stand up to him. He'll back down.

"Your date is wrong by exactly one week," Throwbach
went on. "As I've told you before, false optimism in an
intelligence officer can be fatal. I've been reading my history too."

"You mean, sir...?"

"I mean if I went by your logic, World War III would
be lost before we could even finish digging in."

But my God! thought Blivens wildly. That's 51 days!
That means I'll be here to fight this madman's war for him!

It did indeed, and the rest of Throwbach's words went
past him unheard as he sank into despondency. And these
words carried instructions which the entire command
would do well to execute with the utmost speed. A command decision had been made, and on the way they carried it out, Throwbach was certain, might depend the out-
come of World War III.

4

In the town of Chilly it did not take long for the increased activity at the depot to be noticed. Madame Régine,
patronne of the Rosy Bar, was perhaps the first to sense it,
since it was already four o'clock on Saturday afternoon and
not one of her regular American clientele had appeared.
Her girls fidgeted like tethered fillies in a storm. Liliane,
the blonde, strolled from window to window seeking a
better view down the empty street, while black-haired
Carmen rolled her necklace beads so tightly around her
fingers that the string broke and true-to-life pearls rolled
across the floor.

Madame Régine slammed her account ledger down.

"The dirty pigs! They won't get away with it, you'll see.
I'll go to my friend M. Dupuis on the *Conseil Municipal*."

"What is it, Madame?" cringed Odile the kitchen maid, fearful for her job whenever Madame Régine had one of her tantrums.

"Putting my place off limits, that's what," shouted Régine. "The most honest establishment that has ever catered to American fighting men, just because that pinched-mouth Colonel's wife had to interfere. Why, you'd think my girls weren't clean! Ask any honest soldier if he ever caught anything in my place!"

"Where are you going?" Odile asked as her mistress threw on her coat.

"To my friend on the *Conseil Municipal*! To *M. le Sous-Préfet* himself if I have to! They can't do this to me!"

But Madame Régine could see as soon as she had driven two blocks in her brand-new Peugeot that hers was not the only establishment deprived of its GI clientele. Not an American was visible anywhere. The streets, filled with local citizenry on a Saturday afternoon, appeared to her deserted. So something was amiss. But what?

Madame Régine now drove not to the office of M. Dupuis, her great and good friend at the *Hôtel de Ville*, but instead to an elegant salon de coiffure situated on the main street just off the *Place de la Libération* and bearing the name Chez Lucette on a chic sign. Parking illegally before a driveway, she strode resolutely into the salon, where some of Chilly's most style-conscious ladies sat under the dryers.

"Régine, my dear," chirped a well-rounded figure from beneath a nest of yellow curls which almost belied her age, "What a surprise! But you know I can't take you on a Saturday afternoon without an appointment. This is my busiest day."

"It should be mine too," said Régine darkly, "but it isn't. Come, I wish to speak to you in private."

Lucette's eyes widened in anticipation under her false eyelashes. In a flutter she led the visitor through a door behind the cash register and into a dressing room.

"I'll come straight to the point," said Régine grimly. "There isn't a single customer at my place. Worse than that, there doesn't seem to be a single American in the entire town. Something must be keeping them all on restriction, and who would know better what that something might be than you?"

Lucette relaxed with a sad but conspiratorial smile. The excitement of suspense was replaced by the joy of possessing superior knowledge. Her eyes shone brightly as she began.

"Well, all I can say is this. On Saturdays, like the others, Harley usually works until noon. Then in the afternoon he comes to my apartment to rest. Of course, on Saturdays I have no time for anything but work, as you can see. But it is such a comfort to know there is a man at home, and so I usually manage to absent myself long enough to go upstairs to see that all is well...."

"You needn't go into your amatory schedule with Major Shirk," Régine interrupted her. "The whole town sets its watches by it. And by now everyone must have seen, as I have, that his car is not here and been led to suppose, as I have, that you therefore have not had to go upstairs, as you usually do, to see that all is well. This much is obvious. What I don't know—unless you have had a lovers' quarrel, which is none of my business—is why."

"As I was saying," Lucette resumed testily, "that is what usually happens. Today, however," and her voice dropped and her eyelashes quivered, "I had a phone call."

"Aha! And what did he have to say?"

Lucette paused dramatically. "I'm not sure I should tell you. He said it was a secret."

"And since when do you have a better right to the secrets of the Americans than I?" exploded Madame Régine.

"Why, if I were to write down the secrets I hear from the girls at my place, I could open an intelligence service of my own. The Americans should give me a medal that I haven't done so already. Sometimes I think they take advantage of me because they know I run an honest house. So don't say you can't tell me what he said because it's a secret."

"Well, it isn't so much what he said as what he didn't say. For instance, when I asked him why he wouldn't be here this weekend, he merely said 'I can't tell you a thing. Just wait and see. In fifty-one days you'll know everything there is to know about it.'"

"Fifty-one days? What does that mean?"

"All I know is what it means to me—fifty-one days without Harley."

"You mean they're all restricted for fifty-one days? My business will be ruined!"

"He didn't exactly say he was restricted. He said he didn't think he'd have much time to see me because there was going to be so much work at the depot."

"But that's ridiculous. One does not restrict a company of young men for fifty-one days—especially Americans. Why, they will be like wild animals. No decent woman in Chilly will be safe. What will they do to my girls? For that matter, what will my girls do without them? They'll leave me and go to some camp in Germany, that's what. Probably to that K-Town place where they won't have the protection of French laws. And then what will happen to the Rosy Bar—and to me?"

Lucette sighed. "My dear, how do you think I feel? Say what you like, a girl gets used to having a man around the house on Saturday afternoons. Frankly, it relaxes the nerves."

Madame Régine's face bore an expression of grim resolve. "All I know is that fifty-one days is too long for the boys who visit my place, and it is too long for me. I'm going to find out, first, what is going on that is so secret and, second, what I have to do to put a stop to it. After all, it isn't as if they were at sea for six months in the Navy!"

5

The streets of Chilly-sur-Chize were silent that Saturday night; silent too the interior of the Rosy Bar despite the juke box's blaring; silent Lucette's darkened apartment. Local youths who heretofore had limited their deviltry to hooting at the girls in the cinema suddenly found themselves masters of the town's principal streets, yet too timid from force of habit to seize control from the absent Americans.

Sunday was the same. Though the morning outdoor market, never heavily patronized by Americans, was its usual bustling self, the gossip today was centered on a single subject: the strange goings-on at the depot. To some it was a blessed reminder of what Chilly once had been, but to others a dreadful foretaste of what it might once again become, if ever the Americans should leave. Restaurants, even the one-star Ecu d'Or, had waiters standing around with nothing to do, and some of the lesser-known places also failed to fill their tables. Afternoon driving on the country roads and on the Route Nationale was no less uneventful than in those parts of France where no Americans were stationed. And spectators at the weekly Franco-American softball game, never a serious challenger to a French soccer match, turned away dejectedly when it became apparent the Americans would not appear.

It was only on Monday, however, that the full effects of the new situation began to be felt. French employees of Chilly QM Depot, arriving at work at eight o'clock by bicycle, by car, by bus, and on foot, were met at the gate by armed military policemen—not, as occasionally in the past, to check identity cards summarily despite perfect first-name familiarity with the employee in question, but this time to perform the most minute search of clothing and personal possessions ever ordered in the memory of the oldest worker. Good-humored raillery, so useful in the past in overcoming resentment at this frisking, turned to bitterness as personal possessions were closely examined and even confiscated. Such was the case when Auguste Pinard's newly-filled bottle of red wine was removed from his knapsack and placed with the MPs for safe-keeping.

"What do you think I've got in it?" protested Pinard, his face even redder than usual, "dynamite to blow up the depot?"

"That's Auguste's secret weapon," suggested one.

"It's the atom bomb," offered another.

"No liquor on the post," said the MP. "That's the order."

"That's not liquor, that's my lunch," cried Pinard. "What am I supposed to drink with my meal?"

"At lunchtime you can get your bottle and drink it off the post. This is a place for work. Colonel Throwbach's orders."

The answer was totally unsatisfactory to Auguste Pinard and his fellow wine-drinkers, for whom only half of each bottle was normally consumed at lunchtime, the other half being used to maintain morale and efficiency during the rest of the day.

But they were not the only disgruntled workers. Joseph Blot revolted when he was handed a shovel and told to join a gang of men who were digging what looked like a trench in the field outside the depot.

"I am not ditch digger," said Blot with dignity. "I am waroozman," he added, pronouncing in his own fashion the function of warehouseman.

"This is more important today," the sergeant told him. "And you will not be a ditch digger."

"It looks like a ditch to me, and the digging of ditches is not in my job description."

"It's ditch-digging or nothing. Which will it be?"

"It is not ditch-digging. I go to personnel office."

But Blot and others like him got scant consolation from the personnel office. It seemed there was urgent work of some kind to be done—classified work—and the Civilian Personnel Officer had authorized the use of all available hands. Moreover, in addition to the ditch, which would extend entirely around the depot, carpenters were sawing beams which were to be used to build some kind of scaffolding along the walls.

"This is the Far West," declared one Frenchman scornfully. "What are they expecting—redskins?"

Employee resistance, however, did not prevent or delay execution of Project X, as the work came to be called. Before the first week had passed, the ditch around the perimeter of the depot had begun to assume the proportions of a World War I trench, while the wooden scaffolding had definitely begun to look like a series of watch towers.

Yet the employees' puzzlement was nothing to that of a pair of bland, unobtrusive individuals who arrived during the first week by train from Paris. According to the information they furnished to Armand, the desk clerk at the Hôtel Beau Site, they were commercial travelers. They took a room on the top floor with an unobstructed view over the peaceful valley of the river Chize, including the site of Chilly QM Depot and the ridge beyond. To Armand they appeared hardly different from others of their profession who had passed through Chilly, except for the fact that few but the most affluent ever stopped at the Beau Site, easily Chilly's most expensive hotel. But this pair had one or two heavy suitcases, which the desk clerk, with the help of a chambermaid, found to contain some sort of electronic equipment. Who in Chilly, Armand asked himself, would be interested in such an expensive radio? Certainly the two or three radio shops in town handled nothing as complex as this set, which looked more like a short-wave transmitter than anything else. But since the suitcases never seemed to leave the room when one of the pair went out (they never went out together, even to eat; one remained in the room at all times) and since they were most discreet in their movements and never bothered other guests, Armand concluded they were merely a pair of radio "hams," as he knew the terms from his reading of American novels. For Armand was a devotee of detective and spy novels. A translation from the *américain* usually could be found beneath the reception desk, and whenever the manager was absent Armand could be observed following the progression of some fictional but sinister train of events between the covers of a paperback novel.

In fairness to Armand, however, he never allowed his passion for spy novels to interfere with his daily tasks. In fact, he kept the two concepts entirely separate. He was fully aware that spy novels were pure entertainment intended to divert the minds of those engaged in the world's more serious tasks. He was sure that none of the events he read of ever actually occurred in real life, certainly not in Chilly-sur-Chize. Therefore, once the mystery of the two strangers with the ham radio was clear in his mind, he concluded they must be selling something else and so forgot about them. He didn't notice, for instance, that the high-powered binoculars which had hung from the neck of one of them on arrival never left the room, nor did he see that soon one of them returned at night with workman's clothes on underneath his coat and traces of mud on his shoes. And of course he could not guess that this man's steps often took him to a café frequented by Nick, the bartender at the Officers' Club. Armand, of course, was a model of discretion. He performed his tasks at the hotel admirably and saved his imagination for the lurid contents of his beloved spy novels.

6

Thus did the mysterious fifty-one days shrink to thirty, then fifteen, then five, as the fever of work mounted at Chilly QM Depot and economic activity in town ground to a relative standstill.

True to Madame Régine's predictions, the absence of American uniforms in town had a drastic effect on her operations. At first she thought of lowering her prices in an effort to regain the French clientele she had scornfully let go when the Americans had arrived. But by now the rather blatant notoriety of the Rosy Bar had made patronage by the settled element of the French population somewhat hazardous. As for the French military, gaining their patronage would have required such a drastic cut in her rates that she rejected the idea outright.

The inevitable consequences followed. Liliane, the blonde, was the first to leave. Easily the Rosy Bar's hardest-working girl, Liliane's frequent comings and goings via a discreet corridor to the hotel above (which was also owned by Madame Régine) had been one of the sources of the joy and good-fellowship which had reigned at Régine's. Her work had been tiring and, from her frank admission, lacking in emotional rewards, but the forced inactivity and the lack of income were worse, convincing her that a temporary removal to K-Town in Germany would not be so bad after all. As an eastern Lorrainer she could speak German, and as a French girl she felt she would enjoy a certain popularity among the more prosperous German element as well as among the American military.

The alternative chosen by Carmen, though not involving the lure of foreign lands, was no less fraught with uncertainty. Carmen, despite her raven locks and acquired Spanish mannerisms, was a local girl who remembered the hills and dales around Chilly as the scene of her childhood romps. So, donning sturdy boots to keep out the moisture of the fields, she set forth to seek out at the source the company denied her at the Rosy Bar by Colonel Throwbach's cruel restriction.

Her clientele, it turned out, was more than willing to go half way to meet her, and so the trenches being dug for war were now called upon to serve as the scene of more friendly activities. As anyone less headstrong than Carmen might have suspected, however, the trenches by their very nature were less private than might have been wished, and it was not too long before Carmen was in the outraged custody of the local police. Not through any indiscretion of her own, let it be said, for Carmen was a modest girl who preferred conversations *en tête-à-tête* with one gentleman at a time. However, the peculiarity of the situation, plus the loss of her income at the Rosy Bar, had led her to accept, against her better judgment, the company of a somewhat larger number of admirers, if not simultaneously then at least in rapid succession and even in something of a line. As a result, the trench was soon filled with so many soldiers awaiting their turn that detection by the authorities became inevitable. It was not the first Military Policeman who gave the alarm, for he had enough *savoir faire* to take a place in line himself. But when the Sergeant of the Guard, making his rounds in ill humor after an altercation with his wife, not only found two men not at their posts but came upon them and a half dozen others in the trench outside the wall, Carmen's hospitable activities came to an end, as did her freedom.

None of this improved Madame Régine's financial situation. With both Carmen and Liliane gone and the remaining three girls ready to leave, the Rosy Bar was at a low ebb. Yet her problems were as nothing beside the state in which she found her friend Lucette. At the chic beauty salon dissension had replaced harmony, and one girl had already left over an unprovoked scolding by her increasingly irritable *patronne*. For Lucette was no longer her old self. Losing weight and living on her nerves, she had become a veritable harpy. As a result, not only was she losing her employees, but even her clientele was beginning to go elsewhere. In fact, the next time Régine visited her, there was a noticeable lack of activity.

"This must be your lucky day, my dear," she chirped bravely. "There just happens to have been a last-minute cancellation. So we can fit you in, after all."

But Régine was not here to have her hair done this time either, as she explained when they were alone.

"I have been to M. Dupuis at the *Hôtel de Ville*," she began. "He had nothing to say about the situation—nothing. You can imagine I was not taken in, and so I casually mentioned an old rival of his, *M. le Sous-Préfet*. M. Dupuis would do anything to prevent me from renewing my friendship with *M. le Sous-Préfet*, and that is how he came to tell me the story."

Lucette, who was in a highly nervous state, broke in.

"I know the story already, my dear. It's some foolish war game of the Americans—what they would do if the Russians came. Ha! You can see they were not here in 1940! This much everyone knows. What we want to know is when it will all be over. Until then Harley is gone, and my life has become a living hell!"

"Courage, my dear," said Régine. "You mentioned fifty-one days of unavailability, and that was more than a month ago. The time will soon be up, and he will be yours again."

"Soon, ha! Each day is longer than the one before. And the nights! Don't speak to me of the nights!"

"Actually," Régine went on, "I sometimes think we are so used to Americans that we overlook some very attractive men right here in town. I've found M. *le Sous-Préfet*, for instance, to be a much more youthful man than one might think."

"I thought M. Dupuis gave you all the information you needed to keep you from going to the *Sous-Préfet*."

Regine shrugged. "I needed confirmation and action too. And let me tell you, M. *le Sous-Préfet* is a man of action. He is reporting the whole affair to M. *le Préfet* himself, who is contacting the Ministry, which is contacting the Allied Forces. Believe me, the American Army will hear of this at the highest levels. Then we shall see if the Rosy Bar is to be deprived of its American clientele."

7

By now, Chilly Quartermaster Depot had taken on the appearance of a fortress under siege. The ditch had become a trench, and the trench was becoming a moat, with heavy rains raising the water level and creating a permanent stream, which threatened to become an arm of the Chize river. As for the watch towers, catwalks had been built along the walls so that men could now circle the depot. Colonel Throwbach was seen in a staff car visiting the 17th-century fort built by Louis XIV's military engineer Vauban in a nearby town, and his intentions became clearer when a young lieutenant appeared there with a request for the plans. The Americans, people concluded, were here to stay.

But why would they fortify the depot just to protect a stock of uniforms and GI boots and mess kits? No, there must be something else, something the Americans weren't talking about. What indeed, it was decided one evening at the *Café du Commerce*, if not *La Bombe*?

The group among whom the fearful words were spoken broke up for the evening in good-natured raillery; but the words were out, echoing silently in the minds of all. A vague uneasiness had been replaced by a shared suspicion, which now became a certainty. Men in Chilly eyed each other knowingly when the depot was mentioned. Employees of the depot were questioned in a roundabout way at first, then ostracized when radiological contamination was mentioned. A new guest arrived at the Hôtel Beau Site and took a room adjoining the one occupied by the men with the binoculars and the radio.

Chilly, in truth, seethed with rumor on the eve of the fifty-first day. Mervin Throwbach, his office converted into a Command Post, remained in constant contact with the War Room across the hall. To the War Room came reports from the four Watch Towers, the main defense line in the trench and the forward outpost on the ridges east of town.

The Colonel himself made the rounds in a final inspection to insure that nothing had been overlooked. It had rained all day, and the roads leading to the depot were a sea of mud. But Throwbach, red-eyed from lack of sleep, wanted to satisfy himself that everything possible had been done. Whatever else might happen the next day, he knew Chilly QM Depot would be ready.

At the end of his inspection and leaving word to be awakened before dawn, when the alert would bring the long convoy of unsuspecting dependants sleepy-eyed from their quarters in the town and the surrounding countryside to the safety of prepared bunks and mess kits at the depot, Mervin Throwbach retired to a few hours of well-earned rest.

8

Who can say what might have happened the following day, if...? If Madame Régine had not been deprived of her clientele, would she have gone to her friend M. Dupuis the Municipal Councillor and then to *M. le Sous-Préfet*? If

Lucette had not been deprived of the visits of Major Harley Shirk, would she have been able to reveal the crucial date to Régine? If Armand the desk clerk had not been addicted to spy novels, would he have paid more attention to the suspicious lodgers? Would the lodgers themselves have drawn different conclusions had one of them not been able to secure work at the depot? Would the date chosen for the attack have been a different one had Homer Blivens not been thinking of his imminent permanent change of station?

These and other questions like them are the small change of history, the unforeseen minutiae which shape and alter great events. And though we may laugh at Mervin Throwbach for overlooking them in his pursuit of historical determinism, we cannot laugh at the ultimate question we must face: did the preparations at Chilly Quartermaster Depot warn the faceless planners in the secret corridors of power somewhere in the Kremlin that their schemes had been laid bare and thereby force the master plan to be modified, rewritten, or even dropped, perhaps forever?

In short, did Mervin Throwbach, Colonel, QM-USAR (now retired) single-handedly prevent World War III? And as the unfolding of events on that fateful day proceeds, let us keep in mind that this man, singled out for ridicule and disgrace, in truth may have been a martyr in the cause of preparedness, one of the unsung few to whom a callous and ungrateful world owes so much.

9

Break then, day! Disclose through sheets of rain the spectacle of a handful of weary men in the act of defending freedom—the eagle-eyed guards in the watch towers, the uncomplaining foot-soldiers ankle-deep in water in the trenches, the long line of ranch wagons and minibuses and sports cars bogged in the mud before the depot, at their wheels the courageous mothers, true daughters of pioneer women, leading their crying children through the mire to safety. Light up, finally, the steely gaze in the care-worn face of him who planned it all and saw it through to the end. Cast, if possible, the tiniest ray, the littlest tip of the dawn's rosy finger on the stony features of the man who stands now, fixed forever at the door of his Command Post, listening to the sound of the airplane's engines, wondering if it will mean friend or foe, the joy of recognition or the blast of instant annihilation—but ready, ready and unafraid: a soldier!

It wasn't an airplane, it was a helicopter circling overhead, not to drop some lethal chemical or biological agent upon the heads of the sturdy garrison beneath but rather to pay a visit from Mount Olympus, in fact from the senior deity himself, come to untangle the web of confusion wrought by the rain-soaked players in this bucolic drama. Like the *deus ex machina* of old, the god in the machine was here not to destroy but to rescue his earthling faithful from the evil results of their own folly.

So as the modern day *machina* hovered over the hardstand with the big white "H" in the middle of the depot area, the words US ARMY became visible to all, and a great roar of welcome rose up. Then when the motor fell silent and the giant wings ceased to turn, the portals opened and the grizzled *deus* with the two stars on his helmet emerged and majestically descended to earth.

And now, his moment come at last, Colonel Mervin Throwbach stepped forward, saluted smartly, and reported:

"Sir, Chilly Quartermaster Depot is ready!"

There was an interval of dead silence as the gaunt diety returned the salute and then, hands on hips, looked at the preparations all around him and back at the man responsible for them. His voice was not loud when he spoke the words, but it was perfectly audible to the one for whom they were intended, and for the sake of posterity they may be quoted here, exactly as he spoke them:

"Throwbach, will you tell me what in the goddamned [expletive] hell is going on around here?"

The rest followed inevitably: the simple explanation, the incredulous rejoinder, the protestation, the rising tone, the curt order, the salute and the departure of the helicopter.

It was all over in a minute. Colonel Throwbach was relieved of his command, summarily but authoritatively, and the written special order which followed added nothing to the weight of that one spoken phrase. By the time the papers arrived Mervin Throwbach had already assigned men to fill in the trench and remove the watch towers and dig the stranded ranch wagons out of the mud. He'd already paid a farewell call on the mayor and been accorded a hurriedly-planned going-away party at the Officers' Club. In fact, by that time he was already gone and a new team was busily restoring the depot to its peacetime mission. The crisis was past. There would be no World War III, at least not on that day.

Yet what crisis of such proportions passes without leaving some trace of its passage? At the Rosy Bar, despite the return of its former clientele, despite the extensive renovations after that first wild night when the restrictions were lifted, not everything was as before. Carmen was back, unsubdued though far more circumspect, but Liliane was gone forever, to the state of matrimony in Germany with an American soldier. And the bar itself was greatly enlarged with more hostesses to accommodate an American clientele which was no longer local but came from distant installations in France and even from the legendary K-Town in Germany, so great was its renown. For Madame Régine's new friendship with *M. le Sous-Préfet* was bearing fruit and, as if in some strange compensation for her recent sacrifices, was to make of her a woman of some importance in the community.

The Hôtel Beau Site lost its three longterm guests, suddenly and despite payment of another month's rent in advance. But this was of little concern to Armand the desk clerk, since his fictional hero had just survived a combat with a giant squid and was preparing now to be launched into orbit in pursuit of a master criminal.

As for Lucette, it might be supposed that the departure of Major Shirk—for he did depart along with Major Blivens and others of Colonel Throwbach's principal staff—would have plunged her into disconsolate mourning and achieved the ruin of her business. Not a bit of it. In the midst of her grief her Gallic pragmatism and her friendship with Madame Régine were to rescue her. For Régine, never a woman to leave loose ends lying about, was able to convince her of the multiple advantages of a gentleman friend on the *Conseil Municipal* whose presence would not be at the mercy of a whim of the Pentagon and who, in addition, wielded some influence in the town of Chilly. And since M. Dupuis would be his own master and was in no way under the control of the American military, complete harmony soon became evident at the chic beauty salon not only on Saturday afternoons but on more than one afternoon during the week as well.

Thus did peace return to Chilly-sur-Chize. And thus were the sentiments of the local inhabitants vindicated, that in spite of its many inconveniences to them, the American presence at Chilly QM Depot was, after all, not such a bad thing.